Break
in Case of
Emergency

Jessica Winter

THE BOROUGH PRESS

The Borough Press
An imprint of HarperCollins *Publishers*
1 London Bridge Street
London SE1 9GF

www.harpercollins.co.uk

This paperback edition 2017
1

First published in Great Britain by HarperCollins *Publishers* 2016

A catalogue record for this book
is available from the British Library

ISBN: 978–0–00–813213–2

This novel is entirely a work of fiction.
The names, characters and incidents portrayed in it, while at times based on
historical events and figures, are the work of the author's imagination.

Printed and bound in Great Britain by
Clays Ltd, St Ives plc

MIX
Paper from
responsible sources
FSC
www.fsc.org
FSC™ C007454

FSC™ is a non-profit international organisation established to promote
the responsible management of the world's forests. Products carrying the
FSC label are independently certified to assure consumers that they come
from forests that are managed to meet the social, economic and
ecological needs of present and future generations,
and other controlled sources.

Find out more about HarperCollins and the environment at
www.harpercollins.co.uk/green

JESSICA WINTER is features editor at *Slate* and formerly the culture editor at *Time*. Her writing has appeared in the *New York Times*, the *Guardian*, *Bookforum*, the *Believer*, and many other publications. She lives in Brooklyn.

Praise for *Break in Case of Emergency*:

'Extremely funny – a satirical masterpiece that is tender and existentially-minded as well. I loved it!' ELIZABETH MCKENZIE, author of *The Portable Veblen*

'Very smart and juicy and weird and entertaining ... it reads like a chick lit plot written by Franzen' CURTIS SITTENFELD, author of *Eligible*

'Winter's novel is extremely good, because it is so well written ... an extraordinary debut' *Guardian*

'One of the smartest stories about friendship you're likely to read this year ... Winter takes in feminism and fertility issues while skewering celebrity philanthropy and celebrating friendships; it's brilliantly funny and hugely moving' *Elle UK*

'If you need a New York map of our times, have Jessica Winter become your cartographer. Sassy, sarcastic and sleek, this is a wonderfully brash appraisal of how we live' COLUM MCCANN

'Enth

'Hilarious ... the personal and workplace plots are woven together beautifully. Read, cringe, laugh, relate' *Lenny*

'A funny and moving commentary on that point in a woman's life when everything seems to come into question' *New York Times*

'Curious, captivating' *Kirkus Reviews*

'If you're wondering what it's like to live in New York when you're young, just buy Jessica Winter's book. It's funny, satirical, and deftly written' MIKE SCHUR, co-creator of *Parks and Recreation*

'A beautifully wry story about a woman who just wasn't made for these times' *Red*

'In this cutting commentary on workplace toxicity and how its tendrils can strangle relationships, Winter uses humour to illuminate the state of modern work, family, and friendship. She does a stellar job' *Elle.com*

'A wry look at the in-betweener stage of going into your thirties' *Grazia*

'Wry and unerringly sharp, *Break in Case of Emergency* is a smart look at so-called "first-world problems" – and a reminder that, first-world or not, they have a tendency to wreak havoc on our lives in a way that, at least for a moment, feels entirely insurmountable' *Refinery29*

'Entertaining and smartly satirical ... This is both a biting lampoon of workplace politics and a heartfelt search for meaning in modern life' *Publishers Weekly*

For Adrian

We flatter ourselves by thinking this compulsion to please others an attractive trait: a gift for imaginative empathy, evidence of our willingness to give.

— Joan Didion, "On Self-Respect"

Everything behind those French doors is full and meaningful. The gestures, the glances, the conversation that can't be heard. How do you get to be so full? And so full of only meaningful things?

— Zadie Smith, *NW*

Spring

Our Focus Is Focus Itself

"It's hard to reproduce those kind of results if—oh, sorry," Jen said, realizing a beat too late that the rest of the room had gone quiet.

Leora Infinitas had already taken her place at the head of the table. For one silent-screaming moment, it looked as if she were attempting to rip her own face off, but in fact she was tugging at her eyelash extensions under the placid gaze of the members of her board, who were seated in a corner conference room at the headquarters of the Leora Infinitas Foundation, also known as LIFt.

Jen scanned the other women around the jade-and-walnut table, festooned with crystal-and-bamboo vases filled with fresh-cut gerbera daisies and flamingo lilies, selected at Leora's request for their air-filtering qualities and replaced every day, even on days when the conference room was not in use, which was most days. The other women sat in tranquil anticipation as Leora yanked with greater urgency at her right eyelid using the pincer of her thumb and forefinger, as if trying to thread a needle with her own flesh. The rain against LIFt's floor-to-ceiling windows chattered like a gathering crowd, even as the white noise that pumped in from every ceiling at LIFt—an undulating *whhooooossshhhhh,* an airless air-conditioning—began to hush.

Jen shivered. Even a month into her tenure at LIFt, her body still misapprehended the *whhooooossshhhhh* as an Arctic blast that required shuddering adjustments to her internal thermostat.

Leora Infinitas's lashes now lay on the tabletop before her, a squashed yet glamorous bug. Without them, Leora looked at once diminished and more beautiful. Flecks of glue balanced on her eyelids. She blinked rapidly and stared into the table, searching the lacquer for the script, the incantation, hidden below its glinting surface.

"I don't like the idea of limiting ourselves," Leora finally said. "I'm a big believer in not settling for twenty-four hours in a day."

Rain shattered against the windows, the applause track of a sitcom. A head nodded; a pair of lips buzzed "Mmm."

A pen tapping on the table stilled itself.

The flowers stood beguiled in their vases.

The electrons in the air murmured to one another in grave consultation, then telepathically cabled the message to the rest of the room that Leora, in twenty-one words, had concluded her opening statements. It would be up to her braintrust to, to borrow Leora's phrasing, "advance the conversation."

Whhooooosssshhhhh

"*Whhooo* is to say," intoned Donna, the board chair and one of Leora's closest friends, "that there are not twenty-*five* hours in a day?"

"Ha, right, who decided *that*, anyway?" asked board member Sunny, who was also Leora's personal assistant.

"We always said we'd have a start-up mentality," Leora said. She peered down at the squashed eyelash bug. Soundlessly, Sunny materialized at her side, palmed it into a cupped tissue, and evanesced back into her seat.

"Start-ups never sleep," Leora continued. "Metaphorically speaking."

"Totally," Sunny said, nodding with her entire head and neck, the tissue of squashed eyelash bug clasped in her hand. *Totally* was something Sunny said a lot whenever Leora spoke. Sunny's *totally* was so total that it became two words. *Toe tally.*

"But at the same time, why bother doing everything if you're not doing everything *in. The right. Way*," Leora asked.

"Mmmmm," Sunny moaned.

Donna squared her shoulders. "I think that, right now, at this moment in the young history of LIFt—and especially at this perilous moment in our global economy—our focus is *focus itself*," she said. Her voice was deep and stern, the vowels round and sonorous as church bells. Her hands sculpted the air. Multiple bangles on each of her wrists clinked together in a wind chime of assent. "But shining a light on certain ideas *now* doesn't mean that *other* worthy ideas are left to languish and wilt in the dark forever."

Sunny was slow-motion headbanging.

"We must focus on those projects that feel most immediate to us," Donna continued. "This sensation of the year two thousand and nine leaping bravely into spring after such a bitter winter—what does that *feel* like? Let's capture it; let's hold that moment and transform it. We can return to other, more timeless ideas later—a wellspring of creativity that will nourish us when we feel depleted from giving birth to our first idea-children. And we *cannot* be afraid."

"I love it!" Sunny said, clenching a fist to her sternum. "Donna, you are amazing."

"Karina," Leora said imperiously to LIFt's executive director, seated to her right. "What would you prioritize?"

Karina, who had been raking her fingers through her hair and then twisting the strands, raking and twisting, tossed her hair over her shoulder and widened her eyes, as if absorbing the shock and import of a happy epiphany. "I'm going to second what you're saying, Leora: focus, focus, *focus*," she said. "The only way we can possibly limit ourselves is by taking on too much at once. We're empowering ourselves by making the choice *to make choices*. The newness of the foundation and the uncertainty of the historical moment—we can see them as *dares*. Dares to be bold, dares to *make* decisions and *own* those decisions."

Jen stifled a smile and looked down at her open notebook, where she'd written BOARD MEETING NOTES with her fountain pen and gradually added serifs and flourishes until the letters became a row of gerbera daisies and flamingo lilies. From the first time they'd met, Jen recognized Karina as a master of the filibuster, but she hadn't yet seen Karina cast the spell on Leora—the gift of shrouding any and every topic in a fluffy word cloud of reiterative agreement until the original query was swallowed up in the woozy vapor of resounding enthusiasm for an unstated but sublime goal.

Karina shook her head wonderingly and peered into a dazzling middle distance, taking in a new horizon line. "I'm really jazzed about this," she said. "I can't wait."

Forty-five minutes later, as the meeting did not adjourn but rather transitioned into a discussion of Leora's daughter's Bikram instructor's ayahuasca retreats in Oaxaca, Jen's line of gerbera daisies and flamingo lilies had sprouted into a garden of vines and ivy that plumed across both open pages of her notebook, speckled with topiary animals and actual bounding cats. The stippled-sketch form of Jen's toddler goddaughter, Millie, peeked around a flowering espalier with a little fistful of poppies, a wreath of gardenias and eucalyptus atop her black curls.

Jen closed the notebook, rose, and began to leave the room, but hovered at the head of the table beside Leora. She had resolved to hover in awkward mid-stride, resulting in a slight lurching motion that stirred up a gruesomely intact memory of balking on the pitcher's mound in Little League, with the bases loaded, on ball four. Jen had not yet been introduced to Leora, and keenly wanted to introduce herself now, but just as keenly wanted not to disrupt Leora's Oaxaca anecdote, which involved a surreally vivid dream—induced by a midnight snack of *chapulines* and chocolate *mole*—wherein a *mercado* stall reassembled itself as an animatronic giant and began *clank-clank*ing toward Leora, embroidered tunics and colorful straw handbags winging down from its bionic shoulders in a confetti of symbolism.

"You know, *mercado,* machines, merchandise, mechanical reproduction—the moment was just so *rich* in meaning," Leora was saying. "I don't have the *machinery* to deconstruct it."

"Haha *wow*," Sunny said.

Swaying on her feet, Jen tried to catch Karina's eye to plead mutely for an assist. But in each of the rapt faces around the table, Jen recognized the temporary tunnel vision that she herself had adapted and perfected in high school as an overtaxed waitress at a casual-dining franchise. She arranged a grin on her face that was intended to convey merry diffidence and backed out of the room.

Looking Busy

"Do you want to talk about it?" Daisy asked when Jen returned to her desk.

Jen flopped theatrically into the chair behind her desk. "Wait, I have no idea why I just did that," she said. "I've been sitting for *days*." She stood up, then sat down again, more daintily.

"We don't have to talk about it if you don't want to," Daisy said. "You only infiltrated a board meeting."

Daisy was flipping through a perfect-bound, magazinelike tome titled *Fur-Lined Teacup: Animals • Fashion • Feminism*. The cover depicted, against a white backdrop, an impassive Russian blue cat in a trilby.

"I infiltrated nothing—they just needed someone to take notes," Jen said. "And it would be my honor to talk about it. Leora broke her toe paragliding in Turks and Caicos, which her guru told her was a metaphor for a fundamental incompatibility between her *jingmai* and her *luomai*, so when the nail falls off her toe she has to wear it in a titanium locket around her neck until Mercury enters Virgo. Karina was at a party with the Russian billionaire who is building the cyborg clone of himself, and he asked her what she was going to bequeath to her brain in her will and she said 'fish oil,' and then he asked her out on a date. Donna bought a tapestry in Siem Reap and had it made into a pantsuit. Sunny has a new pizza stone."

Daisy tore out a page from *Fur-Lined Teacup* and handed it to Jen. It depicted a llama lounging in a square gazebo, reading a book.

"Is that llama wearing bifocals?" Jen asked, rubbing her fingers along the creamy, textured paper stock.

"Are they all still talking about the financial apocalypse?" Daisy asked.

"Of course," Jen said, handing the page back to Daisy. "All anyone ever does is talk about the financial apocalypse. Sunny is putting some money into gold. Leora said she's still considering letting a couple of her house staff go because of the financial apocalypse."

"Do you think she'll let us go because of the financial apocalypse?" Daisy asked, picking up a pair of scissors.

"Not if we keep looking busy," Jen said, watching as Daisy cut a careful silhouette around the bookish llama's ears.

Real Jobs and Other Jobs

Before LIFt, Jen had worked as a communications officer at the revered Federloss Family Foundation, which focused on women's reproductive health initiatives in developing countries. When the foundation was blindsided by the compound effects of the economic crisis and significant investments impaled on Bernard Madoff's Ponzi schemes, Jen couldn't help but admire the balletic elegance of its subsequent budgetary adjustments, which absorbed the trauma by eliminating only positions, not the future budgets of pending initiatives. Midwife training schemes and prenatal-care pilot programs would go forward untouched. Jen's dental coverage and pretax deferred savings program would not.

"I always thought that if I ever got laid off I would at least enjoy a degree of purgative moral outrage," Jen said to her husband, Jim, on the day in January she was let go. She was calling him from the street just outside the foundation's dowdy offices in the East Thirties, one unmittened hand clasping her woolen coat to her unscarfed throat, the other clasping her phone to her unhatted ear. "I always thought there would be tears and recriminations. Rending of garments. But these layoffs are judicious and correct. I would have absolutely laid me off."

"It kind of takes all the fun out of it," Jim said.

Jen turned her face into the wind and squinted at the street, naked trees standing mournful watch over blackened geodes of day-old slush and stalled, sagging cars. "There's no one anywhere," she said. "Everyone's gone home. Does anyone live here anymore?"

Despite her statements to the contrary, Jen would have absolutely not laid herself off, because her salary was a rounding error, an irrelevant scrawl of marginalia in any organization's bookkeeping. Just the rent on Jen and Jim's two-bedroom apartment in Flatbush, the Brooklyn neighborhood where Jim taught fifth grade at a local public school, was equivalent to well over half of her monthly take-home pay. The apartment had been advertised as being located within the historic boundaries of Ditmas Park, home to a smorgasbord of Victorian and Queen Anne and neo-Tudor and Colonial Revival detached houses in various states of grandeur and disrepair, but you could not have found a single Spanish tile roof or Ionic column or stone lion guardsman on Jen and Jim's block, not a balustrade nor a gabled dormer nor a single oriel window, just a hulking quadrant of hundred-unit brick boxes whose signature architectural flourishes were the air-conditioning units—replete with company logo—installed beneath each window, which gave the reiterative impression that these buildings were not family residences at all but instead warehouses-cum-marketing experiments in service of FEDDERS AIR CONDITIONING.

Not Ditmas Park, as Jim took to calling their immediate area, was home to a Ditmas Avenue but not to a park or parklike domain, a source of perverse delight to Jim.

"The name itself is a broken promise," Jim had said, "and thus it's an honest and forthright guarantee of all the broken promises that Not Ditmas Park can offer its citizens in terms of amenities, community spirit, and educational opportunity. The name tells a meta-lie in service of a greater truth."

"It's smart to get in on the ground floor of an emerging district," the real estate agent had said. "Or, in this case, the *fourth* floor. You guys are ahead of the curve!"

"We don't really need the second bedroom," Jen had told the real estate agent. "But, you know, we're married now, and—"

"And *aspirations*," said the real estate agent with a wink. "You're young!"

"We're not that young," Jen said.

Their closest subway station stood atop a perpetually dripping overground train line, where the fronts included a dollar store, a liquor store, and a "development corporation"; the indignities of time, weather, and pigeon droppings had chiseled the development corporation's fabric awning into a trompe l'oeil of corrugated tin. What Jen and Jim guessed to be an exposed sewer pipe snaked past one end of the hoarding fence around the train tracks. Behind the plaza sat a mysterious brick-and-concrete hut that evoked an armored-car repair depot near Checkpoint Charlie. The annihilating climate of Eastern Bloc filthy-slipshod brutalism was encapsulated in their nearest post office, which looked and smelled like it had been excavated from the rubble of a gas main explosion, replete with broken metal locks hanging from its doors and service windows, as if smashed in haste to rescue trapped survivors.

Jen and Jim lived within cardboard-thin walls and floors and ceilings unencumbered by insulation, all echoing beams and sound-conducting metal. If you pushed back a chair or Franny the cat batted your keys off the coffee table, the downstairs neighbors heard it. If you coughed or flushed a toilet, your upstairs neighbors heard it. To play recorded music with a bass line was a premeditated act of revenge. Residents who rarely met one another's eyes in the elevator or vestibule would register displeasure with their neighbors' squeaky hinges and furniture-rattling footfalls by leaving cans of WD-40 and fuzzy bedroom slippers on one another's welcome mats, offerings shot through with the sinister supplication of a cat dropping a headless field mouse on the back porch. Jen and Jim gingerly maneuvered around on their toes at all times to avert the wrath of their downstairs neighbor, a replica in pallid flesh-folds of an Easter Island statue perched in a motorized wheelchair who had spent much of Jen and Jim's move-in weekend pounding her own ceiling with a broom handle in protest.

The building's architectural quirks struck Jen as most problematic on late Saturday evenings, when the upstairs neighbors' ungulate children repaired to their grandparents' house and their parents would celebrate their reprieve with a thumping multiroom sexual odyssey—what Jim called their "weekly all-hands meeting"—often scored to *Buena Vista Social Club* or, on at least one harrowing occasion, Raffi's *Singable Songs for the Very Young*, whose material provided a ready template for marching band–style refrains that the neighbors synced with recognizably percussive motions.

FIVE! LITTLE! SPECKLED! FROGS!
SAT! ON A! SPECKLED! LOG!
EATING! THE MOST! DELICIOUS! BUGS!

Then, occasionally, what sounded like a lamp would *chank* to the floor or a bedside table would *whomp* over on its side, followed by the scrabbling of either a small dog's or a large cat's paws as it fled for safety to another room.

"Should we tell them?" Jen asked Jim late one night as they lay in bed, eyes wide in the dark, as the woman upstairs improvised a bellowing descant to her husband's rapid Raffian melody. "It's like they're invading their own privacy."

ONE! JUMPED! INTO! THE POOL!
WHERE! IT! WAS NICE! AND COOL!
THEN! THEREWEREFOURGREENSPECKLEDFROGS

"I'm just glad they're happy," Jim said. Their downstairs neighbor broomed her ceiling, just once, as if in warning.

After the end of her Federloss job, Jen might have assumed that she and Jim would be giving their neighbors more opportunities to invade their privacy now that she was unencumbered by the everyday stresses and timesucks of gainful employment. But Jen and Jim convened fewer all-hands meetings during her enforced sabbatical, for no reason that either could have pinpointed, save perhaps for a sheepishness that floated around the post-layoff Jen like a twilight cloud of gnats. She began too many emails—even to Meg, even to Pam—with "I know you must be totally busy, but I just wondered . . ." She thanked friends too profusely—even Meg, even Pam—when they met for coffee or a drink, and Jen always insisted on paying. She avoided parties, because she'd "have nothing to say."

"I just find it hard to do small talk if I can't account for my time," Jen said to Meg on the phone.

"Right," Meg replied, "because there's always a velvet rope and a horde of squealing fans around the guy at the party who wants to talk about *his job*."

Jen kept an Excel spreadsheet on her elderly laptop titled REAL JOBS AND OTHER JOBS. At first, tapping through fingerless gloves at a kitchen table made dizzy on its oak-finish-and-particleboard haunches by the humidity swings of too many New York City summers, Jen applied for only REAL JOBS: grantwriting, speechwriting, communications work for any worthy cause she could find. But as the winter grew colder and bleaker, she put in for more and more OTHER JOBS. She applied to write copy for the Feminist Porn Collective, but belatedly discovered that she would be paid mainly in feminist porn. She landed an interview to be the research assistant to an elderly romance novelist and semireclusive candle-wax heiress, only to find out ex post facto that the novelist had employed a total of six research assistants over forty years, and each was a white male with a poetry MFA and/or a direct or family connection to Phillips Exeter Academy. She drafted a few speeches for a third-party mayoral candidate whose campaign platform included the abolishment of both private schools and gender designations on government forms. She acted as writing tutor to the sixteen-year-old son of a well-known entertainment lawyer, until she refused to help him forge a Vyvanse prescription, whereupon the teen told his mother (untruthfully) that Jen had absconded with his Modafinil prescription.

Jen did not disclose to her charge that she herself had a prescription for a similar cognitive enhancer, Animexa, which she renewed at increasingly irregular intervals following the loss of her blue-chip Federloss Foundation health insurance.

"You live in a fake neighborhood," the sixteen-year-old had informed Jen one day.

"Ditmas Park?" Jen replied. "It's real. I've been there."

"You live," the sixteen-year-old said, "in a real estate agent's neologism."

This bothered Jen, mostly because the decision to live in a real estate agent's neologism had originally been a marker of grown-up prudence and long-term thinking: The mindful marrieds enter their thirties, conserve their resources, steadily pay down their student loans, live well within their means, reserve space for a hypothetical tiny future boarder.

"Feather your nest," the real estate agent had said.

Now, even living in a real estate agent's neologism seemed like a grim necessity bordering on presumptuous overreach, regardless of the scuffed thirdhand furniture, the chewed gum–like residue constantly and mysteriously accumulating between the kitchen tiles, the canoe-sized kitchen separated by a cheap flapping strip of countertop from the deluxe canoe–sized living room, the dry rot in the windowsills, the closet doors eight inches too narrow for their frames. Even Franny the cat seemed like a luxury, all those unmonetized hours logged napping and grooming.

Jen began writing down every single purchase she made in her notebook. With the same fountain pen, she also drew a picture of each item. Her student loan debit was represented one month by a graduation cap, another month by the hand-forged wrought-iron gate her college class had walked through on commencement day. Cat-food purchases were represented by drawings of Franny in various states of odalisque repose. Jen made stippled pencil drawings of toothpaste tubes and physics-defying stacks of little tissue packets from the pharmacy and curlicuing cornucopias from modest grocery runs.

The first entry in Jen's notebook was the price of the notebook.

Inside the open notebook, Jen drew a picture of the open notebook, then another inside that one and another, collapsing infinitely into the center.

That

"So, any news?" Jen's mom asked.

Jen's mom never telephoned her, but if Jen did not call at regular intervals, Jen's mom would complain to Jen's dad, who would then send an email to Jen asking why she was ignoring her mother. The subject heading of these emails was "Your Mother."

(Jen's mom became agitated, however, if Jen telephoned her too frequently. "Enough! I'm *fine*," she'd say in lieu of greeting if one of Jen's calls followed another too closely. The acceptable interval between calls widened and narrowed at will.)

"Any news on work, you mean?" Jen asked. "Not just yet."

"Could that Meg find you a job?"

Meg was a program director at the Bluff Foundation for Justice and Human Rights, a private behemoth so agelessly fortified by old money that its temporary hiring freeze was itself a metric of dire economic crisis.

"Meg has been really helpful," Jen said. "But obviously I don't want to put it all on her to find me a job—"

"Fine, fine," Jen's mom broke in. "Anyway."

Jen never knew if her mother's conversational style was symptomatic of mere incuriosity or rather of an extreme wariness of any social transaction remotely resembling confrontation, which presumably included most exchanges of words. At cousins' weddings and sisters-in-law's baby showers, Jen watched with dismay as her mother attempted to mingle with people she'd known all their lives: arms folded in front of her as a shield, chin pulled defensively to her neck, poorly conditioned limbic system misinterpreting a niece's attempts to inquire about her protracted kitchen renovation for a passive-aggressive face-off between two opposing parties.

"Could that Pam help you?" Jen's mom asked.

Jen had been dating Jim for nearly two years before he ceased being *that Jim.*

"That Pam always helps me, in her way," Jen replied.

Pam

A few weeks into her post-Federloss unemployment, Jen had started spending several afternoons a week at Pam's place. This pleased Jim, because Pam and her boyfriend, Paulo, were artists, and Jim thought of Jen as an artist, too.

"I was never *an artist*," Jen would say. "I never *made art.* I drew things. I painted things. People."

Pam and Paulo rented a cheap cavernous space in Greenpoint close to Newtown Creek, the site of one of the largest underground oil-and-chemical spills in history. On the walk from the G train stop to Pam's, Jen could never discount the possibility that her air sacs were swelling with some kind of fine fecal mist of gamma rays and chlorinated benzene byproducts, a carcinogenic ambience that Pam enthusiastically leveraged in last-minute rental negotiations with their absentee landlord. The front half of Pam and Paulo's space, which was about the size of Jen and Jim's entire apartment and shared a wall with a tavern, served as a studio by day and a gallery by night. Paulo had divided the back half into four narrow, windowless "rooms" created by particleboard partitions that stopped two feet short of the ceilings. Pam and Paulo slept in the largest partition, while a transient cast of roommates—tourists and students and the hollow-eyed recent survivors of imploded live-in relationships—took up monthly or quarterly residence in the other three spaces.

In the front studio, the drafting table, the kitchen table, and a futon relocated from the master bedroom were currently paired with miniature towers made of stools, pillows, and stacks of oversized books. Each stack was jerry-rigged to support Pam's leg, which had been crushed in a hit-and-run the previous year when a delivery van made a squealing right turn and threw her from her bicycle. Three operations and hundreds of hours of physical therapy later, the leg—which looked perfectly normal at first glance, and both shiny-swollen and shrunken at second glance—was still grinding and wheezing in its sockets. Jen imagined that Pam's powers of concentration were such that she'd occasionally see a drop of perspiration splat onto her laptop, and finally notice that the usual dull ache in her leg had escalated into jangling agony, thudding away at the double-glazed windows of Pam's flow state as her conscious mind deliquesced into oneness with Final Cut Pro or the Artnet biography of Sigmar Polke.

Jen and Pam had met their freshman year of college in a drawing class, where Pam had been impressed by Jen's hyperrealistic technical abilities and Jen had been enchanted by Pam's impassive terribleness—her wobbly, allegedly one-point-perspective *Still Life with Cranberry Vodka and Froot Loops* had so appalled their drawing teacher that he accused Pam of exploiting his class for another taught by his ex-girlfriend, "Kitsch-Kraft and Outsider Art: Toward a Deliberately Bad Avant-Garde."

Later, though, Jen experienced the growing recognition that Pam was "a real artist."

"You're like a *real artist*," Jen blurted out drunkenly to Pam the first time they went to a party together.

Jen's talent-spotting acumen was confirmed their junior year, when Pam started convincing people to allow her to take their picture first thing in the morning, before they got out of bed, before they even fully awakened. Pam would then mock up the unairbrushed, usually unflattering photograph as a faux magazine cover, billboard, or author's jacket photo. The photos, taken in weak dawn light, were dusky, pearly, sometimes slightly out of focus; the best ones looked like secrets or accidents, or secret accidents. Pam called the pictures Wakes.

She started with the people who spent the most time under the roof of the drafty, creaking, badly wired hundred-year-old Colonial house that Meg, Pam, and Jen rented four blocks from campus. The first Wake, of Pam's then-boyfriend, looked like a seventies rock star's mug shot: alarmed and defiant, dazed and hairy. In the second Wake, a puffy-faced Jen ducks bashfully away from the camera; her face is captured in three-quarter profile, her hand blurring upward to check for traces of dried sleep.

The third Wake, of Meg—who was Jen's friend first, whom Jen had introduced to Pam at the "You're a real artist" party, which it often occurred to Jen to point out, though she never did—was the revelation. A double gash of mattress marks swooped across Meg's right cheekbone like a panther's caress. Her hair, which usually fell in computer-generated gentle waves, swirled and crashed around her heart-shaped face. Meg's lips fell slightly open; the strap of her tank top wiped sideward, tracing the curve of her shoulder. Instead of ducking away from Pam's camera, the half-asleep Meg leaned into it sensuously, chin forward, eyes heavy and intrigued.

Pam knew what she had. She blew up the picture big enough to swallow an entire gallery wall at her end-of-semester show. It was a stunning photograph, raw and gorgeous and discomfiting in its intimacy. That it was a stunning photograph of *Meg*—old-money Meg, moderately-famous-last-name-demi-campus-celebrity Meg, Phi Beta Kappa—as-a-first-semester-junior Meg, paragon-of-the-public-service-community Meg—made the photograph an event.

Now everyone wanted a Wake. The campus weekly kept an issue-to-issue tally of everyone who had a Wake and should have a Wake and desperately wanted a Wake, and also a regularly updated online ranking of existing Wakes, with Meg permanently and ceremoniously lodged at No. 1. Pam won a grant to create a single-edition magazine composed of nothing but Wakes. Clem Bernadine, editor of the campus humor magazine, submitted his shirtless and chaotic Wake as his yearbook picture. Joseph Potter, a beloved tenured professor of theater studies, used his one-eye-closed Wake as the jacket photo to his book *Dre Gardens: Hip-Hop, New Money, and the Performance of the Self.*

Pam was now intuitively aware of her genius for talking people into doing things that were not ostensibly in their interest. For her senior thesis project, she convinced the university to allow her to change the signage on several sites around campus to verbatim transcriptions of graffiti from the men's bathrooms at the art school. Instead of directions to the buttery or the law library or the Women's Center, visitors during Parents' Weekend puzzled over commands and epigraphs such as STOP DRAWING D'S AND DRAW BIG TITTIES INSTEAD and SILENCE IS GOLDEN BUT DUCT TAPE IS SILVER and SINCE WRITING ON TOILET WALLS IS DONE NEITHER FOR CRITICAL ACCLAIM NOR FINANCIAL SUCCESS, IT IS THE PUREST FORM OF ART—DISCUSS, all presented in the university's elegant house typography, Demimonde Condensed Blackletter. (The sign outside the university art gallery's parking lot, which temporarily read FIRST-YEAR BOYS ARE TOY BOYS, may have caused the most consternation.) Pam also kitted out a trailer outside the art school as a fake "visitor's center" and filled it with mock posters and brochures advertising the art school. The promotional materials glowed with wholesome and bright-eyed ambassadors of the future of contemporary art, lounging on the campus green or peering rapturously at the art gallery's resident Pollock, their thoughts and hopes amplified in Demimonde Condensed Blackletter captions along the lines of DON'T JUDGE ME I ONLY NEEDED MONEY FOR COLLEGE or I HAD SEX WITH YR TRASH CAN IT WAS OKAY.

"I heard some guy call it 'interventionist art,' but that made you sound like a substance-abuse counselor," Meg said to Pam at her senior thesis show. Meg was looking over Jen's shoulder at a thick, glossy "informational packet" that Jen held in her hands, titled STOP WRITING YOUR NAMES HERE HALF THESE PEOPLE ARE BROKEN UP ALREADY.

"Arbitration," Pam said. "If anyone asks, say this is arbitration."

Pam had continued in this arbitrative vein for the entirety of her postcollegiate art career, year after year producing little that was sellable and less that was sold, and occasionally running into a spot of potentially career-enhancing trouble, as when she used grant money to purchase a month's lease on a storefront next to a real estate agent's office, painted the storefront to appear indistinguishable from the real estate agent's, and posted property advertisements in the window that looked identical to the real estate agent's—that is, until you looked closer at the descriptions, which were written in Pam's recognizably run-on polemical style:

Panache! This dazzling new build destroyed three neoclassical buildings and a park and a dog run Now it's a fifteen-story tower block Steps from Boutiques Bathed in Light No one making less than 500% of the median local income can afford a studio here Turnkey terrific!!!

"It's a commentary on gentrification," Pam explained to Meg, whom Pam called for legal advice after receiving a cease-and-desist letter from the adjoining real estate agent.

To support herself, Pam presumably chugged along on enough one-off adjunct teaching jobs, freelance writing assignments, guest-curator gigs, and other odds and ends to get by. Pam and Jen never spoke of money, and to judge by the frigid winter temperatures in Pam's quasi-legal abode, the smelly-damp bathroom she shared with a revolving door of lost-seeming strangers, and her static college-era wardrobe of holey leggings and faded Champion sweatshirts, Pam didn't have any.

"Do you want to know how I know I'm not an artist?" Jen asked Jim one night, after coming home from one of her unemployed afternoons at Pam's. "Because I couldn't live like Pam lives."

"I doubt Pam needs you feeling sorry for her," Jim said.

"I don't feel sorry for her!" Jen said. "I feel sorry for me!"

"Pam and Paulo are doing fine," Jim said. "I liked that show they did about gentrification."

"That was Pam's show," Jen said. Paulo made large, gooey clumps of things that gelatinized in her memory. He'd tie together dolls, tree branches, and tire irons into a stakelike arrangement and then pour gallons of red paint over it, or lace stacks of 1980s-era issues of *The Economist* with strings of Christmas lights that were also looped around the necks of vintage lawn jockeys sourced on eBay, and then pour gallons of resin over it.

"And I know Pam and Paulo are doing fine!" Jen continued. "That's my whole point! I would *not* be fine, if I were them. But they are fine. More than fine."

Pam had enlisted Jen's collaboration on her current work-in-progress, although Pam was reticent about its exact nature. All Jen could glean about the project was her own role in it: to paint a series of five-by-four-foot portraits based on the grinning, healthy specimens in the promotional materials for WellnessSolutions, a health insurance company.

"So you just have to make sure you have a senior citizen, a new mom, and an apple-cheeked teen," Pam told Jen, handing over the Wellness-Solutions brochures, "and they should look *maniacally happy.*"

In college, Jen painted larger-than-life photorealistic portraits of classmates, teachers, and celebrities: She projected a photograph onto a canvas, traced the main features in pencil, then painted in oil over the tracings. The aspirations toward extreme verisimilitude owed largely to an indelible nightmare Jen had as a freshman in which her first-year painting class was violently purged and repopulated by the blurry wraiths of Gerhard Richter's Baader-Meinhof series. Though she would have admitted this to no one, Jen suspected that she had allowed her portraits to become so big because the ideas they contained were so small. Perhaps they didn't even contain ideas so much as self-projections, as wobbly and coarse-grained as the mechanical projections that propped up her technique. There was an element of self-portraiture in the grinning nervousness, the anxiety of obedience, that could start creeping around her subjects' mouths in the transition from photograph to canvas, in the obsequious gleam of the eye that might twinkle in the canvas but not in the photograph.

In Jen's mind, she appropriated the outside of her work from photographs and the inside of her work from herself, and others mistook this for creativity.

"You are a fabulous copyist, Jen," said one of her professors. For that class, Jen had painted identical twins in the Diane Arbus mode, and titled the work *Biological Inheritance*.

"You are an *astonishing* technician," said another of her professors. "But what else are you?"

"I reproduce things," Jen would say. "Things that already exist. I don't even reproduce things—I reproduce reproductions of things."

"Jen saying her art is not art is the most Jen thing that ever happened," Meg would say.

"Jen, why do you make art if it's not art?" Pam asked.

"Pam just made you into a koan, Jen," Meg said.

"Why is your whole life a lie, Jen?" Pam asked.

"Hey, Pam," Meg said, "do you think we could get Jen to put herself down about how much she puts herself down?"

"Hey, Meg," Pam said, "if a snake ate its own tail, do you think Jen would apologize to the snake?"

Avoidance

Jen couldn't go to Pam's every day just because she was unemployed; or she probably could have, but she didn't want Pam to feel responsible for finding ways to occupy her time. She needed to construct another rudder for her amorphous days, in which anxiety and sloth wrestled with each other only to reach a shaky alliance, usually culminating in a despondent, thrashing nap. Anxiety and sloth made a formidable team of antagonists because their shared goal was avoidance: avoidance of the gaping maw of job-posting sites; avoidance of other people with their helpful advice and compliments and solidarity, all of which Jen's brain translated into prayers for the dying; avoidance of the immediate outdoor environment, which was bitterly cold and covered in the scattering stacks of uncollected trash and unidentified melting black shit that signified the liminal space between winter and spring in Not Ditmas Park.

Jen decided that the rudder would be a daily deadline: By the time Jim returned home from school, at around five p.m., Jen would have X number of cover letters written, Y job-research tasks fulfilled, Z closets or drawers cleaned out. And she would have drawings to show to Jim, and maybe even paintings.

Jim's support of Jen's dormant art career was as unconditional as it was uncorroborated, and it had maintained that sincerity ever since they'd first met, a year after college, when they both taught at the same summer enrichment program for children of low-income families in southeast Brooklyn. In the final blasting-oven days of August, Jen had presented each of their kids with a crayon-on-construction-paper portrait of him- or herself, carefully rolled into a scroll and tied with a blue silk ribbon like a diploma.

"Maybe that was presumptuous of me," Jen had said to Jim as they watched their students ripple and zigzag out the classroom door one last time, a few of the portraits strewn on the cracked linoleum behind them, others rolled inside clementine-sized fists and *thwack*ing proximate shoulders. "It's not like any of our kids were asking for the priceless gift of my artistic expression, like it's some kind of reward. And drawing someone's face is such an intimate act. Literally holding up a mirror to someone takes a lot of mutual trust. It's a kind of disclosure. I mean, who am I to tell them what they look like?"

"Do you want to go on a date with me?" Jim replied.

His faith-based position on Jen's real artistic calling extended itself even to casual introductions at parties: "Please meet my wife, Jen; she's an artist!" His stance wholly lacked in passive-aggression or latent accusation. To him it was simply a statement of fact, and the factual basis of the statement had no statute of limitations.

"You should use your free time to paint," Jim would say during Jen's unemployment. "Or at least do some drawing."

"I should," Jen would say.

"Just don't *make any art*," Jim would say.

Sometimes Jim would come home to a new end table constructed out of stray dowels and disused neckties, two rhubarb pies cooling on the kitchen counter (one crust made with shortening, one not), and a calligraphic note—each letter written in alternating shades of glitter pen—informing him that Jen had volunteered to take the Aggression-Challenged Mixed Breeds at their local animal shelter for a walk. Upon her return, Jen would have much to download on a really interesting *Guardian* piece she'd read on the new patriarch of the Russian Orthodox Church and his stance on female clerics, and another really interesting *Guardian* piece she'd read on the civil conflict in Puthuk-kudiyiruppu, Sri Lanka.

Sometimes Jim would come home to the entire contents of their bookcase redistributed across the floor of the front room in short stacks, as if an inept soldier had begun fortifying his trench too late before the shelling started, and down the hall, his wife asleep on their bed—the bed itself sandbagged by half the contents of their closet—in gym socks and her bridesmaid's dress from a cousin's wedding.

"Are you home?" she asked, stirring from her nap in a flutter of tulle as Jim sat down gently on the edge of the bed. "Are you sick? Is it dark?"

The Emergency Fund

There did exist what Jen and Jim called an "emergency fund," parked in a liquid savings account that currently held $12,771.43, the amount that Jim's mother had left him when she died after taxes plus several years of accrued interest at a median rate of 1.25 percent. They had always intended to add more than interest to it, as the fund was meant to provide extra feathering for the nest of the hypothetical tiny future boarder.

"There's always the emergency fund," Jim would say whenever Jen fretted about money.

"No, there isn't," Jen would say.

"There's no emergency fund?" Jim asked the first time.

"There's no emergency," Jen said the first time.

They might have considered asking Jen's parents for help, which Jen had done once before, as a twenty-three-year-old museum assistant facing a surprise tax bill. She had marked down the maximum number of exemptions on her W-4, mistaking "exemptions" for "deductions," and thus assuming she would be paying her tax bill as she went. That mistake, combined with the fact that it hadn't occurred to her that she'd have to pay taxes on the $5,000 art fellowship she'd won on graduation, meant that she found herself, on the second tax return of her postcollegiate life, owing the IRS $8,000.

"Which is incidentally still less than what Lily Bart owes Gus Trenor at the end of *The House of Mirth*," Pam pointed out to Jen at the time. "And that's not even adjusting for inflation."

Jen did not mention her tax bill to Meg.

When Jen asked her father for help, he offered to loan her the money at the current median rate for mortgage loans, which at that time hung around 7.5 percent. Two years, fixed rate. But first, Jen's dad said, he needed to get sign-offs from Jen's two brothers, because they might want a matching gift, which would only be fair.

"A matching *loan*, you mean," Pam said. "You would all get matching loans."

"I asked him that—my dad sees it as a gift," Jen said. "He thinks he could do better than 7.5 percent in the markets, you see. So he would be coming out behind even with the interest."

"Wait, he's an investor?"

"He's an associate district sales manager for a regional chain of sporting-goods stores."

"Oh, right."

Pam's dad was an auto mechanic. On a road trip their senior year, after the stick on their borrowed manual-transmission heap fell slack and flailing on the freeway, Jen and Meg had watched Pam crawl under the car and pop the gear linkage into place.

"I'm sure he could get you a great deal on Champion sweatshirts, so long as you make your purchase somewhere in southern Ohio," Jen said.

"What is his deal, though?" Pam asked.

"He's into self-sufficiency," Jen said. "That's his deal. He grew up poor in a tough home. Both my parents, they just didn't know things; they didn't grow up with things. They used to keep the books in our house in a closet because they thought that was where they go. They didn't know about fruit. Did you know that I was in college the first time I ever had an orange? Meg offered me an orange and I asked for a knife to cut it with."

"I don't remember that," Pam said. Jen thought it was sweet that Pam assumed she would have been there.

There were things that Jen could say to Pam that she couldn't say to Meg.

"Could you ask your mom for help?" Pam asked.

"Well, you know my mom," Jen said. "I mean, you don't, and that's kind of the point—she's in the picture, but she's sort of blurred in the background, like you flap the Polaroid around and that patch just never comes into focus. It's always felt like she's been in another room. Talking to her is like pressing your ear to a wall."

There was more Jen wanted to say, but she didn't, because Pam's own mother had died of cancer when Pam was a child.

"You should paint your mom," Pam said.

"Anyway," Jen said. "So my dad always comes back to 'No one gave me anything and I turned out fine'—that kind of thing. Standing alone in the world. I respect that. Fairness is important to him."

"Fairness isn't necessarily incompatible with generosity," Pam said.

"It is if you decide that fairness is the same as math."

"Yeah. Or chemistry. Right? If you're balancing a chemical equation, a little generosity is the same as cheating. Faking."

"A rectangle doesn't just shave a bit off two sides and loan the extra to a triangle so that the triangle can achieve her dream of becoming a square." Jen semaphored the shapes with her hands.

"The rectangle must stay a rectangle," Pam said.

Many weeks into her unemployment, Jen had a single-scene dream in which she opened the front door to her apartment to the sight of Franny, shaved to the skin, sitting startled at their doorstep upon a mat woven of her own downy calico fur. Instead of WELCOME, the mat read FEATHER YOUR NEST.

Meg

Around Valentine's Day, Meg and Jen met for an early-evening drink at Tommy's Bar in Midtown. The bartender was also the owner, and was also Tommy. Generations of Magic Marker graffiti covered the walls above the ripped, sticky leather booths. Supertramp was the most recent addition to the jukebox.

"So I don't know whether this counts as a REAL JOB or an OTHER JOB," Meg said, "but I'll let you decide."

In her nubby wool suit—black velvet collar, pencil skirt—and her glossy sweep of hair and her subliminal makeup (cheekbones dusted pink by an eternal cosmetic winter, liner applied so subtly that it simply supplanted the real curve of her upper lids), Meg personified brisk and frictionless glamour. She had always projected this, even in college, even during finals week—the undergraduate uniform of jeans, sweatpants, and puffer jackets on Meg became a form of drag. And Meg almost always seemed to have an egg timer ticking behind her eyes, long before gainful employment or law school or marriage or motherhood had placed any real-world requisitions on her time-management protocols. Even during the first carefree week of term or at Friday-night house parties, it was there: a buzz of impatience, palpable and exquisitely controlled. At eighteen and nineteen, Jen had found the buzz annoying, even egocentric. At twenty and beyond, she had learned to envy it—the way that Meg could apportion units of time like the facets of a jewel that she was coolly and constantly appraising. Jen saw it as a true measure of self-respect.

"Wait, before you tell me, I just have to say, thank you so much for hanging out tonight," Jen said. "Especially on a school night. Millie won't wander into traffic or anything?" Millie, Jen's goddaughter, was Meg's uncannily considerate and beatific two-year-old. Even Millie's tantrums had a tidy, meditative quality.

"She's good. Marc and I have her tethered in the back garden," Meg said. "The neighbors toss meat over the fence if she cries."

"And how's Marc?"

"Ask him yourself," said Meg, gesturing toward a disheveled man in a dun trenchcoat with his head on the bar. Meg's actual Marc was at home, where, since losing his finance job, he pursued various woodworking-related hobbies involving custom picture frames for Millie's finger paintings and carved mallard ducks. His trust fund (private equity) dwarfed Meg's own sizeable one (boiler equipment, mostly, but also television production royalties). Jen had always tried to displace her envy of their bottomless security by reflecting it back on herself as an intriguing hypothetical—how her idea of labor would change if it could be alienated from capital. If ambition were the only means of appraisal.

"Okay, so Bluff Senior, Charles Bluff, Big Cheese Bluff, recently completed an amicable divorce," Meg explained, "and one of the many consolation prizes for the Mrs. Bluff is that she's starting her own foundation. She's even borrowing a couple of our people to get started. It's unclear, but it sounds like she might be into the sensational, big-headline items in women's-rights philanthropy—sex trafficking, FGM, and also stuff like 'women's empowerment,' micro-enterprise, self-esteem . . ." Meg trailed off.

"Sounds promising!" Jen said.

"It's . . . diffuse, at best. They're looking for a communications person. Best-case scenario, you get a blank slate and fill it in however you want. Worst-case scenario, it's a silly stopgap until the dark times are over. Either way, though, would it be weird to be employed by a divorce settlement?"

"What's actually weird is that I think last month Jim and I spent more money on cat food than people food," Jen said, swallowing. She had once again broken a rule she'd tried to set for conversations with Meg: that talking about something being expensive was sometimes okay, but talking about *money*—actual units of currency unto themselves, as opposed to how many units of those currency might be required to make a particular purchase—was not okay.

"Well, let me get you hooked up with the hiring people," Meg said. "And send me your résumé again—you changed the font on it, right?"

"Yes," Jen said. Meg felt that the loops on the *g*'s and *q*'s on a previous iteration of Jen's résumé were too large, connoting flightiness, and that the spacing between characters was too ample, connoting stand-offishness.

"And wait a second," Meg said. "You know who the Mrs. Bluff is, right?"

"Um," Jen said. "She's on TV?"

Who She Is to You

Leora Infinitas, aka the Mrs. Bluff, the founder of LIFt, was born Leeza Infanzia in Jacksonville, Florida, in 1960, on the same day John F. Kennedy was elected president of the United States. As Ruby Stevens-Meisel—pseudonymous sole proprietor of the gossip and philosophy website *DOPENHAUER* and her generation's leading Infinitas scholar—wrote in her magnum opus, "Leora Infinitas Is the Fulcrum of the Universe," "The fates chose an auspicious day to launch a life that would know both triumph and tragedy. One of the first tragedies—and first opportunities for triumph—was one of nomenclature. *Leeza Infanzia* was a name both bombastic and belittling—*Leeza* a bastardized diminutive, and when paired with *Infanzia* taking on the bathos of a Raphael Madonna-and-child rendered as a refrigerator magnet."

"I was chubby. I wasn't cute," Leora Infinitas once said of her childhood self. "I wasn't an easy child to love, visually."

Barely out of her teens, Leeza Infanzia moved to Los Angeles, signing up for acting and dance auditions under her new name, Leora Infinitas. "Her name, its meaning, was now a speech act: *I am infinite light*," Stevens-Meisel wrote. "She is beacon and power source; she is an illuminated manuscript. And yet this new text knowingly slant-rhymed with *Leeza Infanzia*—not leaving Leeza in the dark but rather shining a light through the palimpsest that is *Leora Infinitas,* paying tribute to the young woman who was not (yet) a mother, who first had to give (re)birth to herself."

Leora Infinitas got bit roles in procedural television dramas and could be spotted, for three and a half seconds, two dancers behind Lionel Richie in the "All Night Long" video. Her breakthrough role arrived at the end of the 1980s: Trudy Wheeler née Gunderson, the brassy, no-nonsense wife to a nutty inventor and mother to his two sons on the sitcom *Father of Invention* née *Inventing the Wheelers.* Trudy spent the next eight years tripping over circuit boards powering cold-fusion experiments conducted on vintage Blue Comet train sets and prat-falling over domino structures that climaxed in the fusion of copper wire and silver nitrate. And each time Trudy found a fleet of white lab mice using her pantry as a buffet spread or that the boys had swapped her shampoo for disappearing ink, at the moment of recognition, she would deliver her catchphrase: "I am out; I am dunzo."

The genius of Leora Infinitas—or the part of her genius that helped make her a muse for drag performers, but only once *Father of Invention* had moldered in syndication for years, "only once the wine of Leora had aged," Stevens-Meisel wrote, "only once the complex chemical equation of Leora had intensified its flavor compounds"—was in her ability to find variation upon variation in those mere seven syllables. "I am out; I am dunzo" could deliver rat-tat-tat staccato frustration. "I am out; I am dunzo" could sound a howl of despair. "I am out; I am dunzo" could be a sigh of exhaustion, or a bleat of coquettish bemusement, or a fond surrender to the ineffable lovability of her three charges, no matter how many times they exploded her oven.

Celebrity-magazine editors and talk-show bookers relished the visual contrast between Trudy-Leora (patterned sweatshirts, high-waisted jeans) and Leora-Leora, who wore lots of red: red lips, red stilettos, diaphanous bias-cut red silk, a biker jacket in artery blast. Over time, the contrast faded. In later seasons of *Father of Invention*, the viewer may have paused over why Trudy would need five-inch stilettos and a blowout to clean the always-exploding oven. By then Leora had married Brent Simons, the twenty-five-years-older creator of the show and its equally lucrative spinoff *Son of a Gunderson*, and Leora had borne his two youngest children on a schedule that mapped onto *Father of Invention*'s summer hiatus. "In all things," Stevens-Meisel wrote, "Leora had a sense of timing—or like light itself, she transcended time."

Leora Infinitas, sitcom star, won wacky supporting parts in ensemble comedy films, voice-over roles in video games, her own jewelry and makeup lines. Her divorce from Simons was amicable, save for one spectacular conflagration over a koi pond surrounded by faux-Bernini figures depicting moments of sexual enslavement in Roman mythology, a conflict simultaneously so melodramatic, so inane, and so at odds with its otherwise affable context that Ruby Stevens-Meisel hypothesized that the whole episode was a bit of publicity-enhancing theater ahead of the premiere of her new reality show, *Leora's World*, a hypnotic chronicle of her flinty encounters with her staff and/or friends, with her sulky pair of preteen daughters, and with her would-be colleagues in her nascent quest to become a "philanthropy innovator."

When Leora and Brent Simons split up, the tabloid headlines read DUNZO. When she married Charles Bluff—he of the railroad Bluffs, he of the onetime-third-largest-private-landowners-in-the-northeast– United States Bluffs, he of the impeccable Bluff Foundation Bluffs, to which all other would-be boldface philanthropy innovators aspired— the headlines read DUNZO NO MORE. The chasm of class was a subtext of both the marriage and *Leora's World* itself, most noticeably during the second season's sixth episode, which was built around Leora's thwarted efforts to corner the septuagenarian financier's widow, revered art patron, *Mayflower* and Mitford descendant, and noted shy person Flossie Durbin at a hospital benefit. After filming, representatives of Mrs. Durbin—a trustee of the Bluff Foundation who also happened to blog semiannually about art shows she'd seen and liked—had personally interceded with Charles Bluff to have all references to Mrs. Durbin excised from the final broadcast.

"What this strange and bowdlerized episode tells us," Stevens-Meisel wrote in one of her exhaustive scene-by-scene recaps of *Leora's World*, "is that even a six-carat imprimatur of legal entry into a Citadel of extreme wealth and privilege cannot succeed in dazzling its true residents. Leora's world is not one and the same with that forbidding fortress—she may be *in* it, but she is not (yet) *of* it."

Like Trudy, the Leora of *Leora's World* had her very own catchphrase, uttered spontaneously a few times to a soon-to-be-fired wedding planner, and then encouraged by producers. The catchphrase: "Who am I to you?" While "I am out; I am dunzo" was subject to endless variation, "Who am I to you?" had one correct intonation: the smallest susurrating pause on the *Who*, the *am I to you* a torrent, a rapids. The catchphrase nailed Leora's charisma—it was both narcissistic and solicitous; it demanded an account of her Leora-ness and acknowledged her need for acknowledgment. "Examined over five seasons of *Leora's World, Who am I to you?* interrogated the erosion of a woman's identity when that identity has been built on beauty, desirability—the currency of youth," Stevens-Meisel wrote. "By the end of the show's run, however, Leora's newfound identity as a philanthropic innovator with a sparkling new foundation had rendered the question moot. We no longer lived in *Leora's World*. Now Leora belonged to the world."

Foundations

The Leora Infinitas Foundation, also known as LIFt, will work tirelessly to support women's education, entrepreneurship, and empowerment all over the world. We will acknowledge that no matter where they are on the planet—in a village in sub-Saharan Africa, in a corner office in Shanghai, or at a kitchen table in Des Moines—women share the same hopes, the same dreams for themselves and their children. We may sometimes seem far apart culturally and geographically, but our similarities are so much vaster than our differences. We women—all of us women—can own the means of production, with a cross-platform multimedia foundation. We can lift each other up.

That's what the "LIFt Yourself" concept is all about. Women in the developing world and women here "at home," fulfilling their dreams, helping one another fulfill those dreams, and discovering our common ground.

Speaking personally for a moment: I take this word *foundation* literally. This is the foundation of everything I do: communication, conversation, transformation. It is the foundation of my identity as a woman, as a mother, as a communicator. One message across all platforms, consistent, solid, through and through.

—from the first draft of the "Proposed Platform of the
Leora Infinitas Foundation (LIFt)," by Leora Infinitas in
collaboration with Donna Skinner

Indulge Me

Karina—LIFt
Friday, March 27 5:15 PM
To: Jen <Jenski1848@gmail.com>
Subject: Happiness!

Dearest Jen, I'm so thrilled you've accepted the position here at LIFt. I'm sure Leora is sorry she couldn't make it for our chat, but I'm also sure she's just so amped to meet you. Promise me that, on your first day, you'll let me take you out for a proper lunch—an old-school, glamorous, steak-and-wine lunch. We should celebrate! Indulge me? xo K.

Jen <Jenski1848@gmail.com>
Friday, March 27 5:19 PM
To: Karina—LIFt
Subject: Re: Happiness!

Karina,

I'd be thrilled to! I'm so excited to be joining LIFt. You've already extended such a warm welcome! Very grateful—and looking forward to lunch.

All my best,

Jen

Solidarity

"Remember," Meg had said, "don't accept the first offer."

"Number one," Jen had said, "obviously I won't, and two, we are not there yet."

"Just don't accept the first offer. Write that on your hand. Leave notes around the house. Chant it before you go to sleep."

"Oh my God," Jen had said.

"You negotiated, yes?" Meg was saying now. Jen could hear Millie trilling in the background over the phone line.

"Um," Jen said.

"You didn't."

"I'm unemployed! Or I was."

"So you just took whatever they offered?"

"What position was I in to negotiate? Did I have a matching offer from the unemployment office?"

"A lot of places would have rescinded the offer the moment you accepted without negotiating. They would see it—and look, I'm not necessarily agreeing with this, I'm just telling you—they would see it as a sign that you're—that you're not—well, it doesn't matter."

"No, what? A sign that I'm not what?"

"It doesn't matter. I'm sorry. This is good news. I'm happy for you. I am."

"You have to finish that sentence. A sign that I'm not what?"

Meg sighed. Millie hooted. "That you're not a *fighter*, that you don't fight for yourself. Which in your case is *not true*. I'm just saying."

"But wait," Jen said. "Isn't it a sign of solidarity with the organization to take less money from them? Like I'm looking out for their best interests at a time of financial uncertainty? You could see it that way, couldn't you?"

"Yes," Meg said, "you could choose to see it that way."

Oof

Jen <Jenski1848@gmail.com>
Monday, April 6 9:14 AM
To: Karina—LIFt
Subject: Re: Happiness!

Good morning, Karina! I was having trouble getting buzzed in, so I sneaked in with a UPS guy—hope that's okay! I've parked myself on a couch in reception. Do you happen to know where my desk is located? Or someone else who could help? Sorry to bother you with these mundane matters. And most important: Are we still on for lunch today? Thanks!—Jen

Break in Case of Emergency

Jen <Jenski1848@gmail.com>
Monday, April 6 11:47 AM
To: Karina—LIFt
Subject: Re: Happiness!

Hey Karina, I knocked on your door earlier, but I think you were on a call.
My wonderful new colleague Daisy found a cubicle for me and is helping me
get on the grid. Let me know when you have time to chat today—does lunch
still work? Thanks, Jen

Jen <Jenski1848@gmail.com>
Monday, April 6 3:52 PM
To: Karina—LIFt
Subject: Re: Happiness!

Hey Karina, things are humming along here, but I will need your sign-off
before I can log on to my computer and get set up with email. You might
have noticed that John from building IT has been calling you—his extension
is 25233—and all he needs is a signature to get us going here. Thanks, Jen

Karina—LIFt
Monday, April 6 4:52 PM
To: Jen <Jenski1848@gmail.com>
Subject: Re: Happiness!

Belatedly, welcome, Jen! Sooo glad you're here. Been slammed all day and
need to run—tell Jon yes it's fine—and send me days for lunch. :)

Jen <Jenski1848@gmail.com>
Monday, April 6 4:55 PM
To: Karina—LIFt
Subject: Re: Happiness!

No worries! John does actually need a signature, but it can totally wait until tomorrow. For lunch, how about tomorrow, Wednesday, or Thursday? Have a great evening! Thanks, Jen

Jen <Jenski1848@gmail.com>
Tuesday, April 7 9:22 AM
To: Karina—LIFt
Subject: Re: Happiness!

Hey Karina, great to chat with you in person, even if briefly! Will definitely get that memo to Sunny about responding to the board's latest brainstorms— really excited to dig in there. You asked me again to send you days for lunch— how about Wednesday? Also, not sure if your original proposal of "steak and wine" was intended as a literal menu or not, but I've never been to Staley's Steakhouse, and I'd be tickled to experience it for the first time. The buttery leather booths, the all-star mural of celebrity caricatures on the walls, the presence of octogenarian talent agents—it all screams old-school cheeseball glamour, at least to me. If we want something lighter, there's a really good vegan place—and by that I do mean "really good," not just "really good for a vegan place"—one block up from Staley's where the un-burger is better than the un-un thing and the cashew ice cream rivals the hard stuff. Or, if this lovely weather holds, we could just grab-and-go from the dumpling truck and sit in the plaza! Looking forward—Jen

Jen <Jenski1848@gmail.com>
Wednesday, April 8 11:38 AM
To: Karina—LIFt
Subject: Re: Happiness!

Hey Karina, are we still on for lunch today?

Karina—LIFt
Wednesday, April 8 12:59 PM
To: Jen <Jenski1848@gmail.com>
Subject: Re: Happiness!

Oof, today is tough—Friday better

Jen <Jenski1848@gmail.com>
Wednesday, April 8 1:02 PM
To: Karina—LIFt
Subject: Re: Happiness!

Sure thing.

Jen—LIFt
Thursday, April 9 4:45 PM
To: Karina—LIFt
Subject: Hello!

Hey Karina, just wanted to let you know that I'm now the proud owner of
an in-house email handle. We still on for lunch tomorrow?

Karina—LIFt
Thursday, April 9 8:58 PM
To: Jen—LIFt
Subject: Re: Hello!

Sure. I'm not a big lunch eater—coffee instead?

Jen—LIFt
Thursday, April 9 9:03 PM
To: Karina—LIFt
Subject: Re: Hello!

Of course. Let's see ... Baccalá has one of those patented stir-brewer machines for minimum acidity—I'm not much of a coffee snob, but drinking that stuff makes me feel like I'm in Monti, about to hop on a Vespa. Q.E.D. is a six-block hike but worth it for the cantuccios, and for the adorable ancient lady who makes the cantuccios. And last time I grabbed a latte at Cake Walk I saw Natalie Portman filming a movie nearby, which is an endorsement unto itself!

Karina—LIFt
Thursday, April 9 10:07 PM
To: Jen—LIFt
Subject: Re: Hello!

There's a Starbucks half a block from the office

Jen—LIFt
Thursday, April 9 10:10 PM
To: Karina—LIFt
Subject: Re: Hello!

Easy enough! Around 3 or 4? That's when I usually need a caffeine infusion.

Karina—LIFt
Thursday, April 9 10:12 PM
To: Jen—LIFt
Subject: Re: Hello!

Let's say 9.30, I have a call at 10

Jen—LIFt
Thursday, April 9 10:14 PM
To: Karina—LIFt
Subject: Re: Hello!

Perfect.

Jen—LIFt
Friday, April 10 9:45 AM
To: Karina—LIFt
Subject: Re: Hello!

Hey, Karina, just wanted to make sure you remembered our coffee date!

Jen—LIFt
Thursday, April 10 10:07 AM
To: Karina—LIFt
Subject: Re: Hello!

Hey, Karina, it's just after 10 and I know you had an important call, so I'm
going to head over to the office—see you soon!

Special Projects

LIFt leased part of an upper floor of a midcentury skyscraper, one whose date of completion coincided with the apotheosis of America's postwar white-man's utopia, an industrial ecstasy synonymous with its Midtown Manhattan location and expressed in the vast and echoing lobby—one that strived for timelessness in its haphazard signifiers, in its Art Deco–ish brassy trims and flourishes, and in the Works Progress Administration swagger of the Diego Rivera–manqué mural behind the elevator bank, in which bulbous-muscled iron workers bore aloft a boyish-looking potentate: yellow forelock, three-piece suit. Once upon a time, salons and way stations and anterooms had hugged the lobby like a golden horseshoe. There was the dining room with the glass chandelier supposedly custom-crafted for Mamie Eisenhower and, mounted on a wall like a stag's head, the jewel-encrusted suit of armor supposedly stolen from the Kremlin, each of which came with bottomless permutations of tales about the past-resident banker, broker, or blueblood newspaper editor who had acquired the items and how. There was the carpeted, split-level commissary, with its subsidized prime rib and its free booze after six p.m. and all day Friday. There were the oddly apportioned conference rooms, dotted with alcoves and tiny partitions. By some historical accounts, these vaults and bowers provided randy executives and their conquests with points of rendezvous that promised both a necessary sense of discretion and a frisson of sex-in-public excitement.

But Jen only knew all this from pictures. The dining room was now a mobile-phone storefront. The dim, sex-soaked recesses of the conference rooms were now the fluorescent-lit dressing rooms of a T.J.Maxx. Nobody knew where the mural had gone. The lobby had shrunk radically in size over the last decade, as the building's owners partitioned it first for a Japanese steakhouse, then an American steakhouse, and then an Outback Steakhouse.

"Are you ever in the lobby," Daisy once asked Jen, "when you stop and think you can smell the burning flesh of end-stage capitalism?"

"No," Jen replied, "but are you ever in the lobby when you hold up your keycard to the sensor on the turnstile, and instead of a beep, you hear the bleating of a little lost lamb being led to slaughter?"

"Yes," Daisy replied.

Jen and Daisy worked at the geographic center of LIFt's operations, in what Jen estimated to be the precise spot on the entire office floor that was simultaneously farthest away from the women's bathroom, farthest from the main exit, and farthest from the nearest unobstructed window. They shared a cubicle wall, which Daisy interpreted as a canvas for her rotating collages of Shetland ponies wearing Shetland-wool sweaters, baby sloths in tiny macramé hats, and root vegetables that resembled religious icons. Sometimes Daisy would engage the baby sloths in a visual dialogue with photos cut out of gossip magazines of disheveled starlets exiting various nightclubs.

Jen's title at LIFt was Communications Manager and Co-Director, Special Projects. Daisy's title at LIFt was Senior Program Officer and Co-Director, Special Projects. Neither of them could have always stated with certainty which projects they were intended to manage, officiate, or codirect, or which qualities made any particular project special. LIFt convened sporadic meetings, wherein Karina condensed her cumuli of verbiage while finger-combing her hair and Donna riffed on *vision* and *intentionality* and *passion* and Sunny headbanged and Jen, always by last-minute request, took notes as well as tried to think of something to say to introduce whatever new memo that Karina or Sunny had most recently asked her to draw up, whether it was the "Old Programs" memo or the "New Programs" memo or the "Building on Past Success" memo or the "International Applications of the 'LIFt Yourself' Concept" memo or the "Programs to 'LIFt Yourself'" memo— until Leora had another appointment or, occasionally, when it became clear that Leora would not be attending at all or, on one occasion, when Sunny realized ten minutes after the scheduled start of the meeting that at that very moment Leora was in Dubai, presiding at the opening of a jewelry store as part of the promotional tour for her skin-care line, LeoraDiance™.

As volubly pointless as these memos and meetings tended to be, preparing the memos occupied the bulk of Jen's hours in the office, and the meetings themselves represented Jen's only in-person time with the women she assumed were busy running LIFt. Donna, Karina, and Sunny had a block of offices on the south side of the floor, with Leora's corner suite tucked safely behind Sunny's perch. Jen and Daisy were stationed on the east side of the floor, estranged from the rest of the LIFt braintrust by a giant stack of empty filing cabinets, a row of empty offices, and an underpopulated maze of cubicles occupied by a smattering of other indeterminately engaged LIFt contractors, most reliably Petra, a freelance graphic designer whose metonym was the black extension cord that snaked from an electrical socket above the ladies' room sink down to the linoleum floor and under the handicap stall, where it powered the *HUNGH-guk HUNGH-guk* of Petra's breast pump twenty to twenty-five minutes at a time, three to four times a day.

The glare from the reflected light of the glass-and-titanium bee-hive skin of the building opposite made Jen and Daisy's computer screens effectively inoperative between nine-thirty and ten-thirty a.m. each day.

If Karina was in the office, her door was closed.

Jen—LIFt
Wednesday, May 20 10:15 AM
To: Karina—LIFt
Subject: Hi!

Hey Karina,
I know you've been super-busy, but I was wondering if you might be able to spare even a few minutes in the next few days to discuss what I should be prioritizing going forward. I'm raring to get started, but want to make sure I'm pointed in the right direction first. Let me know when works for you. Thanks,

Karina! And we should include Daisy, too—she's awesome and I know she has tons of smart ideas and research.

> Looking forward,
> Jen

> Jen—LIFt
> Thursday, May 21 5:12 PM
> To: Karina—LIFt
> Subject: FW: Hi!

> Hey Karina, sorry to be a pest about this, just wanted to make sure you received my message from yesterday—thanks!—Jen
> —————Forwarded message—————

Major Brainstorm Mode

Daisy was on Facebook playing Socialist Revolution, where she'd just been appointed the mayor of the Politburo Standing Commission on Internal Affairs. Jen had her earbuds in to watch a video of Leora's recent interview with British socialite and "roving entertainment correspondent" Suzy Coxswain, who had made recurring appearances on *Father of Invention* as Fiona, Trudy's ribald Cockney friend.

> *Suzy Coxswain:* LIFt Foundation—it kind of sounds like makeup, haha!
> *Leora Infinitas:* Well, it's not the LIFt Foundation—it's just LIFt. *Foundation* is the *F* in *LIFt*.

Suzy Coxswain: Too bad, haha! I could use a bit of a lift, haha. Feeling a bit *jowly.*

Leora Infinitas: You are beautiful, Suzy, inside and out.

Suzy Coxswain: Oh, bless.

Leora Infinitas: And that's the message of LIFt. If that sounds cheesy, well, call me cheesy! What's wrong with being a little cheesy, anyway—what are we so afraid of?

Suzy Coxswain: Well—

Leora Infinitas: You know, Suzy, I think a lot about the word *integration.* Because women can feel torn in so many different directions. Maybe a woman is grappling with not liking what she sees in the mirror in the morning. And maybe she's having problems with a friend, or some kind of a conflict at work. *And* maybe she just saw something on the news about the, you know, the humanitarian crisis in Somalia, and feeling so helpless because she wants to *do* something, but she doesn't know what.

Suzy Coxswain: She just doesn't know! Not even where to start!

Leora Infinitas: Right. *All* of these things are important. We can't rank them. What we can do is, number one, *integrate* them, and number two, start a conversation about them with other women. That's what LIFt is about. You have children, of course, Suzy?

Suzy Coxswain: Do I! Three boys, still holding out for that girl, haha.

Leora Infinitas: Okay, so motherhood is a fundamental strength that we somehow twist into a fundamental conflict: Am I a woman first or a mother first? Well, my answer is *yes.* What comes first, home or work or the world outside my window? My answer is *yes.* How does being a mother influence my ethics? My answer is *yes.* How do I put my children first *and* put the children of the developing world first, too? My answer is *yes.*

Suzy Coxswain: Well, sure, but okay, playing devil's advocate for a moment—your kids are *your* kids. They're yours; they're different, haha.

Leora Infinitas: I don't see them as so different. And I don't see
  other women as so different from you and me, Suzy. I think if
  we come together we can be everybody's mother. I know that
  sounds so presumptuous!

"Daisy," Jen said without removing her earbuds.

"Hang on, I've been denounced as a Trotskyite," Daisy said.

"I think you need to see this," Jen said.

"Am I bothering you ladies?"

Jen turned in her seat to see Karina standing inches away, shrugging emphatically into a lightweight trench coat. "Karina, hi!" Jen exclaimed at a high pitch. She pawed at the buds in her ears, swatting them to the floor. As she reached over to pick them up, the wheels of her chair rolled over the cord, trapping the earbuds on the carpet. Jen paused for a second, doubled over, then hoisted her ass off the seat, pushed up at the bottom of the seat with her left hand until the wheels left the carpet, and grabbed the buds with her right hand. Jen moved to sit up again, but again the cord went taut before she was fully upright, this time because it had wound itself around the stem of the chair. Jen folded the buds in her lap and looked up at Karina from this slightly hunched position.

"How many kulaks do you think are left in that village, Comrade Daisy?" Karina was asking in the tone of a saucy conspirator, leaning jauntily against the stack of empty filing cabinets that loomed behind Jen's desk.

Daisy looked over her shoulder, nodded at Karina, and turned back to her computer screen.

Karina winked at Jen and mouthed *Love her!*, rolling her eyes and lashing her tongue across her front teeth on *Love*. Jen wondered if Karina was being sarcastic or sincere, and also if Karina herself knew.

"Sorry for stalking you with all the emails!" Jen said. She hoped her temporary hunchback scanned as warm, inviting body language—a plant leaning toward light.

Karina cocked her head and clucked neutrally. "Hey, can't knock persistence."

"So, what I was thinking—" Jen started.

"All I can tell you is that we—the board, the staff, the whole team—we are in major brainstorm-and-research mode right now," Karina said. "Lightning and thunder, fire and brimstone, category-five brainstorms. And research. And I've gotta say"—Karina pulled her bottom lip down from clenched teeth and looked sidelong with bugged-out eyes, as if she were being groped against her will—"Leora does *naahht* seem too happy with how we've been stormin' her brain so far."

"Oh, wow, okay, we can fix that," Jen said, nodding rapidly, bugging out her eyes in mirroring solidarity. Karina looked over Jen's stooped shoulder, and Jen wondered if Leora and Suzy were still bantering silently on the screen behind her. "Any specifics on what Leora isn't happy with?" Jen asked, maneuvering her chair slightly with the aim of using her own bent head to block her computer screen from Karina's view. "Does she want ideas about messaging for our programs, or messaging ideas for the website itself—should I prioritize one over the other?"

"I really don't see why we need to *exclude*," said Karina, her gaze still trained over Jen's shoulder. "She just wants more ideas, more research. The more the merrier."

"Right, of course, but what about all the ideas and research I've—we've submitted so far?" Jen asked, bobbing and weaving her head slightly in an attempt to cover more of the screen space behind her.

"Nobody's knocking your work, Jen," Karina said. "It's *not* about that, okay?"

"Oh, no, I wasn't saying that—sorry, I'm not being clear. I guess if I knew which ideas and research Leora liked and disliked so far— whether or not the research and ideas were mine!—then I would know how to proceed from here," Jen said. "I mean, she's so busy, maybe she hasn't even gotten to them yet, which would be totally understandable, obviously—"

"Your work is *good*," Karina said. "Like anything else, there's stuff that really sparkles and stuff that could be better."

"Right, okay, thanks, that's good to hear," Jen said. "What could be better?"

"Well, I'm not a mind reader—you'd have to ask Leora," Karina said.

"That would be great, actually—I can ask Sunny to set up some time."

"*Naahht* too sure she'd have the bandwidth for something like that right now," Karina said. "Though I can certainly *try* to bring it up with her."

"You know," Jen said, "it's crazy, but Leora and I still haven't even met!" The second this fell out, Jen realized the error she had made.

Karina nodded pensively. "You know, I'm curious. If you are asked for three ideas on how to message a LIFt concept, do you come up with ten ideas, and present what you think are the best three? Or do you only come up with three ideas and just present those?"

"Oh, gosh, I don't know. It depends."

"Interesting. So sometimes you're just presenting the first things that pop into your head? Kinda seat-of-the-pants?"

"Oh, no, I wouldn't do that. There's probably always a whittling process."

"Interesting. But then there's the question of how you determine the best three out of ten. How do you know that you're not hiding your brightest light under a bushel? Do you trust us to see the ideas you want to hide?"

"Oh, it's not about hiding—it's always different." Jen sat up straight, still holding the earbud cord, severing it with a muffled *pop*. "You know, I'm sorry to harp on this"—Jen laughed right here, as she often did with Karina, and Jen always imagined these laughs as having mass and taking up space, but plush mass, deferential mass, a comfy cushion to soften any demand or contradictory opinion—"but it would be so amazing, just in terms of time management, to have a little bit of feedback on all the work I've done so far. I mean, if that's possible. I completely understand if—"

"I'm giving you feedback right now," Karina said.

"Of course, but—"

"Here's your feedback in a nutshell: More, more, more!" Karina said. "How's that for a vote of confidence? Just assume that there's an *insatiable* appetite for your ideas and your efforts right now. What you have to remember around messaging is that this is a *collaboration*."

"Oh, sure, I know—wait, what does that mean?"

"It means that we don't hunker down in our hidey-holes guarding our turf. We're all in this together, sharing ideas, bouncing ideas off one another. Collaboration and sharing."

"I didn't—"

"I've *gotta* run, Jen," Karina said, turning to leave and waggling her fingers over her shoulder. "Gotta tend to the spawn."

Jen cushion-laughed. "Oh, for sure, you've gotta do that!"

The Existential Question of Why We Are Here

Leora Infinitas's fondness for fortuitous acronyms began but did not end with the name of her foundation, and often a LIFt initiative began and ended with the spark of an inspired abbreviation. Leora proposed a proposal for an "edu-preneurial summit" on the global rise of web-based autodidacticism, to be called Women Inspired for Self-Education (WISE). She proposed a proposal for a series of webinars "reintroducing busy women across the world to their neglected love affair with the REM cycle," to be called Women's Initiative for Sleep Hygiene (WISH). She proposed a proposal for a Skype-enabled encounter group session covering seven continents—"McMurdo Station, we haven't forgotten you!" Sunny exclaimed—on "kicking our sex drives into top gear," to be called Women Empowered to Love their Libido (WELL). This bounty of acronyms took a turn toward the demotic after Leora, having just served as grand marshal at a drag queen parade in Grand Rapids, Michigan, returned to the LIFt offices with an idea for a body-acceptance campaign, to be called the Women's Endeavor for Realism and Kindness! (WERK!).

"Have you ever suspected that you had a fake job at a fake organization, and you could be found out at any time?" Jen asked Jim.

"If I ever did, a ten-year-old who hasn't eaten breakfast at home in a year would kick me in the shins and snap me out of it," Jim said.

Karina would relay Leora's ideas to Jen and Daisy, and Jen and Daisy would then spend many hours researching potential LIFt grantees doing work that overlapped with Leora's acronym du jour and writing bulleted, footnoted summaries of each potential grantee and coming up with copy and branding and infographics and focus-grouping for the proposed projects, even though they knew that the acronyms were ends in themselves—game plans for a Game Over. Daisy, much more than Jen, reacted to Leora's bounty of acronyms in a spirit of reciprocity. She ideated "a mosaic of learned spiritual responses to the existential question of why we are here" called the Women's Ontology of Nurturing Karma (WONK) as well as a pan-global crafts-and-baked-goods bazaar called the Women's Harvest of Outrageous Awesomeness (WHOA). Seizing the opportunity presented by one of Leora's ever-more-infrequent office visits, Daisy walked right up to Leora outside the ladies' room to pitch her acronyms—a bold, possibly unprecedented move by a non–board member, and one that Jen watched from across the office while gnawing on alternate thumbnails.

"She's nicer than everyone says," Daisy later reported.

Nonetheless, Leora had rejected WONK and WHOA on the spot, calling out WHOA in particular as "jejune." Jen and Daisy didn't know what *jejune* meant until they looked it up.

"Maybe not knowing what *jejune* means is a symptom of being *jejune*," Daisy said.

Daisy later turned her attentions from acronyms to anagrams— spending the better part of one weekend crossing out the letters of LEORA INFINITAS FOUNDATION to create ADROIT FELON IS IN A FOUNTAIN—but not before designing and silkscreening T-shirts advertising Women in Crisis Constructing Acronyms (WICCA), illustrated with a kitten in a witch's hat scrambling the letters on a Scrabble board.

Zen Rand

Jen climbed off her paint-splattered stepladder, rotating her shoulder in its socket and stifling a mewl of pain. She had been standing atop the stepladder at the back of Pam's studio for two hours straight, the elbow of her painting arm propped in her opposite palm, doing minutely detailed blending brushwork on a head-and-shoulders portrait of an enormous happy teen: floppy, rust-colored cowlick; glinting rectangle-smile full of braces; the color of his hoodie a spectacularly verdant marriage of cadmium yellow and ultramarine. Coaxing a person out of a driver's license photo or a magazine clipping and onto the canvas, finding the fabric of its shadows and inventing its light, was scary and exciting. She loved the loamy certitude of unmixed oils, their textures of soil and blood tissue, and the sense of unthinking command and casual mastery she felt in mixing them. She loved the unalloyed physicality of tracing the final images' outlines in graphite, of laying down the underpainting and base coats. But once she had found the shadows and the light and the colors, and all she had left were the hours upon hours of documenting—transcribing—what she had already found, then a portrait could become at times a maddening exercise in high-level painting-by-numbers: cognitively demanding enough to forestall zoning out, but not nearly demanding enough to assuage an internal tedium that, mixed with increasing physical discomfort, began to quake in a manner not unlike that of rage.

"We should go outside," said Pam, pitching her voice across the room and above the *shish-shish* leaking out of her earbuds. She sat in silhouette against the late-spring sun shining through the studio's front windows. She wore a coffee-colored romper and a headband festooned with miniature plastic sunflowers and a pair of stacked-heel clogs, the purpose of which was mostly ornamental. Her leg, a latticework of healing scars wrapped in a Navajo blanket, was propped on another stepladder and a stack of old *Vogues* as she tapped steadily away on her laptop.

Jen had already made vague, gentle entreaties about what greater artistic good her jumbo portraits would be serving: the redheaded teen orthodontics patient, the randy-looking senior couple, the ecstatic-looking doctor draped in a hijab and a stethoscope. But Pam just as vaguely and gently rebuffed these entreaties. Through sheer proximity and osmosis, Jen had deduced that Pam's new project had something to do with her cycling accident and her subsequent, interminable dealings with WellnessSolutions, her health insurance provider.

Jen walked across the echoing studio and lay down on a yoga mat stranded on the floor next to Pam. She arched her back into an askew bridge pose and stared at the pert upside-down chin and the froggy upside-down legs, respectively, of a giddy mother holding her giddy infant—the portrait Jen had finished the previous weekend, propped against another wall.

"We should go outside," Jen agreed, her pelvis jutting crookedly into the stale studio air. "I just need to clean my brushes first."

"So you haven't told me anything yet about Leora Infinitas," Pam said, typing, earbuds still in place.

"I haven't actually met her. I've been in the same room with her."

"Tell me about that."

"Top contender for hall-of-fame moment so far is when she took a lengthy call from her professional organizer during a staff meeting."

"That's astonishing," Pam said flatly, typing.

"I think she just forgot she wasn't alone, or whatever her version of alone is."

"Do you like Leora Infinitas?"

"I guess so. I at least get the impression that she's trying to do good."

"Do good for who?"

"Her aims are—diffuse," Jen said. "Hopefully she'll narrow her focus down as she gets her bearings."

"Shouldn't you be working for, like, Melinda Gates, or the Ford Foundation?" asked Pam, taking out her earbuds and setting her laptop on the floor. "Or maybe you don't even have to work for anyone. You and Meg could just start your own thing."

"Someday we'll all be working for Meg," Jen said.

"I always imagined the two of you teaming up and changing the world," Pam said. "I still do."

Pam's deadpan mien, almost monotone voice, and refined aesthetics bought her a wider margin for occasional sentimentality than Jen might have tolerated in others, particularly because Pam's affect was so spare and inscrutable that it was difficult to reconcile it with any excess of tenderness, even for her two closest friends.

Each of the three of them had always paired off the other two as a dyad, a clean deuce—spiritual twins who had accepted a false triplet into their orbit out of the very qualities of magnanimity and open-mindedness that they shared as eternal monozygotic double-souls. To Meg, Pam and Jen were the artists, the creatives; to Pam, Meg and Jen were the Samaritan wonks, advocating with serene forcefulness on behalf of the less fortunate.

But to Jen, Meg and Pam were the competents. Their stores of education and know-how took shape in Jen's mind like a rambling country estate, forever revealing new trapdoors and hidden parlors and Escher-like staircases descending toward a secret bookcase wall behind which lay another library, another music room. In college, both of them could whip up a borderline delicious four a.m. dinner from whatever scraps and remnants happened to be in the pantry of wherever they were smoking pot and watching a VHS marathon of *Twin Peaks* that particular Saturday night. Both of them could repair a torn hem with some thread and a safety pin; both could tie a man's tie and play "Love Will Tear Us Apart" on the piano and knew how to finagle the connection on a blown fuse by wrapping tin foil around it. They remembered the names of birds and plants and rock formations. They had read everything. It was teenaged Meg who taught Jen the basics of how a charitable foundation should be run. It was teenaged Pam who taught Jen how to scale a skillful small portrait onto a giant canvas.

And both of them, it seemed to Jen, somehow cultivated entire other galaxies of social ties—not just a smattering of a few other close friends and a larger group of fond acquaintances, as Jen had maintained in the decade after college, but discrete worlds unto themselves. Pam pursued email-and-coffee-date relationships with any artist, writer, or random person at a party she found interesting, with no fear of her interest going unreciprocated or being misinterpreted as a romantic overture; before her accident, she seemed to make the time to attend every opening, every reading, every event relevant to her ambitions. Meg arranged her regular reunions with her friends from boarding school and closely manned her complex circuit board of professional contacts, all of whom seemed to invite Meg to their weddings and their children's weddings.

Jen's guiding image of Meg and Pam, though the passage of years had faded and likely altered it, was of the two of them platonically entwined on a sofa at a crowded off-campus house party, heads pressed together, murmuring to each other as they people-watched, as if they were invisible to everyone else who was surreptitiously watching them back, including then-current boyfriends—nervously hovering, faintly aroused—and Jen.

"JEN!" Meg called as she noticed Jen opening a beer at the drinks table. Meg unwrapped herself from Pam and reached her arms out. "Salt of my earth, fire of my loins." Her voice was softened, not quite slurred, by beer and fatigue.

"Jeennnniieeeee," Pam called, clapping her palms on her knees as Jen moved to settle herself at their feet. "I want to braid your hair."

Her fingers, like Meg's voice, were thickened with alcohol, but she managed a hairline braid that rolled along the back of Jen's neck and finished in a loose yet intricate knot. Jen slept facedown for two nights to keep it.

Jen sat up on the mat in Pam's studio, stretched her legs flat, and reached out to touch her toes. "I think Meg could change the world," she said. "I don't know that Leora will. She could, if she wanted to. She has the money and the contacts. She means well." Jen pulled her knees up to her chest and dropped her head against them. "And that could have, you know," she said, her voice muffled in her thighs, "a good effect on lots of things."

"I watched *Leora's World* a lot when I was laid up," Pam said. "I even read her autobiography."

"Why in the world did you do that?"

"I couldn't watch TV all day and I needed easy things to read. It was entertaining. It was quite something, actually."

"I have to admit, her worldview is this weird jumble of Buddhism and libertarianism."

"It's like a yoga teacher rewriting *The Fountainhead*."

"Yes! My colleague Daisy calls it 'Zen Rand.' Like, 'Let me help you discover that the government shouldn't help you and neither should I because nobody helped me, but I'm starting a foundation to help people anyway. Namaste.'"

"Right," Pam said. "But lots of people helped her."

"Yeah," Jen said, "but maybe charisma is measured in contradictions."

"Whatever, I'm happy for you," Pam said. "I am."

"Thanks," Jen said, looking up at Pam.

"You know, get out of it whatever you can get out of it," Pam said.

"Yeah."

"So we don't have to talk about this if you don't want to talk about it, but just in case you do want to talk about it," Pam said, "do you want to talk about the Project?"

The Project

Pam was the only person not assigned to the Project who knew about its existence. Jen and Jim were the Project's principal architects ("I prefer *product managers*," Jim said). By mutual tacit agreement, Jen and

Jim never spoke in explicit terms about it; the first, unspoken rule of the Project was not to call any procedure, implement, or site related to the Project by its actual name. Jen and Jim had grown fastidious about this rule without interrogating why they had ever instated it in the first place. In the beginning it was just a nervous tic, or a way of imagining themselves apart from their situation. Now the rule was like protective outer gear. A shield against inclement weather. A prophylactic.

They embarked on the Project with some degree of ambivalence, propelled forward largely because Jen, having breached the threshold of thirty without yet crossing the Rubicon of thirty-five, thus found herself in the epoch that women's magazines, morning talk shows, mutual acquaintances, miscellaneous cousins and sisters-in-law, and occasional prolix strangers on the subway had agreed on as the preferred window for all Project launches. Jen and Jim's ambivalence tipped into bland relief when the Project did not launch immediately, granting them more time to adjust to the idea of a hypothetical tiny future boarder. But as month after month passed, and as months somehow metastasized into years, relief curdled into tantric panic. They had not known what they wanted, or how much they wanted it, until they discovered that it was not necessarily theirs for the taking.

At first, Jen and Jim worked on the Project in the traditional manner: by themselves, in secret, mostly at home. After about a year, they had tapped outside consultants with medical degrees to explore methods for expediting the Project. The Project halted during Jen's sojourn in the valley of joblessness, but gainful employment and, more to the point, gainful employer-provided health insurance had redoubled her enthusiasm for the Project. They referred to Jen's many Project-related appointments as "trips to the henhouse" and sometimes as "black-box testing." Jim's significantly less frequent Project-related obligations were "swim meets" or occasionally "speed trials."

Gainful employment and gainful employer-provided health insurance had also redoubled Jen's enthusiasm for her Animexa prescription, although licensed professionals had warned her that even small doses of central-nervous-system stimulants would be incompatible with Project completion. Meanwhile, Jim prepared for his swim meets by taking up a diet of sautéed spinach and lean chicken and adopting an at-home wardrobe of size-too-large boxer shorts and the occasional sarong, all the better for producing "new obsolete stock" stored at sub-zero temperatures in "Han Solo's Carbonite Tomb."

Jen told herself that she had designated Pam as the Project's sole outside observer because she knew all Pam would do is lend an ear, observe without judgment. She knew that Pam's still-ongoing medical odyssey would keep in check Jen's self-pity or irritation about the end-less trips back and forth to the henhouse. Jen also knew that if she had designated the only other viable candidate, Meg, as a Project observer, that Meg probably would have urged her to take trips instead to a newer, swankier, more high-tech, probably out-of-network henhouse, and switch to a diet largely made up of kale, cranberries, almonds, and peanut butter, and do other things for which Jen had no energy such as acupuncture and cognitive behavioral therapy and not chewing gum and not occasionally breaking off half an Animexa tablet before writing a research memo for an upcoming LIFt meeting.

But if Jen was being honest, she would admit she picked Pam, not Meg, because she doubted Pam-the-real-artist was interested in a Project of her own—and even if Pam was interested, she would be in an even worse financial position than Jen to undertake one.

Business

"That Sharon is having another baby," Jen's mom was saying. "Did you see the reveal?"

Sharon was one of Jen's sisters-in-law. After seven years of marriage to Jen's brother and two children and one incubating fetus, Sharon had not yet danced into Jen's mother's affections with sufficient vigor to shake off the *that*. Betsy, Jen's other sister-in-law, had shed the *that* just three and a half years and two children in. Jim theorized that Sharon lagged behind Betsy because Jen's mother preferred what she saw as Betsy's homespun and low-budget approach to the social-media arms race of gender-reveal cakes, a war that Sharon waged by proxy on multiple tiers with hand-piped fleur-de-lis, blowtorched meringue, and frosting carved and shaped into pink-and-blue pairs of pacifiers, partridges, and baby booties.

"I don't think she makes those herself," Jen's mom said, her tone sniffing of conspiracy. "I think she has *outside help*."

"Mom, of course she does," Jen said. "You can't make your own gender-reveal cake. It defeats the purpose of having a gender reveal."

"Hmmpf," Jen's mom said.

"You know," Jen said, trying to keep her tone playful, "you have got to be the only mother of a married childless woman I know who doesn't give her daughter a hard time about delivering grandchildren on schedule."

Jen's mom was silent. "It's none of my business," she said after a moment.

"I guess there's no pressure on me, huh, since your boys have been so prolific."

"It's none of my business," Jen's mom said again.

"It can be your business if you want it to be," Jen said. "I don't mind if you ask me about it. It would be nice to—"

"That's your private business," Jen's mom said with finality.

Jen had never asked her mother for her privacy, and Jen's mother freely gave it to her nonetheless.

This Sex Thing

"Hey, Jen." Karina was standing directly behind Jen, slouching against the empty filing cabinets, holding a slim folder between two fingers, as if it were sticky or flammable.

Jen carefully took out her new earbuds, set them carefully on her desk, and turned carefully away from her computer screen, which currently showed the Grand Rapids Miss Congeniality, Lady Sally Mineola, wrapped in a roller-derby bondage ensemble—helmet estranged from the top of her wig line by a teetering Marie Antoinette pouf—and sipping champagne from a stiletto held in the teeth of a heavily muscled man wearing nothing but Y-fronts, tanning oil, and a bejeweled *luchador* mask.

"Leora sure has fun friends!" Jen said brightly.

"No idea, no idea," Karina said. "None of my business."

"Oh, just so you know, this is for WERK!, the—"

"You were a little late again getting in this morning," Karina said. "Everything okay?"

"Oh, yes," Jen said. "I had a doctor's appointment."

"Another one, yes, I can see that," Karina said, chinning toward the cotton ball plastered to the crook of Jen's arm with a Band-Aid. "Hope all is well?"

"Ah, this is nothing, just a bit of medieval bloodletting to balance the humors, no biggie."

"Phlebotomy," Daisy said from behind the cubicle wall.

"Phlebotomy," Jen said.

"Good to know," Karina said. "In the future, though, do make sure to give the team a heads-up if you're going to be late. Otherwise we'll be worried about you."

"I did—"

"We need to discuss this, uh, *sex thing* you wrote up," Karina said. "Leora is a little, well, let's just say she's not happy."

"Sex thing?"

" 'Not happy' *may* be a bit of an understatement," Karina said.

"What sex thing?"

"It was for"—Karina checked her notes—"Women Empowered to Love their Libido. W-E-L-L, WELL." She set the folder down on the filing cabinet and dusted her fingers, as if some grime or grit had rubbed off.

"Oh, that one was fun. There's actually quite a wonderful program happening in—"

"This is not how you should be spending your time," Karina said. "I'm frankly surprised that you couldn't come to that conclusion on your own." Karina tilted her head and shook it slightly as she gazed at Jen, more in sorrow than in anger.

"Ah, got it," Jen said.

"You need to remember—and gosh, this is a good reminder for me, too, and for all of us—that we need to leave ourselves a lot of room to be able to speak to a lot of different people, with different, oh, you know, *standards of discourse*—not to get all college-seminar-intellectual on ya."

"Oh, no, not at all, I got it," Jen said.

"You got it," Karina said.

"Totally got it," Jen said.

Karina blinked twice and folded her arms. "Is that it?" Karina asked. "Anything you want to tell me?"

"About—women's sexual empowerment?"

Karina puffed sharply through her nose. "Just trying to make sure we're all on the same page now," she said. "You know, I don't know what really happened here, but it's important that we're on the right track, that we know what direction we're headed in."

"What happened," Jen said, "so far as I can tell, is that you asked me to work on an idea that came from Leora and the board, and now Leora has decided that she doesn't like the idea. Right?" Jen smiled and laughed to indicate that she was happy and engaged and LIFting herself, no matter what kinds of challenges or friendly misunderstandings might present themselves along the way.

"Interesting way to put it," Karina said.

Jen laughed again for reasons unknown to her.

"I just think it's good to keep in mind that we need to be careful," Karina said. "We have to set the highest standards for ourselves, and then *raise* those standards. You know, it's so amazing to work at an organization like LIFt, where we can just let our imaginations go wild, and in service of a greater good—it's just such an amazing opportunity, that freedom. But with that freedom comes responsibility. Especially with hot-button issues like sex, relationships, female sexuality, reproductive . . . *issues*. Do you know what I mean?"

"Totally," Jen said. "Totally hear you, totally agree. It's great to have feedback! But just to be clear—you asked—I was asked to work on this. I didn't go off and make it my own thing. I can show you the email you sent—I mean, the email I received—"

"You don't have to do that."

"No, it will only take a few seconds, just so we can reconstruct—" Jen started to turn back to her computer.

"Please, don't let me distract you any longer from Lady Sally Mineola, 'Rebelle Without a Flaw,'" Karina said.

Jen turned back. "Ha, you got me there, but I just wanted to make sure we—"

"Look, *no one* is blaming you, Jen," Karina said. "It's *not* about blame. You haven't been here long and you've already made a big impact. I'm proud of you! I just wanted you to know that Leora, well, she just expects us to reach a little higher." Karina reached up her hand and waved like a pageant contestant. "She would never want us to settle for the lowest common denominator."

"Well, I admit it wasn't my favorite idea of the stack so far," Jen said, in a spirit of agreement and same-page-ness.

"Well, there you go—there's a lesson in this: Trust your instincts. That's a key message for us to send as an organization, but we can only *send* the message if we ourselves have gotten the message! So if you're working on a project and you don't think it's working, speak up. We can collaborate on a solution, or we can walk hand in hand back to the drawing board." Karina was nodding now, but regret still shone in her eyes.

"Sure thing, Karina, thanks for that."

"Awesome. You're a smart cookie, Jen," Karina said. "You don't have to prove that to anyone. But you do have to trust yourself. It's just so important."

"So true," Jen said, but Karina was already walking away.

Summer

The Garden of Earthly Delights

Saturdays and Sundays at the henhouse were always the most crowded, for reasons Jen couldn't comprehend. Jim speculated that other clients of the henhouse had cracked some code of inbound logistics, allowing them to time their production orders so as to pursue their respective Projects without interfering with a high-pressure workweek.

"It's possible, right?" Jim murmured, shifting in his beige seat at the beige back wall of the beige-carpeted waiting room. "Like how female roommates sync up their menstrual cycles."

"That is a myth," Jen said.

If one of Jen's visits fell on a weekday, sometimes she could get out of the henhouse in time to get to LIFt by nine a.m. But not always, and never when it was Jim's day of the month to come in. Too much had to happen.

First, they would wait for Jim's name to be called. The name-calling nurse was invariably the most petite and sweetest-looking staffer on duty that morning, and would read from the sign-in log apologetically, half smiling, half cringing.

"We should have pseudonyms," Jim whispered. *"Noms de guerre."*

"Don't worry, we both have generic names," Jen said. "No one will ever know who we are."

Jen spotted one of Pam and Paulo's onetime temporary roommates across the waiting room. The roommate had arrived too late to snag a seat, and instead leaned against a wall, arms crossed over the dark leather satchel held to her chest, and wearing not the telltale hunted, haunted look that marked out most of Pam and Paulo's tenants, but the calm, empty expression that most visitors to the henhouse cultivated.

Jen looked away, heat in her cheeks. Embarrassment, she had

learned through hours of study in the henhouse waiting room, was conspicuous. Whispering, too, was conspicuous, because of its correlation with embarrassment; most henhouse clients, if they spoke to one another at all, opted for a low conversational hum. In impassivity lay anonymity. The key was to present not a closed book, but an open book full of bright, blank pages.

"We should use our porn names," Jim whispered. "You have a great porn name." Jen's porn name was Cuddles Greenacres. Jim's porn name was Fishy Thirty-second.

When Jim finally heard his name, he would ease his way past piles of crossed legs and close-squeezed chairs toward the nurse, who would usher him through two sets of doors and down a beige-on-beige hallway into a small, windowless room, its beigeness somehow more profoundly beige. Jen was not permitted inside the room, and had only fragmentary, Jim-filtered impressions of it: the scent of water damage and fruity air freshener, the listing stacks of cracked DVD cases, the streaked screen of the television bolted to the wall, the box of disposable plastic sheets for covering the recliner chair that didn't recline, the green exit buzzer next to the doorknob that visitors such as Jim were not permitted to touch. The plastic vase of dead flowers.

"In the henhouse, I'm a patient," Jen once said to Jim. "But are you—a client?"

"I'm an executive assistant," Jim replied.

Usually Jim would rejoin Jen in the waiting room after just three to five minutes inside the Garden of Earthly Delights.

"BACK OF THE NET," Jim texted Jen from the Garden of Earthly Delights during Project Acute Phase No. 1, before he reappeared in the waiting room wearing his best bright, blank expression.

"SWISH," Jim texted Jen from the Garden of Earthly Delights during Project Acute Phase No. 2.

"TYGER TYGER BURNING BRIGHT," Jim texted Jen from the Garden of Earthly Delights during Project Acute Phase No. 4.

There was one instance, during Project Acute Phase No. 3, that Jim did not return for more than twenty minutes, no texts.

"Sorry," he said, sitting down next to Jen. His brow was shiny with sweat. "Delay with the production order."

Jen rubbed his back reassuringly. "But it shipped?"

Jim swigged from a bottle of water with a lustiness tipped with anguish. "Ohhh, it shipped." He exhaled. "Delivery truck got held up by three nurses discussing last night's episode of *The Bachelor*."

"The nurses were *in the Garden*?!?"

"No, no, they were just outside the gates of the Garden. Right at the door. If they'd come into the Garden, I'd have texted you to ask permission."

"That's so romantic, honey."

Perhaps an hour later, Jen would be called in to a different room, where a physician would administer Jim's speed-trial results. Jim named this room Eugenics Incorporated. Jen didn't like that name at all.

Inside Eugenics Incorporated, a henhouse staffer always presented Jen with paperwork recording Jim's speed-trial results for Jen's confirmation and signature. One staffer in particular always handed over the paperwork with a countenance of blushing pride, as if she couldn't believe her luck—and the numbers *were* excellent, as all that spinach-eating and sarong-wearing had given Jim the aquatic profile of a sprightly teenager. But the results also carried a more troubling message, as Jen would reflect afterward during her assigned five to ten minutes of repose on the examining table, legs flung superstitiously up in the air.

Here is the swimmer.

Where is the shore?

It was understood—although a henhouse staffer always reminded Jen of the understanding, just to be sure—that Jen and Jim were to convene as many all-hands meetings as possible during the forty-eight hours immediately following Jen's trip to Eugenics Incorporated.

Confirmation that yet another round of visits to the henhouse would be necessary came in the form of what Jen had rather unimaginatively named the Monthly Adverse Development. At seven a.m. the morning after every Development, Jen found herself in line with the other henhouse regulars, filling in the identical admission form she had the previous month, proffering her arm for an identical round of phlebotomy, receiving an identical-looking prescription for an even higher dose of Sermoxal. The Sermoxal prescribed to Jen in service of the Project had thickened and exploded the Adversity of said Monthly Developments, draining and choking off her serotonin, scrambling her beta-endorphin, crashing the servers of her frontal lobes, and stoking a sourceless, objectless rage that throbbed inside her at a cellular level. The rage wasn't even always subcutaneous; Jen could break out in a sweat from it, her hypothalamus triggered for thermoregulation simply because, say, Jim had left a half-spooned yogurt cup on the bedroom floor or because the upstairs neighbors had installed a pop-up bowling alley directly above Jen and Jim's bedroom, open from six a.m.

"This isn't me," Jen said to Jim in their kitchen one morning. "I'm not really upset about anything. My nervous system is just misfiring."

"But it's perfectly okay to be upset," Jim said. "You've been through a lot, and—"

"I'm *not* upset," Jen barked, slamming her fist onto the countertop. A strip of veneer, peeling away from the countertop's edge, flapped in distress. In the silence that followed—silent save for her downstairs neighbor's howls of protest—Jen stared in puzzlement at her unclenching fist, and thought it entirely possible that another entity had taken up temporary residence in her body, although not the entity she had anticipated or wished for.

Directly above Jen and Jim, a screaming child began jumping up and down in place, feet landing flat on the tiles to command maximum surface area.

If Your Skull Was a Club

Waiting for Jim during his first, mercifully brief sojourn in the Garden of Earthly Delights, Jen absentmindedly looked up from her careworn copy of the September 2008 issue of *Condé Nast Portfolio* and saw her first-floor neighbors, Nadya and Natasha, seated directly across from her. Jen locked eyes with Nadya, then Natasha, then looked down again.

Jen never would have admitted this to herself, much less to anyone else, but if an electroencephalograph had been able to translate the tickertape of mentalese launched by the Nadya-and-Natasha sighting, the Chyron caption scrolling behind Jen's eyes would have read: *They are older than you and rounder than you and they come from somewhere else and they spoke another language first You are ahead of them You were always ahead of them You will be fine It will all work out You will be fine You will be fine You will be fine*

It was in moments like these that Jen found herself recoiling from her own mind.

"What's the Woody Allen line? 'I would never want to belong to any club that would have me as a member'?" Jen asked Jim once. "Do you ever feel like that about your own brain? Like, if your skull was a club, you wouldn't try to get in?"

"Groucho Marx said that," Jim said.

Now, months later, sitting in the same beige seat in the same freezing beige waiting room—the soothing constancy of its climate maintained by poor insulation in winter and, now, an overzealous air-conditioning unit in summer—with the same copy of *Condé Nast Portfolio* visible in the same scuffed magazine rack hanging next to the same sooty windowsill, waiting for Jim as he journeyed through the Garden of Earthly Delights in service of Project Acute Phase No. We've-Lost-Track-by-Now, Jen shivered in her sleeveless dress and sandals and checked her phone for the first time since the previous evening. Her hands trembling, she found herself scrolling through a long email thread on her apartment building's listserv, swiping past variations and permutations of "Congratulations!" and "So happy for you!" and "Mazel tov!" to the originating email from Nadya, who thought maybe people had noticed Natasha looking a little different lately and anyway she just wanted everyone officially to know their happy news and thank you so much.

Jen returned her phone to her tote bag, dropped her chin to her chest, and wrapped her bare arms tightly around herself, organizing her body in a more compact, better-calibrated, more heat-efficient form.

But this more hospitable form was itself conspicuous, so she unwrapped her arms, fished *The New Yorker* out of her tote bag, opened it to a random page, and pretended to read, clenching her teeth, squeezing her crossed legs together in an awkward hug of goose-bumpy limbs.

Then she rolled up *The New Yorker*, stuffed it into her tote, fished out her phone, and tapped out a "Congratulations from Jen and Jim on the fourth floor!" and stared at the screen, contemplating whether or not to add more exclamation points, whether they would enhance or belittle the enthusiasm conveyed in her joyous reply-all.

She decided on four exclamation points, then deleted one of them, then sent.

You will be fine It will all work out You will be fine You will be fine You will be

Evidence

The train from the henhouse to LIFt halted without explanation two stops from the station closest to the office, so Jen speed-walked seventeen blocks to work in the hazy, sweet-sick morning heat. As she hustled into the elevator, the viscose lining of her dress clung to her with what she hoped was not an indecent moistness. In the henhouse, Jen's constricted veins had cowered from two different nurses, and so a third—older, less openly stumped by Jen's venous incompetence—had slipped a series of smaller needles just under her skin, pushing in and out in search of purchase. Jen watched blood leak and seep from her veins into the surrounding tissue as the nurse threaded and pulled, threaded and pulled, a brackish purple blooming under her skin. She imagined the needle as an anteater, flicking its spiked tongue every which way on a promising lump of tree roots. No, better: She imagined her blood as a tiny sea creature—some as-yet-undiscovered species of amniotic ray—easing through her body's channels, caressing over her capillaries, pulsing and blooming with oxygen, with messy, colorful life.

In the elevator, perspiration wallowed at the base of her spine and streaked down the backs of her thighs. Heat and sweat had begun to peel the Band-Aids away from the wilted cotton balls stuck in the crooks of her arms. As the elevator pinged into place on the thirty-eighth floor, she ripped the bandages off simultaneously in a crossed-arm choreographic move—a little private flourish visible only to Jen and the unblinking eye of the security camera—and stuffed them into her tote bag as the elevator doors *gug-flump*ed open.

She had gotten up so early, and she was late.

It's All About the Team

She had gotten up so early, again, and she was late, again. Weeks, months, had gone like this.

"Jen, look, the last thing we want is for people to feel as though they're punching in and out on a clock," Karina was saying. "On the other hand, a team can't start out on the field a man down, can they?"

The atmosphere at LIFt rumbled with agitation in triplicate. So far as Jen could tell, Leora Infinitas was 1) not satisfied with the pace of progress at LIFt; 2) not frequently available to communicate with her staff at LIFt about her unhappiness with the pace of progress at LIFt; and 3) not forthcoming about the projects on which her staff were meant to be making progress. Leora's discontent had not filtered from her board down to the rest of the staff by any direct means. Instead it had faded in slowly, like a hissing ambient static.

Whhooooossshhhhh

You could hear it even when Leora wasn't in the office, which was most days. Today, Leora was with Sunny in San Diego, giving a talk titled "The Work-Love Balance."

"Leora Infinitas and her new-ish foundation have been exhorting women worldwide to 'LIFt Yourself,' which in their view requires the usual menu of charity and volunteer work as well as savvy career choices: *If you love what you do, you never have to work*," wrote *DOPENHAUER*'s Ruby Stevens-Meisel, who often made note even of Leora's most mundane public appearances. "The 'work-love balance' is therefore a zero-sum game—an aggressive reformulation of Karl Marx's zero-sum theory of wealth, labor, and power, although one that Leora, the people's polemicist, would never put in such academic terms."

"I know, I *was* late, I'm sorry," Jen was saying to Karina. She was finding her breath and her hands were shivering and she was smiling so hard her face hurt. "I had a—"

"A team can't start out with a *woman* down on the field, I should say." Draped across the empty filing cabinet behind Jen's desk, Karina rested her chin thoughtfully on her fist.

Amid other Pavlovian conditioned responses that Jen had acquired since joining LIFt, the sight of Karina leaning against the empty filing cabinets triggered cravings for an Animexa tablet. Karina leaning against the empty filing cabinets conveyed that a memo would have to be conceived and researched and written, or a meeting would have to be convened at which a memo would be formulated or discussed or autopsied or, most likely, ignored. An Animexa tablet replicated and improved on the effects intended by the *whhooooossshhhhh* and by Daisy's noise-canceling headphones. The physical side effects of Animexa were diverse, inconsistent, and, most important, minor—the slightly dilated pupils, the cottonmouth, the clams-on-ice fingers—but to Jen its main pharmacological effects were aural. The drug seemed to create its own sound waves, which were 180 degrees out of phase with any interfering waves signaling boredom, embarrassment, and existential futility.

As Jen reminded herself even now, Animexa's sound waves were also out of phase with the Project, although at that moment it could not have mattered less.

"Right, right, I'm sorry," Jen said. The smile on her face was genuine and absentminded, a smile acknowledging and addressing someone across the room whom only Jen could see. "I had a doctor's appointment. I did email you about it last night. I always—"

"But you would have known about a doctor's appointment before *last night*."

"Well, it's—"

"It has not escaped my attention that all your many, many doctor's appointments are in the morning." Karina's face twitched. Jen's frequent albeit slight tardiness had never, to Jen's knowledge, even remotely impacted a single item of business at LIFt—and indeed she lacked clarity on what, if any, business LIFt had to itemize and her own role in achieving those items of business. And yet Karina's face had just unmistakably twitched, and for a second Jen feared that her tardiness had driven Karina past some critical physiological threshold, that her belated arrival times could somehow jam Karina's feedback nerves, drain her electrolyte supply, jab her myofascial trigger points.

But actually, Karina had winked at her.

"Yes, yes, the morning," Jen said. She remembered her needle marks and bruises, and placed her hands in piano-player position on her knees, elbows pulled in, aiming to hide her wounds or at least cast them in shadow.

"Are you a night owl, Jen?" Karina asked, cocking her head and approximating a tone of friendly conspiracy. "Lot of *late ones*? Not a morning person?"

"Sorry?" Jen hoped that Karina wouldn't wink again.

Karina wriggled her nose, as if jesting with a toddler. "I get it, I get it," she said, bucking her chin at Jen. "*Believe* me, I get it, because I'm pretty nocturnal myself. Or I used to be. Kids are an alarm clock you really can't hit *snooze* on."

"Oh, no, I'm not—I'm not lying—not that I'm accusing you of—sorry—"

"You are so *smiley* this morning," Karina said. "I kind of love it."

"Well—"

"So these *doctor's appointments*," Karina said, enunciating each syllable as if for an audience of lip-readers. She paused and sighed. "Okay, problem-solving time: Maybe you could stagger them out—sneak out early once in a while instead of coming in late."

"This doctor—these—I need to go in the morning. I can always stay at the office late."

Karina shrugged. "Again, it's about the team. Do you expect the rest of the team to stay at the office late?"

"Oh, no, of course not, I just meant—"

"Look, don't even worry about it," Karina said. "It's just something to keep in mind." She tapped her index and middle fingers to her brow. "Nine, ay, em!"

"Got it! Thanks."

"And *oof*, look at those bruises," Karina said. She furrowed her brow in an effort of concern. "You okay? Need some ice?"

Jen didn't look down. "It's nothing. Thanks, though."

"All right, well, I don't mean to pry. But if you ever need to talk about anything, anything at all, I'm always here for you," Karina said, her hands clasped in a prayerful position as she backed away and turned around. "And *stay happy*—look at that smile," Karina added, her back to Jen.

"Thanks very much, Karina," Jen called after her.

"And see ya later, Daisy," Karina said over her shoulder. Daisy, concealed behind the cubicle wall, had been sitting two feet away from them the whole time.

"I think she thinks I'm a drug addict," Jen said, once Karina was out of earshot.

"Uppers or downers?" asked Daisy, from behind the cubicle wall.

"Downers would make you sleep in, right?"

"It depends. Uppers could keep you up all night, so maybe you're a speed freak or on an all-night coke binge, fall asleep around sunrise, and then you get a late start on the day. Or maybe you're zonked on oxycodone all the time, so it's Sunday morning every morning all day."

"Which drugs would make you bruise easily?"

"Heroin. Steroids. Aspirin."

"Maybe I should go public about my struggle with intravenous aspirin addiction."

"You could write an open-letter confession to Karina."

"Dear Karina, I am sorry I was twelve minutes late to work today . . ."

". . . I apologize that my Aspirin Anonymous meeting went late . . ."

". . . Because my sponsor had a slip and raided her kids' bathroom for chewables . . ."

". . . Last week I sneaked an Advil and all I could think was 'I'm whoring around on my one true bride . . . '"

". . . so then I emptied all my aspirin bottles into the ocean, and when the tablets washed up onto the shore they spelled out K-A-R-I-N-A . . ."

"I'm really sorry, but—" Daisy interrupted Jen, but then Jen realized that Daisy was on the phone now, talking to someone else.

"—but I have board members voting against that grant because one of them was over there and his taxi driver said he had three wives, and therefore they don't think gender equality is going to happen there anytime soon," Daisy was saying.

Jen drummed her fingers on her desktop and bounced a little in her seat before she picked up her phone to leave Jim a voicemail. "I'm sorry, I would have called you from the henhouse, but my cell was dead," she said to the voicemail. "I'm also sorry that I didn't go for the test right away. I am *also* also sorry that I am leaving this as a message. But anyway the answer is yes. We did it. Finally. Swish. Back of the net."

Proficiency

"There is some serious motherfucking arbitration going down tonight," Meg said.

Meg, Jen, and Jim clinked their glasses together as the crowd at Pam's opening-night party swirled and heaved around them. Pam had called her show *Break in Case of Emergency,* and as Jen had guessed, it was an elaborate riff on the medical and bureaucratic tribulations Pam had endured after her cycling accident. Pam had had the presence of mind to record virtually every second of more than twenty hours' worth of phone calls with WellnessSolutions and then transcribed them. She had sliced and diced both the recordings and the transcripts to make crazy quilts of health-insurance-provider jargon, stonewalling, who's-on-first bureaucratic script, and mindless pleasantries. She'd then given the edited transcripts to a local drama student with a honeyed baritone to provide the voice-overs for parody WellnessSolutions commercials, which now played on a loop at opposite ends of Pam's studio space. Shot on a borrowed Flip camera, they featured every trope of a WellnessSolutions TV ad campaign: silver-haired retirees dancing in slow motion at their daughter's wedding, a dog running in slow motion across a field, a toddler toddling in slow motion at the seaside. Pam had also hired actors to perform live lip-synchs of the audio edits at three spots around the studio. The actors wore white shirts, black slacks, and headsets, and they paced and smiled and gesticulated, like hosts of a motivational webinar.

The different edits of audio and video mixed and overlapped across space, though not aggressively enough to discourage conversation among the guests, which enhanced the show's feeling of disorientation and information overload. Adding to the sense of claustrophobia were Jen's portraits, which were mounted around the perimeter of the studio. As she'd been working on them one by one, they'd seemed friendly, albeit overbearing; in their final resting place, they were unsettling, menacing.

"Happiness zombies of the uncanny valley," Meg said, approvingly.

"It's like if they smiled any harder, their faces would smash apart, like glass under pressure, to reveal the sputtering robot viscera underneath," Jim said.

"Thanks so much, guys," Jen said.

"You need to contact the billing department to obtain the preauthorization approval code, then contact the billing authorization department to request the preauthorization," a woman just behind them mouthed into her headset.

Toward the back of the gallery was a chuppah constructed of hospital-bed components and wheelchair parts, with a canopy sewn out of hospital gowns; guests were invited to wrap lightbulbs in gauze pads and athletic tape and crush them underfoot. Smack in the center of the exhibit was what looked to be a cross-section of a grocery-store shelf, sliced clean out of a supermarket aisle. It displayed an enigmatic hodgepodge of items: canned beets, canned artichokes, a wine-bottle opener, slabs of vacuum-packed mozzarella, a honeycomb of bone marrow. Each item carried a unit price, a retail price, and a bar code.

"Oh, God," Meg whispered to Jen, "the bone marrow looks like rugelach."

"You would use the Medical Claim Form for out-of-pocket expenses before meeting the deductible, but once you've met the deductible you'd switch to the Medical Benefits Request," a man's voice said behind them.

"Ladies, good evening." Paulo leaned in to Meg and then Jen for a two-cheek kiss. In his standard uniform of rabbinical beard, viscerally splattered overalls, weathered steel-toed boots, and gruff, laconic affect, Paulo usually brought to Jen's mind a muzhik with a graduate degree in philosophy, or a philosophy graduate student dressed as a muzhik for Halloween. In any context—even tonight, with his beard close-trimmed, his overalls swapped for a slouchy blazer and jeans, and his features plumped in a sociable arrangement—Jen always pictured Paulo perched stone-faced atop a Belarus tractor, smoking an ironic pipe.

"You clean up real pretty," Meg said to Paulo.

"I'm a pretty, pretty boy," Paulo replied, showing his teeth and patting his flat belly.

"You're even prettier since the last time we saw you, which I think was at the Turbuleers group show," Jen said.

"I fucking hated that show," Paulo said. "Did you fucking hate that show?"

"I met a rockabilly cowboy," Meg said.

"That cowboy you met, his name is Taige Hammerback, he's from San Jose but he twangs like he's from Texas, and he's in character *all the time*," Paulo said. "He does studio visits like that. He got married like that."

"I remember him well," Meg said. "He finds lots of reasons to take off his cowboy hat to show you his cowboy pompadour."

"He probably has sex with that hat on," Paulo said. "He goes to the grocery store with that hat on. Well, he probably doesn't have to go to the grocery store anymore, because now Taffy French reps him."

"He still has to eat, though," Meg said.

"No, Taffy French can hire people to eat for him," Paulo said.

"Pam worked for Taffy French one summer," Meg said.

"She spent most of it choosing and presenting fabric swatches and wood grains for Taffy French's baby daughter's new high chair," Jen said.

"Wait, was Taige Hammerback the same guy who takes Polaroids of landscapes, and then he glues them into little hand-stitched books, and the books are kind of dirty and dusty, like they've been out cattle ranching?" Meg asked.

"But then he did a thing where he attached Polaroids of Western landscapes to actual cattle, who wandered around in the sun until the Polaroids were totally sunbleached and blank, and then he exhibited the destroyed Polaroids," Jen said.

"It doesn't even matter what Taige Hammerback makes," Paulo said, "because it's all personality-driven. You just come up with a persona and you're more than halfway there."

"So, okay, easy, you just need a persona, Paulo," Jen said.

"Hairy drunkard," Paulo said.

"Hirsute oenophile," Meg said.

"I'm afraid that authorization code has expired, ma'am," a woman's voice behind Jen said.

Over Paulo's shoulder, Jen spotted Jim, who had wandered away to a table labeled "Instructions for Breakage" that was scattered with peanuts, Christmas crackers, and several still-intact piggy banks. He was methodically snapping every bubble on a sheet of bubble wrap.

"Let's go see Pam," Jen said.

Pam was resplendent in a loose topknot and a ruffled, emerald-colored shift, the shortest dress she owned. ("I am going to wear the shortest dress I own," she had told Jen on the phone the night before, "but I can't remember what it is.") The dress—tight and structured when Pam first purchased it, now hanging fashionably loose from her frame—indicated that she'd lost a great deal of weight during her recovery, and what little she'd put back on was lean muscle from physical therapy. Her naturally round face was thinner but not gaunt; now she had more prominent cheekbones and a more severe jawline and, as Leora would say when hawking LeoraLash™, "eyes that pop." A wild, ghastly thought careened into Jen's head: that the accident had been—in some cosmic sense beyond Pam's control but inextricably knit into her destiny—intentional, karmic, a net positive. It had given Pam a compelling backstory and a wellspring of creative fodder, and somewhat improbably, it had raised her conventional-beauty quotient. Even the scars on Pam's model-skinny leg, flat and faded, looked art-directed, geometric. The lines of her legs and the lines on her legs signaled pathos and sex and dangerous youth and discipline and a hard-earned beauty. A glamour of tragedy and luck. Liabilities had shape-shifted into assets. Into a persona.

Jen blinked hard and shook her head almost imperceptibly, as if a drop of water bobbled in her ear canal. Sometimes she felt on the verge of apologizing to others for the faux pas her brain regularly committed.

"You've always been a genius of reappropriation, Pam," Sue Kittredge, one of Pam and Jen's college professors, was saying. "But this time what you are reappropriating is *you*. It's such an act of empowerment. And it's so generous of you to share it with us."

Pam shrugged and smiled. "What can I say—I ran out of other material."

"I think it's a breakthrough," Sue Kittredge said. "So bold. So brave."

"Hi, girls!" Pam exclaimed to Meg and Jen, putting one arm around each of them in a three-way hug. "Thanks for coming, and Jen, thanks for making sure there was some actual art at the art show."

"And *you*, Jen." Sue Kittredge turned to embrace her former student. "These portraits brought back such wonderful memories for me."

"Aw, thanks. It was fun. I don't think you've met my husband, Jim— that's him over there, the guy who just dropped the peanuts, and he seems to be trying to start a conversation with one of the lip-synchers."

"I can certainly understand your frustration, ma'am," a woman's voice said behind them.

"Okay, so Mrs. Flossie Durbin is hovering near the exit," Meg was saying urgently to Pam, "and she never stays at these things longer than twenty minutes. Let's pounce on her now—I can introduce you."

"I don't know," Pam said. "Shouldn't Mrs. Flossie Durbin be free to come and go as she pleases?"

An exponentially more productive blogger than Flossie Durbin, the well-known economics writer Hatch Warren, once crunched the numbers and concluded that a Flossie Durbin blog post—which tended to forgo formal or analytical rigor in favor of declarative brevity—raised the valuation of an artist's work by a median of 18 percent. One past recipient of a Flossie Durbin blog post was Logan Benson, a first-year Yale MFA student who appropriated the tags of anonymous street artists in tapestries in the mille-fleur style. ("Fresh and vibrant," Mrs. Durbin wrote. "The colors are animated but never cloying, the darker tones are haunting but never morbid. A clean balance of raw energy and highly wrought technique. Recommend.") Another time, the recipient was Alex Katz. ("We risk forgetting the exciting audacity of the lonely figurative painter forging his own path in an Abstract Expressionist moment. Who else could have found so much roundness in flatness? Recommend.") Years ago, Mrs. Durbin's personal assistant had sent Pam an email inquiry about staging a Wake, but despite Pam's enthusiastic replies—three emails, three voicemails, and a three-page handwritten letter—the assistant had never followed up.

This was not unusual, and was characteristic of Mrs. Durbin as a study in contrasts: Her enthusiasms seemed as fickle as her influence was glacial, axiomatic, permanent; her moneyed remoteness could pair comfortably with her penchant for turning up at minimally publicized, low-budget gallery openings in inconvenient areas of town; her rarefied provenance and withholding, near-mute public persona could somehow coexist with her enthusiasm for second-generation blogging software. Even the coolest of the cool kids among the overlapping social circles of whatever constituted the city's "underground" art scene—Pam and Paulo among them—regarded Mrs. Flossie Durbin with an amused fondness, a kind of benign condescension that would have vaporized on contact should her finger have ever fallen upon their shoulders in a tap of election.

"Eighteen percent, Pam!" Meg was saying.

"Eighteen percent of zero is still zero," Pam said, taking Meg's arm. "But I'm happy to meet a nice lady."

"I'm amazed that Mrs. Flossie Durbin is even in town in the summer," Jen said to Sue Kittredge as Pam and Meg nudged their way through the crowd toward the exit. She raised her glass, tilting it so that the wine tipped against her lips and back again.

"You know, you haven't changed a bit, Jen," Sue Kittredge said.

"What else are you up to these days? Where can we see more of your work?"

"This is pretty much it! I was just a hired goon for Pam on this," Jen said.

"That can't be true."

"Well, you know how it is—you have the job that pays the bills, you think you'll have time to make things on the side, but over the years, it just kind of slips away," Jen said. "Although, listening to myself, I'm probably just making excuses."

"Do you and your husband have kids yet?"

Jen smiled big and wide. "Nope!" she said.

"In that case, you really do have no excuse. Where do you work?"

"Well, until recently I worked at the, uh, the Federloss Foundation?"

"Where do you work now?"

"I work at, um, a start-up?" Jen said. "I am so sorry, Sue, but I need to run to the ladies' room—I'll come find you later, okay?"

When Jen came out of the bathroom, Jim was jotting down notes in the narrow margins of a copy of *The Nation* in front of the giant teen-aged orthodontics patient, a half-full glass of wine cradled between his forearm and ribs.

"This portrait made me realize something," Jim said as Jen carefully extracted the glass of wine from its precarious berth. "I have this kid in my class, Stevie, who's really happy and cooperative all the time. He's great, but I kind of file him away in a drawer in my mind, like, 'I don't have to worry about this one.' But maybe it's all a front. Maybe it's a façade of happiness masking horror and mania and giant metal weaponry."

"I'm sorry that my picture of a kid with braces made you diagnose Stevie with mental illness," Jen said.

"Stevie doesn't even have braces," Jim said, taking back the glass of wine.

"My whole mouth tastes like braces," Jen said. "Even my tongue." She thrashed her tongue around, attempting to air out her mouth like a musty duvet.

"Oh, wait, you should hold this," Jim said, handing back the glass of wine. "For show."

Jen took it and teethed the rim of the glass intently. "My tongue is mighty, it is made of *iron*," she said.

"Did you tell Pam yet?" Jim asked.

"No, I'm waiting until after the craziness around the show has died down a little."

"You should tell her," Jim said.

"I will totally tell her as soon as—*hi!*"

Meg and Pam stood before them, wearing smiles evocative of the teenaged orthodontics patient and/or Stevie. "Jen," Meg was saying, "Mrs. Durbin wants to talk to *you*."

"Okay, sure!" Jen said, handing the glass of wine to Jim.

"Not right now, because she left, but she wanted you to have this," Pam said, handing Jen a business card. "You're supposed to call her assistant."

"Okay, but why?" Jen asked.

"I'm afraid I cannot provide you with that information at this time, ma'am," a man behind them murmured into his headset.

"Mrs. Flossie Durbin is a woman of few words," Meg said. "But you are definitely, definitely supposed to call her."

"Okay, but what did Mrs. Durbin think of Pam's show?" Jen asked.

"Mrs. Durbin said the show was *proficient*," Pam replied, taking the glass of wine from Jim and draining it triumphantly.

"Holy fuck," Jim said.

"Are you serious?" Jen said.

"I was there, man," Meg said. "I saw it. I heard it."

"Recommend! Recommend!" Jen said.

"This is the greatest night of my life," Pam said. "Let's go smash some lightbulbs."

Signal Problems

The train was all messed up again. The lines frequently refused to venture past the southern tip of the park, thwarted by "planned maintenance" or "signal problems" or other vague but official-sounding exigencies. Jen and Jim waited a while in the muggy night air for a shuttle bus.

"Good God, they sent a cattle car," Jim said when the overcrowded bus rolled into the stop twenty minutes later. "Call the USDA."

"I am dunzo," Jen said. "Let's walk home."

"Are you okay walking past the Deli of Death at"—Jim checked his watch—"one in the morning?"

"No," Jen said, "but if I die tonight, I don't want the last thing I see on earth to be somebody's armpit."

"You'd rather it be a rack full of expired Honey Buns."

Located on an infamous street corner equidistant from the train station and Jen and Jim's apartment, Brancato's Grocery, aka the Deli of Death, was not only the region's preeminent cocaine and methamphetamine marketplace but also a locus of neighborhood nightlife ranging from armed robbery to dogfights to quarterly shootings. Brancato's rarely closed, and the Staffordshire terriers guarding the door after ten p.m. rarely stopped barking.

"It's kind of unfair to call it the Deli of Death, because no one has ever died there," Jen said. "That we know about. Since we've lived here."

Jen's heels made a solitary *clop-clop* on the uneven sidewalk as she walked arm in arm with Jim.

"How are you feeling?" Jim asked.

"I'm fine, fine," Jen said quickly. "Let's not talk about it—we'll jinx it. Wasn't tonight great?" she asked, inhaling the humidity index through her nostrils theatrically. "Great turnout, Pam was on point. Everyone seemed really happy to be there and slightly freaked-out, which is what I think she was going for."

"Mmm-hmm," Jim said. "And that lady, the Fozzie woman. You're going to be best friends with her now."

"Mrs. Flossie Durbin. Yeah, well, I doubt much will come of that."

"You're going to call her, though."

"Sure, sure."

"Maybe I'll call her," Jim said. "We have a lot in common, Flossie Durbin and I. We like the same stuff."

"*Anyway,* I think this was a big night for Pam. This could change everything for her."

Jim said nothing.

"Don't you think?" Jen asked.

"I guess so," Jim said.

"What do you mean?"

"I don't know. Didn't you think it was kind of contrived?"

"The show? No, I thought it was a matter-of-fact way of dealing with a really messy, emotive topic. It was smart and honest."

Jim said nothing.

"What do you mean by *contrived,* anyway?" asked Jen, unlinking her arm from Jim's and turning to look at him. "Anything anybody makes is contrived. By definition."

"It just seemed like she was exploiting it."

"Exploiting the accident? Why shouldn't she exploit it? It happened. It was a big deal. Why shouldn't she have something to say about it?"

"But it's like it precludes anyone from criticizing it. Because if you criticize it, you're criticizing someone who has suffered—no, you're criticizing their *suffering,* actually. And nobody wants to do that, so they praise it."

"But who are all these people praising it?"

"Whoever was there. Mrs. Flossie Durbin. You."

"Well, of course the people at Pam's opening would say nice things about her opening!"

"No, it's not just that. You'll never really know how people really feel about work like that, because the nature of the thing means you have to respond to it in a certain way or you're an asshole."

"But that's not Pam's fault. Is she not supposed to make stuff out of concern that you won't feel comfortable criticizing it?"

"That's not what I meant."

"And wait, back up, I still don't know what you mean by *exploit*. You mean the work is exploitative?"

"Yeah, kind of."

"So it was cynical somehow? And who or what was she exploiting? Herself?"

"You know what, forget it, because you're always going to be better at arguing this stuff than I am."

"Don't be like that, honey. I'm interested in what you think."

"Yeah, well," Jim said.

They walked in *clop-clop* silence. They could hear the dogs barking now.

Initiative

The fatigue was the heel of a hand, pressing steadily and insistently against Jen's forehead, fingers palming and compressing the deflated basketball of her skull, shading her eyes and darkening her field of vision. The fatigue was a chloroform air freshener, affixed someplace under her desk where Jen couldn't reach it, every inhalation of its scent making her eyes water and her nose run and her lower jaw crack under the tensile pressure of gaping, heaving yawns. The fatigue could not, of course, be placated by a second cup of coffee or half an Animexa tablet. Or even a quarter of an Animexa tablet, perhaps ground into a fine dust to be sprinkled in decaffeinated tea or dotted on Jen's tongue for a largely psychosomatic effect. Jen had considered all these possibilities, repeatedly. Sometimes—now—Jen could answer the fatigue only with a supplicant's pose: elbows propped on her desk, face hidden in her hands, the pads of her fingers making pleading circles against her closed, weeping eyes.

"Today is the *day*-eee, ladies! Look sharp!"

Jen splayed her fingers and peered up through them. Sunny was beaming expectantly at Jen and Daisy.

Jen appreciated that Sunny always came around to the front of their cubicles before addressing them, whereas Karina preferred to approach silently from behind and wait until Jen's pheromone-detection radar or latent powers of echolocation intimated her presence. To better anticipate Karina's stealth attacks, Jen had mostly stopped using her earbuds and had changed her computer desktop background from a picture of David Bowie eating breakfast with Mick Ronson to a plain, shiny black. If Jen tilted her screen at an acute angle to her right and made sure her browser and inbox took up only the left two-thirds of the screen, the right one-third could hold up a muddy mirror to Karina's approach, buying Jen an estimated four to seven seconds of advance warning. Of course, Jen forfeited these advantages whenever she prostrated herself before the fatigue.

Daisy, by contrast, had started wearing her bulky noise-canceling headphones most of the day, every day, sometimes even to the bathroom. Tapping Daisy on the shoulder elicited a yelp of surprise, so now whenever Jen wanted Daisy's attention she would send her an email or instant message.

"Hey, Sunny!" Jen said, sniffling. "How's it going?"

Daisy took off her headphones slowly and set them down on her desk, as if she were moving through water.

Sunny was pulsing her hands together in a silent clapping motion. "Are you guys *ready*? Big day, big day."

"Ready for what?" Jen asked, pulling a tissue from its box.

Sunny protruded her eyes and wagged her head. "*Lee, OH, rah,* is here today!" she said, her voice percussive with rebuke. "She'll be here in like an hour. Are you *ready*?"

"Leora has been here before," Daisy said.

"Good one, Daize," Sunny said, giggling. "But there's here and then there's *here*. And is she ever going to be *here*. Are you girls ready to show some initiative on Leora's new initiative?" Sunny called out each syllable of *initiative* like she was counting out the letters in the name of her favored college sports team. Her hands scissored and sliced the air as if in some half-forgotten cheerleading move.

"Um, probably!" Jen said.

"*Probably*? Guys, get excited already! I've been thinking about this all week!"

"So there's a meeting—today?" Jen asked.

Sunny exhaled dramatically, letting her hands fall defeated to her sides, and rolled her eyes heavenward as if in exasperated appeal. "If this is your sense of humor, you'll have to excuse me, 'cause I ain't laughin', kiddo!" Sunny said, laughing, as she walked away.

"I heard Karina talking about this," Daisy said. "Leora is coming in and we're going to lock ourselves in a room until we help the board figure out the future of the organization, or something."

"I see," Jen said.

"I think there was an email, too."

"But—I didn't get the email!"

"So good, you're off the hook," Daisy said.

"Was there an assignment? Are we supposed to *present*? Fuck."

Daisy was staring at the tiny surveillance camera affixed to the nearest ceiling corner, as if she had deduced something in its reflecting eye—something demoralizing and piteous—that she hadn't been looking for.

"I really wouldn't sweat it," Daisy said. "Any of it. Ever."

What Is Your Excuse?

Every staff meeting grew more hands: colorfully accessorized and manicured hands—Jen had lost track of how many—none of them over the age of twenty-four and all of them the goddaughter of a LIFt staffer or the niece of a friend of Leora's or the friend of a child of a LIFt board member. Jen had been introduced to most of them, known each of their names for at least a few seconds or part of a day, each of them rotating in and out a couple of days a week, these unpaid "LIFt collaborators" erratically filling out the previously desolate maze of cubicles that stood between Jen and Daisy and the building's southern corridor of offices. Now, lined up around the conference table, they blurred together despite their high-resolution finish of whitened smiles and poreless skin and sculpted quadriceps and shiny, shiny hair. At first, in their presentation and easeful confidence, Jen classified them as next-generation Megs, except that part of Meg's Meg-ness was in being an outlier; these girls were Megs to a one. They also adjusted the settings on Meg's calm but no-nonsense aptitude to find a brighter and sweeter level; they swapped Meg's dove grays and silken blacks for lime greens and indigos, magentas and piccalillis. One of the girls was wearing a flamingo brooch on a sailor collar. Another wore jodhpurs and a bowler hat. Every one of them had at best an ornamental job and comically inflated job title, and it was endearing to Jen—moving, really—to know that their own superfluity had never crossed their minds or influenced their posture or informed their choice of Crayola-coral lipstick. Not one of them, Jen knew, ever entered a room or took a seat at a table half expecting someone to turn to her and ask the eternal question: *What are you doing here?*

Or maybe the eternal question was *Why do you need to be here?*

Or maybe *Why are you here?* was best and simplest.

Jen couldn't decide.

"She was just an amazing woman. An *amazing* woman," Leora

Infinitas was saying from the head of the table, Donna on her left, Karina on her right. Just as an American president addressing a joint session of Congress might point out a firefighter's widow or plucky small-business owner in the audience as support for a military action or a tax cut, Leora's opening statements to staff meetings always invoked a land mine survivor or famine survivor or Stage IV cancer survivor whom she had met in her newish capacity as a philanthropy innovator. This new acquaintance of Leora's served as a vivid anecdote for her audience and, for Leora, a useful plot device in a journey of fulfilled identity—a catalytic converter of self-actualization. This rhetorical woman-device was usually *amazing*, frequently *phenomenal*, redoubtably *inspiring*, occasionally *rad*.

"And I couldn't help thinking—and look, I'd been two hours cross-legged on a dirt floor with this woman." Leora swallowed and paused to look around the room. "I had laughed with this woman." Pause. "I had cried with this woman." Pause. "I had held this woman's hand and stared into her eyes. And I just felt so *honored* by the power of her presence, the sheer force of her *survival*, and so humbled by it." Pause. "It's a blessing to be humbled." Pause. "It's a gift." Pause. "We forget this. But we can't forget it. It's a *gift* to be humbled."

Jen couldn't gauge for how long she had zoned out. Donna's hands were teepeed, her head bowed deep, her bangles clattering in sympathy. Sunny was openly weeping.

"And I couldn't help thinking," Leora said. "I *couldn't help thinking*—even though all that *thinking* threatened to break, just for a second, that *lunar beam* of concentration and communion between her and myself, even though it took me out of the moment for a moment, only for a moment—Lord knows I'm not perfect—"

"Amen, sister," Sunny said, and sobbed.

"—I couldn't help thinking, *Leora, what is your excuse?*"

Leora stopped and nodded as she looked around the room. A crystalline tear globule hesitated at the edge of each pair of her Leora-Lashes™. Her nostrils flared with a suppressed sob, but she kept it at bay, nodding at her staff, nodding at the jade-top table, blinking, inhaling, exhaling. She shook her head. She swept an inky-black hair extension behind her shoulder. She nodded some more. An argument tossed and turned inside her.

"And later on in, you know, the really *grotesque* comfort of my hotel room," Leora said, her voice breaking and healing itself in one phrase, "later on, that question came up again. *What is your excuse?* The question reverberated through my dreams. In the morning, I heard that question, I felt it, I saw it as if it were written in steam across my bathroom mirror: *What is your excuse?*"

Leora raised her palms toward the ceiling. "Now," she said. "What do I mean by this? What is this question?" Like Donna, she teepeed her hands together on the jade-top table. "What I mean is that if I can look this person in the eye, after all she's shared with me, after all she's been through, and knowing all that, and yet also knowing that she somehow finds the strength to get up in the morning, to work, to provide for her family, to cook and clean and mend and comfort, to care for herself and her babies and her community when the whole world seems to have been so careless with her—has she not earned my gratitude for sharing so much of herself with me?"

She held her hand to her chest. "My *gratitude*. I think we can agree that she's earned it. My *gratitude*, which I log as faithfully as an accountant, ladies, and so should you. Like a doctor keeps a patient's chart, like the captain of a ship keeps a log to show the distance he's come and the miles he's yet to go, the latitude and longitude of my life I mark with *gratitude*, always gratitude. And there, right there, a debit in the gratitude column. Make no mistake."

Jen tried to survey the room without moving her head. She thought of an oil painting with the eyes cut out in a *Scooby-Doo* haunted mansion.

"So how do I pay that debt?" Leora asked. "Well, let's start with how *not* to pay it. Let's start by facing my greatest fear, and my greatest fear is to be ungrateful. To lose track of my gratitude. To run up a gratitude debt." The *t* of *debt* was a puff of air. "How could I be ungrateful? Wouldn't the height of ingratitude be if I did not work to earn, to pay back, what this amazing woman gave me? If she can do all that, if she can be that strong, that powerful—and it is the weakest among us, you see, who must summon the most power, because that power is not simply handed to them—if she can be that powerful, what is stopping *me* from fulfilling *my* full potential? Aren't I required by natural law to do right by her? Do I have a choice not to learn and grow and live a bigger, better life owing to her example? How could I not? Do I even have the option? *Do* I?"

Sunny fled the room in tears. Karina's eyes were full and her nose was red, and both hands clamped a lock of hair to her jugular like a cluster of funereal lilies. Donna's lips and bangles murmured and trembled in prayer. The row of toothpaste smiles and shiny, shiny hair fidgeted as one. Daisy was texting.

"What is your excuse?" Leora repeated. "Now, I'm going to keep asking this of myself. But now we need to ask it of ourselves. We need to ask it *of* LIFt and *as* LIFt, as one voice—many, many voices in one. This woman—this *incredible* woman—posed a challenge to me. She didn't know it, but she did. And this challenge is one I cherish and one I want to pay forward. I want to gift us with a challenge. A challenge to the mind, the body, the spirit. A challenge to look at yourself, and ask yourself, *What can I change?"*

Sunny had returned to the room and sat down again, puffy-eyed and hiccupping. "That's right," she said, her voice a watery tapioca. "That's right."

"And so," Leora said.

Sunny blew her nose and chuckled to herself. Karina reached over and patted Donna on the hand. Donna held three fingers tenderly to her lips as she looked up at Karina, her bangles collapsing in a cathartic heap against the crook of her arm.

"Love," Donna jangled. "Love."

"Now," Leora said after a contemplative pause, "all of you may be asking yourselves: What does all of this mean in practice?"

Jen opened her notebook.

"It means speaking with a louder voice that carries across the seven continents."

"*Yay*-yuh, we even want the damn *penguins* to be singing our song!" Sunny said.

Jen began drawing a singing penguin.

"It means we'll be launching and offering support to a slate of exciting new programs around the world," Leora continued.

Jen turned the page and took her first note of the meeting: *New programs:*

"It means we'll be pushing harder than ever, more creatively than ever, to find the best, most effective, most innovative ways of helping women help themselves, all over the world."

Jen took her second note: *Who was L.I.'s inspirational lady? Name/ country/program?*

"It means we'll be ramping up our communications efforts."

Jen's hand and pen dangled over the page.

"It means having a clear and unified message," Leora continued.

Jen turned back to her singing penguin. Its lower beak, Jen decided, would quaver with vibrato.

"It means sending that message through the best channels, led by a remarkable team of—ah—ah—Julie?"

The women in the room looked around at one another.

"Julie," Leora said. "Is Julie here?"

One of the penguins' implausibly long and dexterous wings, Jen decided, would be clapped soulfully to one ear of its studio headphones.

The social-media intern smiled shyly and raised her hand, wiggling her fingers. "Hi, everyone," she said. "My name is Jules, actually—"

Jen looked up as she realized Leora's mistake, and cushion-laughed. "Oh, sorry, I think you mean—"

"Leora," Donna intoned, "can we talk about messaging for a moment?"

"So let's talk about messaging for a moment," Leora said, without looking at Donna. "Just as *I* was challenged, I want to engage and challenge all our compatriots around the world. Our fellow women deserve to have a new clarity, a new purpose—a new challenge."

Jen shut her notebook and looked out the window.

"We will call it TTC: Total Transformation Challenge," Leora said.

"T-T-C," Donna said. "No more half-measures."

"Spiritually comprehensive," Leora said.

"Holistic," Donna said.

"Catchy!" Sunny said.

"A challenge to the mind, the body, the spirit," Leora said.

"The idea, and stop me if I'm wrong, Leora," Karina said, raking and twisting her hair, "is to issue a challenge to all LIFt allies across the country—allies across the *world*, really—to set themselves a goal in each of these three categories, and they can log their progress on our website. So for one of us, maybe Mind is learning Arabic, Body is setting aside forty-five minutes per day for meditation or yoga, and Spirit is—hmm, what would be a good example of Spirit, Leora?"

Karina's upward-management skills were so impeccable that Jen couldn't tell if Karina was strategically infantilizing herself before Leora or if she honestly couldn't come up with an example.

"Not three categories, though," Leora said sternly. "Seven. We should have seven. Seven has *prana*."

"Seven, it definitely needs to be seven," Karina said, performing a remonstrative once-over of the rest of the group.

"Mind, body, spirit," Leora said. "What else?"

"Soul," Donna said.

"What is soul?" Daisy asked, looking up from her phone.

"Soul is where you *come from* and where you're *aspiring to go*," Donna said.

"But what's the difference between soul and spirit?" Jen asked.

Sunny made a wet noise that may have involved her uvula. "Jen, why so pedantic?" she said.

"Soul and spirit seem too close to me," Leora said.

"You're right, Leora," Sunny said quickly.

"Another one could be relationships," Daisy said.

"The *heart*," Donna corrected her.

"Okay, the heart," Daisy said. "Another one could be space."

"Outer space?" Karina asked, smiling warmly at Daisy.

"No, like, *home*," Daisy said, without returning the smile. "At home. Home space."

"That's five," Sunny said.

"The planet," Karina said. "Our bond of mutual respect with the environment, with Mother Earth."

"Yes and yes," Leora said.

"Ooh, one to go!" Sunny said. "So that's earth, plus mind, body, spirit, heart, space . . ." She was counting on her fingers.

"It's funny," Karina said, pulling her fingers through her hair from the scalp, as if coaxing new brainstorms from her follicles. "I never cared about the environment before I had kids. I mean, why would I? I'll be *dead*."

"Toe tally," Sunny said.

"Work could be the last category," Jen said. "Our keep. How we earn a living—is it fulfilling, is it integrated with the rest of our life, does it meet our creative needs, our spiritual needs, and—and our material needs." She tried to make eye contact with Leora, who was abruptly transfixed by the gigantic diamond cluster perched on her finger.

"Hm," Karina said. "I don't know. I feel like our community would be turning to us to get *away* from the daily grind."

" 'Material needs' seems off-message to me," Sunny said.

"Materialism," Karina said. "Not a good look."

"It's a question," Donna said, "of *vocation* versus *avocation*. Our community thirsts for *avocation*."

Jen was mesmerized by Leora's being mesmerized by her ring.

"Jen?" Karina asked.

"Oh—" Jen started.

"The *mission*," Donna said. "That's a category."

"Isn't the whole thing the mission, though?" Jen asked. "This would be like a mission within a mission."

Leora held her bedazzled hand up in the direction of the closest floor lamp and squinted. "The mission," she said. "I'd say *we've* got one."

"Woot!" Sunny said, bouncing in her seat.

"Total Transformation Challenge," Leora reiterated. "TTC. It's a rallying cry. It's a movement. It's a social media—*thing*. TTC. It's what will be on every woman's lips across the world. We have the power to make it part of our lingua franca. A new phenomenon that we will have created and given to the world, out of gratitude. Say it with me: T-T-C."

"Like Aretha Franklin's 'TCB,'" said Sunny. "Taking care o' *biz*-ness!"

"Like BYOB or NIMBY," Petra said. "I mean, not in terms of meaning, just in terms of everyone knowing what they mean—"

"Like OPP," Daisy said.

Leora dipped her chin in confirmation. "Make it so," she said. "We launch October first."

A Teachable Moment

"So, I *love* the Total Transformation Challenge idea. Needless to say!"

Jen was standing in the doorway to Karina's office. During her tenure at LIFt, she had not yet sat down on Karina's couch, and rarely placed her entire body past the doorframe.

"So great, right?" Karina replied. "Really gives us that focus we've been talking about. And I love how aggressive the launch date is. I think everyone is really pumped about this."

Daisy had a Post-it on which she kept a running list of Karina's verbs of enthusiasm.

pumped
psyched
jazzed
amped
stoked

Then Daisy started making up her own, and kept a list of those, too.

stacked
oomphed
spanched
hoinked
plurged
quorched

Daisy stuck the Post-it on one of the Shetland ponies on her cubicle wall, just beneath the pony's cardigan collar.

"Right, focus, totally," Jen was saying. "Just checking—what relationship does TTC have with our existing international programs?"

Karina smiled. "Absolutely none!" she said. "Do you have a problem with that?"

"No, of course not, sorry!" Jen said, mirroring Karina's smile.

"Is that all?" Karina asked.

"Well, actually, there's one other thing, so sorry to keep you," Jen said. "So I know that Leora is really attuned to acronyms and catchy abbreviations and stuff, which is great—I love the internal rhyme of TTC, by the way! But anyway, I just wanted to point out that this particular acronym, TTC—well, we have some competition for that slot."

"Mm-hmm," Karina said.

Jen nodded encouragingly.

"And?" Karina asked.

"Oh! Sorry. Well, I just know this because I have friends who are new moms or, you know, trying to become new moms—and what am I saying, *you're* a mom, so maybe you know this! But anyway—TTC is online shorthand, apologies if I'm stating the obvious, for 'trying to conceive.'"

"Mm-hmm," Karina said.

"So, I just know from looking at parenting blogs and stuff for inspiration for *our* site—so from doing that, I learned that women identify as TTC if they're asking for advice on fertility issues. And TTC is often a category or a keyword on those sites—a subtopic? I'm sure the audience for those sites would possibly sometimes overlap with ours?" Jen swallowed. An inlet of saliva kept rising under her tongue.

"Mm-hmm," Karina said.

"So you could see how it could be confusing?" Jen's spine was folding forward. She pressed one hip and shoulder against Karina's doorframe.

"Confusing," Karina said, and pressed her lips together.

"Yeah, like if we're talking to our audience about TTC, they might think we're saying something else, like, 'Hey, go make some babies!'"

Jen attempted a cushion-laugh, but the saliva made the laughter gurgle and drown, and a dying sound spurted out instead, like Bertha Mason cackling in Mr. Rochester's attic.

"Mm-hmm," Karina said.

"So, that's all," Jen said, exhaling. She swallowed again.

"It's interesting," Karina said.

"Yeah," Jen said. She could sense her stomach slowly angling a battering ram into place, aimed in the vicinity of her epiglottis.

"It's interesting," Karina said, "that you chose to bring this up now, here, with me. Not in front of the group, not in front of Leora, when we were all exploring these ideas together, as a team. That's an interesting choice. In making that choice, what message are you sending, to me and, more important, to yourself?"

"Sorry?"

"Think about it."

Jen smiled as winningly as she could. She imagined herself in the maw of a trash compactor. One hand at her side reached up to grip Karina's doorframe.

"The only message I'm aware that I'm sending," Jen said brightly, sweat pearling on her philtrum, "is that to many people—many women—TTC stands for 'trying to conceive,' which may confuse people if we decide it stands for Total Transformation Challenge."

Some of the contents of Jen's stomach splashed upward, spraying the back of her esophagus. She coughed delicately into her free hand.

"The message you're sending, *I* would say," Karina replied, "is that you don't trust the give-and-take of the group dynamic, and that you're insecure about sharing your ideas in mixed company."

Karina's words stood in counterpoint to her confidential, just-us-girls tone—the tone of an old friend asking for advice over coffee. Jen wished she could record the conversation so that Pam could enlist one of her actors to lip-synch it.

"So, instead of choosing trust, openness, and confidence, you're falling back on their opposites," Karina continued. "Which is ironic, isn't it? Ironic because we're encouraging women to push *out* of their comfort zones, to speak up for themselves, to think that their ideas actually have merit."

"Right," Jen said. The corners of her mouth twitched and jerked. She estimated that she had forty to sixty seconds before her nose started oozing. "Right. Yes. I can see that."

"It's interesting to think about," Karina said. "Something to keep in mind—the importance of walk-the-walk, you know?"

"Definitely. So—so I'll go ahead and mention the TTC thing to Leora," Jen said. "Better late than never." Karina's office tilted sideways. Jen bent her knees slightly to keep her balance, and they knocked together.

"Don't worry about it, Jen," Karina said. "You've entrusted me with this, and I think this is a teachable moment for both of us."

"Are you sure? I don't want to add to your workload." The words were old leaves in a drainpipe, clotted and slimy.

"Absolutely sure."

Jen swallowed again. "Great, okay, then, thanks, Karina," Jen said. On *Great,* she aimed for a middle C but landed on an F sharp. "And you know"—the first cold beads of sweat punctured Jen's brow, but something compelled her onward—"the acronym thing might not be a big deal. It's not like we're calling it"—here Jen spaced the words out evenly, the better to drive the joke of the acronym straight into the carpet—I'm Very Fabulous, right?"

Bertha Mason let loose a shrill cackle.

"Ha, ha," Karina said evenly.

"Thanks, Karina!" Jen said again.

Jen exited Karina's doorframe in what she intended to look like ebullient hustle. She strode across the office with shoulders squared, passing behind a cubicle row of toothpaste smiles and shiny, shiny hair. She entered the bathroom and felt a passing gratitude that all the stall doors were open.

> *Zero people here*
> *Log a zero in my ledger*
> *Thank you no one*
> *Thanks for no one*
> *Thanks for nothing*

In one swirling and possibly graceful figure eight, Jen slipped inside the handicap stall and shut the door and sank to her knees and yanked her hair back with one hand and leaned the opposite arm against the toilet and heaved, and again, and again. Of all the mistakes she'd made so far that day, her first mistake had been orange juice for breakfast.

Wild Gifts

jenski1848: Hellooo

whatDaisyknew: AHOY AHOY

jenski1848: I love that you're listening to "Protect Ya Neck" at work.

whatDaisyknew: SORRY I'LL TURN IT DOWN

jenski1848: So Karina just told me that Leora wants to do a video series for the TTC launch called "When Bad Things Happen for Good Reasons."

whatDaisyknew: EPISODE ONE: THE ARMENIAN GENOCIDE

jenski1848: I think it's more like "I was injecting heroin between my toes, then my toes fell off, then I opened a rehab clinic, then I used the proceeds from my rehab clinic to buy new bionic toes."

whatDaisyknew: TOE TALLY. HA HA SORRY THAT WAS JEJUNE

jenski1848: Or, you know, a car accident brings two long-lost sisters together, or a near-death experience results in an epiphany, etc., etc.

whatDaisyknew: EPISODE TWO: A WILD GIFT FROM THE JANJAWEED

jenski1848: Can you give me a hand with this and put a call out, email people? Oh and we should probably avoid using the word "bad." "Challenge" or "adversity" or "hurdle," those work. "Journey."

whatDaisyknew: EPISODE THREE: LOOK AT ALL THE PRETTY PINK RIBBONS I CAN WEAR IN THE HAIR I DON'T HAVE BECAUSE OF THE CANCER

jenski1848: Thanks, D.

All-Media Motivational Thingy

"It's insane and depressing to me that you can't get away even for a few days," Meg was saying. "I don't get it."

Meg was grinding spices with a mortar and pestle at her kitchen island while Jen and Millie sat on the floor near her feet, bent over large sheets of construction paper with crayons and markers. Millie was relying heavily on black, purple, and blue to create a thick, raging storm vortex. Jen was drawing an elephant using his trunk to pick from an apple tree.

"Sucko," Millie whispered to her drawing. "Sucko."

"Circle, yeah—you see, these apples are kind of circle-shaped," Jen said. "An apple is round like a circle."

"Sucko," Millie said, scrawling more furiously with her violet crayon.

Together, the three of them plus Buzz, Meg's doleful and red-bandannaed golden retriever, had been hiding from the early-August heat all Sunday afternoon among the cool off-whites and pearly grays of Meg's central-air-conditioned loft. (Jen and Jim had a single air conditioner that turned their bedroom into a walk-in freezer if the bedroom door was closed and that had no discernible effect of any kind if the bedroom door was open. Jim was there now, in a hoodie and fingerless gloves, reading *A Man Without Qualities* underneath a blanket and Franny.)

"It's beautiful. And it's *so big,*" Jen had said after Meg and Marc finished renovating the loft, when Meg was seven months pregnant with Millie. Jen had cringed inside, wishing she'd stopped at "It's beautiful." Pointing out the size of Meg's home veered too close to talking about money; or, more precisely, it veered too close to gawking. Or maybe gawking was just what Jen was doing—because Jen's gaze was, arguably, empirically stupid; this was not a value judgment but simply a statement of fact in re: Jen's lack of money, lack of knowledge of money, lack of upbringing in any remote proximity to money, lack of experience discussing money, lack of a conversion table for translating what someone like Meg meant when she referred to "a lot of money," lack of comprehension of what it was to have money, spend money, or invest money, lack of understanding of what it might mean to point at a giant empty space in one of the most expensive zip codes in the country and not only call dibs but think it a shrewd and even excessively reasonable choice given other, pricier options that were nonetheless also tenable.

"Eh, we'll all be practically living in one room like savages," Meg had said, rubbing her belly with one hand and rapping her knuckles on the counter with the other. "The girl-child will see unspeakable things."

Was the counter—soapstone? Silestone? Jen couldn't remember.

"Seriously, it's ridiculous," Meg was saying now. "You have to come out at least for a few days. I can't imagine the Mrs. Bluff staying in the city in August."

"She's not; Leora is gone all month," said Jen, who was crowning her elephant with a tiara made of honeysuckle. *Honey sucko.* "But she's working from her summer house and has to sign off on everything. The others are gone for a week or two at a time, but they check in, supposedly."

"So why can't you go away and check in?" Meg asked.

"It's complicated," Jen said. "It's partly because this stupid video project fell in my lap. Is that a house, Millie?"

"Behwuh," Millie replied.

"A bear, huh—that's a big bear. Is the bear a boy or a girl?"

"Guw."

"Does she need a house in the storm?"

"Yeah."

"Okay, let's build the bear a house to keep her warm and dry in the storm," Jen said. "I'm hoping things will be calmer after we launch this—whatever it is."

"This all-media motivational thingy," Meg said. "Could Jim come first and you could join us later?"

"Well, Jim has all this administrative stuff to get done ahead of the school year that he didn't have last year," Jen said. This was true, and also irrelevant to the question of whether or not Jen and Jim could spend some time at Meg's summer rental.

"But Jim—" Meg stopped.

"But Jim has the whole summer off and could have gotten it done anytime?" Jen asked. "I've thought the same thing. I wish he—" This time Jen stopped herself. To verbalize her wish that Jim—who spent his summers reading and running, running and reading—would seek out tutoring gigs or freelance writing assignments or anything that might monetize his yearly three-month sabbatical would also veer too close to talking about money.

"Whatever, I still don't get it," Meg said. "Anything you have to do, you can do at the house. And it sets a bad precedent that you're chaining yourself to your desk like this—they'll come to expect that of you, and you have to nip that in the bud."

"You'll have to pardon me, ladies," Jen said.

Jen shut the door behind her in Meg's downstairs bathroom, where she always half expected a man in a tuxedo to hand her a towel, and sat down on the edge of the built-in stone tub. She had lied to Meg, and had erred in predicting that her lie would land clean, would speak for itself, would not demand explanation or amplification.

She tried to remember a time she had ever lied to Meg before, and couldn't.

Every year since college, Meg had invited Jen and Pam—and, later, Meg and Marc had invited Jen and Jim and Pam and Paulo—to some kind of summer retreat: Meg's parents' lakeside house, Marc's parents' place upstate, and for the last few years, a beach house that Meg and Marc rented for the month of August. The first year of the beach house, Jen had tried to pay for herself and Jim, to extract from Meg the price of one-third of one-fourth of the rent—because they only ever stayed for one week, anything more would be too much of an imposition, although Pam did not share this view—and when Meg refused either to provide the sum or to entertain the notion of accepting any money from Jen whatsoever, Jen went online to research comparable rents in the area and, a few stunned minutes later, ceased her online research and silently accepted Meg's generosity.

In each year since, Jen's palpable sheepishness about the rental house and its estimated price tag had channeled itself into monetary overcompensation: a $250 surprise grocery run, a stream of screen-printed hand towels and homemade soaps and other desperate purchases from the quaint little shops in town, and constant, keening offers to buy gas or pay for gas or offer cash for gas up front.

"*Basta*, Jen," Meg said once.

Jen understood Meg's exasperation. She was aware of how her behavior turned what should have been a gift into an off-balance and embarrassing transaction. And still, some coagulated recess of Jen's mind resented Meg for acknowledging her missteps. And when Meg had mentioned the house this year—at this point, it was less an invitation than a reminder—Jen felt a sinking column open inside her like a plunger, trapping a pocket of air at the top of her sternum, and as Meg rattled off dates and times and ideas for day trips, Jen blurted out that she was really sorry, but they probably couldn't come this year.

Jen rose from the edge of Meg's bathtub and saw thick horizontal streaks of charcoal and intestinal pink swipe past her; she gripped the side of the sink until the streaks receded into pinpricks of light and the nausea receded with it. She inhaled through her nose and exhaled through her mouth three times each, flushed the toilet, palmed some water from the faucet, and opened the door.

"Do you need help with anything?" Jen asked Meg, who was still grinding.

"Yeah, I need help with the fact that I want you to come to the house," Meg said. "Just come to the darn house."

"Next year," Jen said. "When things have calmed down. And thank you so much, as always, for—"

"Jenfa. Jenfa." Millie was rubbing Jen's leg and staring plaintively into the middle distance. "Jenfa," she whispered.

"What is it, my love?" Jen asked.

"Sucko," Millie said to a lost horizon. "Wan daw sucko."

"You want to draw a circle? I bet you can draw a circle, sweetheart," said Jen, kneeling down and leaning over a fresh sheet of paper, her lower abdomen touching the tops of her upper thighs. Jen slowly drew a big red circle.

Holding the crayon in her fist, Millie approached the page with the same patience and caution with which she would greet and pet Franny whenever she and her mother paid their infrequent visits to Not Ditmas Park (infrequent only because Jen was constantly deflecting the visits; infrequent because Meg and Millie "shouldn't have to go to the trouble to come all the way from SoHo"). Millie even coached herself using the same mantra she used with Franny: "Jenta, jenta," Millie whispered to her fist.

"You don't have to be gentle," Jen whispered, rubbing her nose against Millie's ear to make her giggle. "You can *attack*."

Millie stuck out her tongue in concentration and pushed her crayon across the page in what was intended as a swooping motion. The completed mark was an off-kilter kiss between greater-than and less-than signs. She tried again and again, layering the page with disembodied Pac-Man maws. Millie squawked admonishments at the page, lowering her head until her nose almost touched the paper, as if she could intimidate it into showing her not the marks her hand actually made but the perfect interlocking rings her mind could see.

Jen reached over to grab an antique miniature globe off a coffee table and showed Millie how to trace around the circular pewter base.

"You know, I never thought about this before, Millie, but it's really hard to draw a circle," Jen said. "You have to know exactly where to start, which is also exactly where you have to end, and you can't really stop to check your work."

Millie teethed her lower lip and turned to Jen, her eyes round. "Fanny," she said, in a grave, confessional whisper. "Fanny."

"Franny's at home with Uncle Jim," Jen said. "But she misses you, and is hoping to see you soon, and she told me to give you this special message. Are you ready?" Jen pressed foreheads with Millie and rolled her tongue against her teeth in a loud purr, and Millie laughed.

"That *is* pretty funny, Millie," Jen said, looking up for Meg. But Meg had laid down the pestle and padded silently across the great room, where she was fast asleep on a sofa.

Jen had looked up too quickly. She ducked her head back down and closed her eyes, waiting for another rushing foam of nausea to recede.

"Daw Fanny, daw Fanny," Millie was saying, laughing and rubbing Jen's arm.

"That's a good idea, sweetie," Jen said, opening her eyes and taking the crayon from Millie. "If we draw Franny, then she'll be here with us."

We Talked About Seven

There was a young rabbi who had rediscovered her dormant faith after the death of her father. There was a medical resident whose elective mastectomy at age thirty-two had turned her into a health-food nut and ultramarathoner. There was a successful real estate agent whose house burned down and sent her into a surprising state of quasi-Buddhist bliss at the loss of her material possessions. There was a young electronics heiress whose brief, DUI-related jail sentence brought her into contact with women serving harsh sentences for minor drug offenses, which led the electronics heiress to enroll in law school to become an advocate for such women. There was an event planner who found her fiancé in bed with a circus performer she had hired for a four-year-old's birthday party, which inspired her to start a popular new dating site.

And there was, to Jen's profound sorrow and regret, a wealthy retired friend of Leora's who had outsourced her favorite horse's daily exercise to a groom because she was so busy with her garden and memoirs, and shortly thereafter the horse had died of colic, which taught Leora's friend an important lesson, as she wrote in an email to Leora, "about the value of remembering to take a breath and look around you so you don't miss anything."

"We're so hard on ourselves. And that's what makes us women great. But it also hurts us sometimes. What doesn't kill us only makes us stronger, and vice versa," Leora once said.

"What kills our horses only makes us stronger," Daisy once said.

For the video project, they had, in Jen's assessment, a decent if not excellent spread of ages, ethnicities, and cultural backgrounds. Geographical diversity among the interviewees wasn't as good, but Donna wanted to do all the interviews and did not wish to travel. Jen had presented photos of each woman to Karina, who often said, "Even if it's weird to talk about it, we always need to think about *optics*. It's just a reality."

They'd booked a video crew and blocked out studio time. Donna had a script for all six interviews that she wouldn't share with anyone else. "It is down on paper," she said, "but it's not yet in the air. The conversation needs to breathe and fly on its own. Ink and tree mulch can't contain it."

For weeks, Jen had been trying to get the roster and budget in front of Karina for her approval. But whenever Jen caught her in person, Karina would ask her to put her questions in an email, which Karina would then ignore, no matter how many times Jen forwarded and forward-forwarded the email to her.

Then Karina had gone on vacation; on her return, she was perpetually "slammed" with other work. In the last few days running up to the shoot, Jen had given up, assuming Karina had given her tacit approval, or her approval-by-forfeit.

Karina—LIFt
Monday, Sept 14 11:14 AM
To: Jen <Jenski1848@gmail.com>
Subject: Shoot tomorrow
Priority: High!

Jen, as discussed, do not proceed with tomorrow's shoot until you have my sign-off.

Jen—LIFt
Monday, Sept 14 11:56 AM
To: Karina—LIFt
Subject: Re: FW: Shoot tomorrow
Priority: High!

Of course—just switching this conversation to my work email. (I don't see messages as quickly on the other email!) I'll be right over with lots of cool stuff for you to check out. I'm excited for you to see what we've cooked up— be there in five.

Karina—LIFt
Monday, Sept 14 11:59 AM
To: Jen—LIFt
Subject: Re: FW: Shoot tomorrow
Priority: High!

Come by in an hour or so instead—I'm swamped right now

"We talked about seven," Karina was saying, head shots and biographical sketches fanned out on her desk before her. It was four-fifty-five p.m., the day before the shoot.

"That's true," Jen said, who wasn't actually sure it was true, "but we have a very strong crop of six."

Karina continued to scowl at a head shot of the crusading socialite. Jen's face burned and itched. She wished she'd remembered to bring her can of ginger ale to Karina's office, imagined pressing the cold, damp metal to her cheek.

"So Petra has dummy screen shots from the six videos in a grid on the landing page for the whole package—I can show you on my computer, if you want."

"Is Petra the one who's always carrying the bag around?" Karina asked.

"Petra is—"

"—I don't know how to make this clearer to you," Karina said. "We talked about seven."

"And we have six," Jen said.

"Seven is Leora's number, and last I checked, I'm pretty sure this is Leora's foundation."

"We shoot tomorrow and we have six."

"Look, Jen, it's up to you whether you see this as a collaboration or not, but that's what it is. Collaboration. Communication. Give-and-take."

"Uh-huh," Jen said.

Karina shrugged. "I don't know what to tell you," she said. "You have work to do. Close the door behind you as you leave."

Who Is "We"?

Jen was sitting at her desk. She couldn't remember how she had gotten from Karina's office to her cubicle. Daisy was on the phone.

"They don't want any of the money to go toward salaries," Daisy was saying into the phone. "Only toward the programs. Yes, I've explained that the salaries are part of the programs. If you want Leora's money, you have to take it for free."

Jen's immediate visual ken had narrowed; the periphery was a retching taupe spatter of molding mushrooms and crusted-over oatmeal and curdling cream. A *wheee* of tinnitus rang in her ears and struggled to harmonize with the background *whhooooosssshhhhh*. She sipped from her can of ginger ale, held the soda in her mouth for a moment before working up the courage to swallow it.

She took a saltine from its package, wetted and worried one corner of the saltine with her teeth, returned the saltine to its package.

She watched her hand pick up the phone. She watched her fingers dial Pam. She knew three numbers by heart: Jim, Meg, Pam.

"You sound upset," Pam was saying.

Jen touched back into the conversation. She'd missed the ringing sound, the exchange of salutations. What had she said beyond hello?

"No, not at all," Jen said.

"I'm sorry that I kind of closed the drapes on the world after the show," Pam said. "I mean, you know this—I always get kind of depressed after an opening. Not depressed, just low. Like, the comedown."

"I know," Jen said. "You just need your space after something so big like that. It's understandable." *Unstanbull.* Jen had to concentrate not to slur her words.

In fact, Pam had scarcely crossed Jen's mind lately. Jen felt a momentary gratitude that her carelessness happened to have synched with Pam's customary spell of post-opening hibernation.

Thanks for no one

Thanks for nothing

"I think it was especially intense this time, maybe because the show was kind of personal?" Pam said. "I haven't really come around to how I feel about that."

"Well, you should feel *great* about the show," Jen said. She placed her elbows on her desk and her face in her palms, phone jammed between her ear and shoulder. Inside her palms, Jen's vision pulsed red and brown, with flickers of narrow bluish-yellow light.

"Is everything okay?" Pam was asking.

Jen had fallen into her palms and crawled out again. "Totally fine, sorry, I'm just being a space cadet," she said. "I haven't been feeling so well." *Feesowull.*

"I'm sorry, lady. That sucks."

"Thanks, I'm okay," Jen said. "I—um—I meant to tell you—I'm—"

"I think there's some weird bug going around," Pam interrupted. "People who usually get colds in winter are getting them now."

"I—" Jen stopped. Not now.

Say nothing thanks for nothing

"Maybe that's it," Jen said. "I'm getting a jump on flu season."

She tried to remember a time she had ever lied to Pam before, and couldn't.

"Yeah, makes me glad I'm a shut-in," Pam said.

"You're not a shut-in. Hey, I was wondering if you could do me a favor."

"I can try."

"So we're doing this video series about women who have overcome adversity—"

"Who is 'we'?" Pam asked.

"Oh, sorry, 'we' is the foundation. LIFt."

"Right, okay."

"So, first of all, I want to be totally honest with you: I'm asking you not just because you're awesome and amazing and I think you'd be perfect for this, but because I'm in a bind. I need to find one more person to participate in the video series by tomorrow—long story, the deadlines got all messed up. I didn't ask you in the first place because I was hesitant about mixing up our friendship with my stuff at work. But even though I'm in a spot now, I promise that I *wouldn't* be asking you now if I didn't think you'd be really, *really* great for this."

"Okay, okay, I get it," Pam said. Jen could hear both affection and irritation in her voice. "What exactly do you need from me?"

"Well, so you'd be on camera talking about—about the accident— your accident—and your recovery from it," Jen said. "So that would be the adversity you had overcome. You could say a lot of the things we've talked about in the last year or so, about how too many healthy people in their twenties and thirties don't have health insurance, how bike safety in the city is atrocious, how the cops don't follow up on drivers who hurt cyclists—all that stuff. You've always wanted people to be more aware of all these things."

"Yeah, I've just never known how to do it," Pam said. "I don't have any community-organizer skills."

"Okay, but you'd be doing that just by talking about it in a public forum like this." Jen could hear a hectoring impatience hardening her voice, and tried to knead it into something softer. A column of sweat streamed across her hairline past her ear on one side, then the other. "You could talk about your art, too."

"I could," Pam said.

"Your story is just so compelling because it really happened to you, and it could happen to anyone," Jen said. A vise was tightening around her skull. "Almost like—like this was a bad thing that happened, but look at the good that could come out of it because you can take con- trol of the situation and make meaning out of it. I mean, *not* that, but something like that."

"That sounds a little Zen Rand to me," Pam said.

"No, no, more matter-of-fact than that," Jen said, without knowing what she meant.

"No, I get it," Pam said, kindly. "So it's a bunch of videos of women overcoming adversity. Who else is being interviewed?"

"Let's see," Jen said. "There's a woman who spent some time in jail for substance-related charges, and now she's in law school because she wants to become an advocate for women in prison on nonviolent drug-related offenses."

"Oh, that's cool," Pam said. "So the adversity she overcame was addiction?"

"Yeah, I think so," Jen said. Gray baubles of sweat were dropping soundlessly onto her desk. Invisible crystals of freezing rain stung her eyes. Her stomach lurched up and over. Her internal organs were calcifying into jagged rocks.

"Jen?"

"Sorry, we cut out for a second. You know, I don't have the exact details on all of the interviewees, but I can get them for you if it's helpful."

"No, that's okay, sounds like a good story," Pam said. "Do you have just the basic info on a couple of the others?"

"Um, there's a woman whose house burned down, and she sort of learned how to let go of her possessions, stop being so materialist."

"That one isn't as good," Pam said.

"Yeah, honestly, I think yours would be the best one, by far," Jen said. She imagined the cord on the phone as the lifeline in her grip as she disappeared into a quicksand of sewage. Revulsion flattened and stretched her facial muscles. "You know, it's obnoxious for me to say this," she said to Pam, "but it could be a really good platform for you. We'll have someone do your hair and makeup, and my colleague Donna will be interviewing you, and she's amazing—"

"Wait, Donna? The life coach?"

Jen's stomach grumbled and reared up again, this time in dire warning. Pam had an excellent memory. She listened to what you said and remembered it. It was one of the reasons Jen loved her.

"Yeah, I know," Jen said, "but she's great, she really is."

"What will the series be called?" Pam asked.

Jen rested her forehead on her desk, two hands pressing the phone to her ear. The sweat on her brow and on her desk caused her to slide forward, mashing her nose against the particleboard. "We're not sure yet," she said.

Jen could hear Pam thinking.

"Can I sleep on it?"

"I—I—I guess you could—but—" Jen stammered. She rested her head across from the phone receiver in a pantomime of sickbed pillow talk.

"You need to know now, I get it," Pam said.

"Well, it's just that we're shooting the interviews tomorrow," Jen said.

"I'll do it," Pam said. "Why not? I'll do it."

Behind the phone, the package of saltines swam into view, and Jen squeezed her eyes shut to make them disappear. Just palpable amid the gusts of nausea that pinned her tightly to her desk surface, Jen discerned a serene and lilting fatalism. She had willed herself to catch a disease, and then she gave it to her friend, as if it were a gift.

Lessons in Zen Rand

Jen could not account for the next twenty-four hours, not even directly after they'd elapsed. She knew there had to have been two legs of a commute, and seven or so hours of sleep, and sweaty, messy attempts at dinner and then breakfast and lunch; there had to have been conference calls and emails; there had to have been bolts to the bathroom; there had to have been some kind of frantic pitch session in Karina's office wherein Jen marketed her friend Pam as a LIFt-worthy package of strength, vulnerability, creativity, tragedy, and good *optics*. She knew she had welcomed Pam into the LIFt offices, ushered her into the soundproof video studio, introduced her to Donna, and coaxed her to submit to the makeup artist's entreaties, "just for a touch-up." But Jen could never have sourced a single specific freeze-frame or intertitle from these twenty-four hours. In her memory's telling, she hung up the phone with Pam and looked up and Pam was standing in front of her desk.

"What the fuck?" Pam said in a stage whisper. Her eyes, framed with heavy mascara and liner, glittered with fury; a horrified smile strained her features. She had turned a deep red, burning through the heavy pancake makeup up to her hairline. Large-eyed and large-mouthed and painted, breathless and zipped up in one of her Champion sweatshirts, her hair raked back in a makeshift knot, she summoned in Jen's addled mind a ballerina who'd been pushed offstage to a skidding stop, still spinning with emotion and adrenaline after a truncated, tumultuous performance.

"Pam, hi, what?"

"What the fuck was that?" Pam was asking. Hissing.

"What's wrong? What happened?" Jen stood, started to reach for Pam's arm, then thought better of it. She sensed Daisy to her left rising from her cubicle and slipping quietly away.

"I just got interrogated on camera about how God himself sent the angel Gabriel down to earth to personally pulverize my bones with his divine truck and teach me an important lesson about owning my power. *The fuck*, Jen?"

"The interview? Pam, I'm sorry—what—"

"You know, this is my own fault. I thought I was going to be talking about fucking health-insurance deductibles and protected bike lanes. I should have known it would be this faux-Buddhist libertarian bullshit."

"Zen Rand," Jen said, almost to herself.

"You *knew*," Pam was saying. She suddenly seemed calmer, more in control of herself. Her affect was reflattening. "You work here. You knew these people. Jennifer, this woman was one step away from telling me I'd invited this into my life to give me a motherfucking *purpose*. Do you know how infuriating that is to me?"

"I can't even imagine, Pam. I'm sorry."

"You tricked me into exploiting myself so that you could finish an assignment."

"*No.* No, Pam, calm down, I would never—"

"I'm perfectly calm." Pam did sound perfectly calm. The red was fading. "You're either too stupid not to know this would happen, or you did this with malice. I have never known you to be stupid, so that leaves malice."

"Pam, no, please, I can explain—"

"I don't need you to explain. I'm leaving now. I can find my own way out."

Jen turned and watched helplessly as Pam walked across the office floor and vanished through the glass doors to the elevator bank. Jen locked eyes with Jules the intern, who had swiveled around in her chair and was scrunching her face into a shoulder-squeeze of sympathy. Jen did not react, and turned and took her seat again. She folded her hands on her desk. She was comfortably seated in a still pocket of time, no turbulence, 70 degrees Fahrenheit, pH balance of seven. This pocket of time would expire in ten to fifteen minutes. The pocket of time walled itself off from dread about the moment of its expiration, the moment that the pocket of time would run out of oxygen; her amygdala would remain sound asleep until then, until the alarm rang. Jen could peer wonderingly at her steady hands with dry eyes and no apprehension. Even the pain in her lower abdomen, which had been building all afternoon, receded a bit. She heard Daisy reinstall herself in her cubicle.

whatDaisyknew: Didn't mean to eavesdrop but is everything ok
jenski1848: Is there someone who could send me a link to the interview
    Donna did with Pam, the last-minute addition?
whatDaisyknew: Sure, I've already seen it, it sort of looks like a hostage
    video shot in a realtor's office in Palm Springs

As the raw video began, Pam was rubbing her teeth with one finger, unaccustomed as she was to lipstick. The makeup artist had already performed a rhinoplasty of contouring. The hairdresser had straightened Pam's hair, which Jen knew must have taken at least an hour or more. Pam was wearing a ruffled tangerine blouse that Jen had never seen before—Jen assumed it was borrowed from Leora's ad-hoc clothing-storage space, which Daisy had stumbled upon one day while searching for padded envelopes and which Petra had then started using instead of the handicapped stall to pump breast milk. The ruffled tangerine blouse was further embellished by a chunky, brassy necklace that Jen recognized from Leora's Opening Statement!™ jewelry line. Off-camera, Donna was asking Pam if she was ready to begin. Jen could hear Donna taking off her bracelets.

All right, good, let's start. So, Pam. It's been nearly a year and a half now. Can you tell us what happened?

Sure—and thanks for having me here today, Donna, and thanks to, um, the foundation. So, let's see, I was riding my bicycle to a gallery on a Saturday afternoon. I was making a turn at an intersection, and, as far as I can piece it together, a van was speeding to make the light, hit me from behind, and threw me from the bike. I'll probably never know exactly what happened, because the van drove away and the cops never really followed up on it.

What were your injuries?

Well, my left leg was shattered. Just wrecked. I had a compound fracture of the femur and a smashed tibia, and my ankle was beyond—I mean, the pedal had slashed clean through it. It was pretty gross. I also dislocated my shoulder and cracked a couple of ribs—but on my right side. So my injuries were ambidextrous, you could say.

Aha, so you had found a new equilibrium!

Ha, yes, you could say that. But it was my leg that was the big problem.

What do you remember of the first days after the accident?

I remember coming in and out of this bluey consciousness—everything seemed underwater and tinted blue, with tinges of red at the edges, like, um, like the curling of fingers, or seaweed. And I remember pain, just excruciating pain, like every cell in my body was being crushed over and over again. The pain was so bad I was surprised I was alive. It was so bad I was sort of in awe of it, you know? Like I could behold it from a slight distance, and I guess I got that distance because of the medication they were giving me. If I had been inside that pain, I would have gone crazy.

But you made it, Pam. You made it. Tell us about your road to recovery.

Well, I don't know how much detail you want me to go into, but they basically had to reassemble my leg, which took a lot of time and operations and then recovery time between the operations. That was, in a way, the most dispiriting part—every time I'd have recovered enough from an operation to start to sort of feel like myself again, another operation would come around the bend. And then I basically had to learn to walk again, with a leg that felt uncomfortably new and unfamiliar, but also old and over it—over *life*, you know? My leg was depressed, which was depressing to me. My leg and I had to get to know each other again. And my two different legs had to learn to get along.

And now?

Things are pretty good. My leg gives me trouble when it's cold, or when it rains. This past winter was hard at times, going up stairs and stuff. And I have a lot of scars on my leg, but I kind of like them now. They've healed and smoothed over, and they're sort of cool-looking. They're a story.

Battle scars.

Something like that. I don't really think of it as a battle. I'm sad that I can't really run like I used to anymore. Maybe someday. I could ride a bike, but I don't want to.

A fear you need to conquer.

Yeah, maybe—well, I don't know about that. I don't know that I need to conquer it, actually. I mean, why would anyone want to get back on a bike after what happened?

What did you learn about yourself during the months you spent recovering?

Well, it's interesting. One thing I didn't know is that the femur is the only bone in the human thigh. Isn't that weird to think about? We've got fourteen bones in our face, twenty-nine bones in our skull, and just that one lonely bone accounting for about a quarter of our height. So, anyway, with a femoral fracture, what happens is—

Pam, I'm going to stop you there—I meant more on a personal level, a spiritual level. What did you learn about yourself during this time?

Oh, okay. Let's see. I don't really know.

We've talked a lot about the physical. What about the metaphysical, the spiritual?

I don't—I don't believe in God, so—

We don't necessarily have to be talking about a god. Let me put it another way: When this accident happened, what did you think the universe was trying to tell you?

I don't know. I don't—it's sort of hard for me to think in those terms. Sorry, I know you need stuff for the interview. Um— huh, I don't know. It was just the thing that happened. I don't think it was, like, a *sign*. Or like a divine message. Is that what you mean?

Maybe you were the message, and this event was the messenger.

Yeah, I don't know.

Because you do have a message, don't you?

Yes, I do. First of all, I want people in their twenties and thirties who don't have health insurance to make sure they have it. The only reason I had health insurance when this happened was because I was at a party one time and I mentioned I didn't have health insurance—it was almost like a brag, like a bit of bravado. Bravada? And this woman I'd just met turned to me and told me about her brother, who was diagnosed with cancer at the age of twenty-six. If he hadn't had health insurance, she said, he would have bankrupted their entire family and their lives never would have been the same. She told me that story and I got health insurance the next day. It wasn't great insurance and it was really expensive and it had a high deductible, but it was something. This accident happened just over a year after that. I want to sort of be like that woman's brother for people who think they can squeeze by without insurance.

The second important issue here is that I think if a pedestrian or cyclist gets hit by a car in the city where I live, or any city, there should be a police investigation, always, without exception. Because in my case—in my case—

—*You put your life into the hands of the justice system, and you felt the justice system let you down.*

Well, no, it didn't even get as far as the courts. I thought I would be in court saying, "This driver was negligent, and the burden is on me to prove it, and I think I can prove it, but it's up to the justice system to decide." But the police were the gatekeepers to the justice system, and they closed the gate. They had multiple witnesses, tire tracks all over the place, even most of the license plate, and they might have even had security-camera footage, but we'll never know because they didn't follow up, they didn't even find out if the footage existed. They probably would have investigated properly if I had died—and isn't that crazy, that *that's* the threshold for an investigation? Death? But instead it was like, "Well, whoops, it was an accident, sucks for you, but what can we do?"

Hey, you know what, Donna, could I do that part over again? I think I can do it more concisely and be more articulate. I shouldn't say "sucks"!

Well, actually, Pam, I was going to stop you anyway, because—keep in mind that we are aiming for a very diverse nationwide audience, so we may not want to drill down so much into specifics on these points, which are very, well, specialized. Police matters and so forth. It might be fruitful to paint with a broader brush. Not so local, you see?

I think so. Yeah, no, you're right, I can boil it down to talking
   points. I should be better at this—I watched so many cable-TV
   talk shows in the hospital.

Okay, let's regroup and start again.

Sounds good.

Pam, what was the message this accident was sending you?

The message I have is—oh, wait, that wasn't your question. Sorry.

*Let's try again. You're doing really well. Okay. Pam, what was the
   higher purpose of this accident? Why did it happen?*

I don't—I don't understand the question, I'm sorry.

Well, do you think the accident happened for a reason?

N-no. No, I don't think the accident happened for a reason. I
   think I've tried to make some good come out of the accident,
   but it didn't happen for a reason.

*But the accident taught you something. So in a sense, couldn't you say
   that it happened for a reason? That, in a way, it had a purpose?*

No. No, the accident did not have a purpose. Two different things
   happened: The accident happened, and then I did things in
   response to it. That's not the same thing as saying that the accident was purposeful—I mean, we keep saying "the accident,"
   but we're talking about an enormous amount of suffering and
   pain, a year of my life in a sense lost to this, part of my body
   literally destroyed. So much pain. So it's hard to talk about it
   like it was a cloud with a silver lining.

What did the pain teach you, Pam?

The pain—the pain didn't teach me anything. Pain is pain. I
   don't . . . yeah.

What I'm hearing from you is that bitterness was consuming you.

Huh. I don't—you know, I—it's weird, because at first I—um—at
   first I—I didn't have much room for emotions. I—I was in
   pain all the time, for a long time, or else out of my mind on
   drugs. There's a kind of—deranging effect of that, like I said
   before. And yeah, so—yeah, once the pain starts turning into
   just plain old severe discomfort and inconvenience, then the

emotions start having room to move in, and you do feel angry, because someone did something terrible to you and there were no consequences.

You wanted revenge?

No, no. No, of course not. I'm not a vengeful—no. I wanted— look, imagine, this terrible thing has happened and no one is helping you make it better. I mean, that's not true, your friends and family are helping and doctors and nurses and physical therapists are helping, and most of those people are being really awesome, but the person responsible for this isn't helping, and he's not being held responsible, and no one seems interested in holding him responsible. It's like—me and my doctors and family and friends were held responsible for a crime we didn't commit. That's it, that's it.

Because you discovered that you are responsible for your own life, and sometimes that's a terrible burden, isn't it?

Well, no, nobody is responsible for her own life, not entirely. You can imagine that you are, but then a truck comes out of nowhere and mows you down! That's actually exactly the opposite of what I'm saying. I didn't invite this into my life.

But you were responsible for your response to the situation.

Well, sure, to a certain point, but I was lucky. I know that's a weird thing to say, given what happened, but it was. I had health insurance. I had love and support. I didn't have a head injury—that right there, that was *fantastic* luck, life-changing luck. Sure, I was wearing a helmet, but nothing I did right then determined whether or not I received a head injury—you could be wearing a helmet and a truck could still come along and crush your skull.

You asked a minute ago if I was consumed with bitterness. I think what I was really consumed with was an obsession to tell people what I'd learned and make them act on it. I wanted young, healthy people to know that they needed health insurance. I wanted cyclists to wear helmets, always. I wanted my representative in Congress and my local police precinct to know that a crime had occurred, a real crime, not just an accident—because an accident can be a crime, and vice versa—and that resulted in gross bodily harm to me and emotional distress to my parents and my boyfriend and my friends. I wanted these powerful people to know that the police, who are entrusted to serve and protect, did not, in my opinion, serve and protect me. I wanted health-insurance companies to know how much completely unnecessary stress and tedium and frustration and worry they put their customers through when their customers are already depleted physically and emotionally—that it amounts to a form of abuse, truly. And I wanted drivers to know how much power they had to hurt people, and to feel sort of—to feel chagrined by that power. To feel the literal shape and weight of that power.

So you felt that the accident had made you a teacher, a leader.

No. I never felt that.

Everything you just said sounds like the words of a teacher and a leader. A teacher and a leader doesn't have to be some wise old man on a mountaintop. What we're talking about is simply the power of sharing our experience so that others can learn from it.

Well, I think it—it gave me a useful anecdote, I'd say.

But not everyone might have seen it that way. Some people might have just closed in on themselves, felt sorry for themselves. They wouldn't have seen it as a teachable moment.

Well, I wouldn't judge them for that. Believe me, I did plenty of feeling sorry for myself during that time.

You invoked the word power *a moment ago. What I'm hearing is that you felt powerless, and you seized this chance to own your power.*

I don't—yeah, I don't know.

Well, can we explore that idea together for a moment, Pam? That idea of empowering yourself in a moment of powerlessness.

I mean, yeah, sure, it gave me something to think about; it gave me an intellectual focus.

So that's what the accident was there to teach you—that you had power, how you could use your power.

I just—this thing happened—and I think—I think the accident gave me the opportunity—no—I think the accident created an occasion for me to say, "This happened to me, and here's what could have been better, and here's what could have been worse, and here's how it could have been prevented." And saying that has involved me talking to people with a certain degree of power: congressmen, community representatives, police representatives. And it still does, because I want change to happen. I want laws to change.

That amazing moment when you realize again that everything happens for a reason.

Okay. Fine. Sure. Yeah.

Do you see that journey we just went on together, Pam? Only a few minutes ago you were saying that this accident had no purpose. But we've realized together that it had a great purpose for you.

No, I just—I was just agreeing with you.

Pardon?

I was just agreeing with you to be polite. I don't want to argue, you know.

We only want the truth here. That's what these conversations are—they're a search for the truth. The truth of your spirit, the truth of your soul, the truth of Pam's purpose here on earth.

Yeah, no, I get that.

So, then, what is your truth, Pam?

I don't know. I really don't know. Um, so do you guys think you have enough material to work with now?

The time-elapsed bar at the bottom of the screen showed about thirty seconds left on the video, but Jen closed the tab, exited the video player, leaned over, and vomited neatly into her wastepaper basket. The ginger ale was amenable, she'd found, but she'd have to remember to chew the saltines more thoroughly.

whatDaisyknew: I'll be right back with some water and paper towels

Jen pushed the wastepaper basket under her desk with her foot and watched the package of saltines. She was surprised to find herself still seated inside the pocket of time, as if pressing play on the video had pressed pause on the autonomic avalanche to come.

"The biker," a deep, familiar voice was saying.

Jen looked up at an out-of-focus image of Donna standing in front of her desk, where Pam had just stood. Donna's face was a picture of heavy-lidded perturbance, as if her umbrage had rudely awakened her from a late-afternoon nap.

"The biker?" Jen asked, guarding Donna from her breath by sipping from her ginger ale.

"The biker."

"The biker," Jen repeated.

"Friend of yours."

"Pam?"

"The biker."

"Are you asking," Jen said, holding her hand over her mouth in what she hoped looked like a pensive gesture, "for general impressions of my friend Pam, whose interview with you didn't go as well as either of you had hoped?"

Donna stared back at her impassively. "You need to put a collar and a leash on that attitude and take it out for a long, hard run."

Jen pressed her lips against the can of ginger ale and pretended to sip to keep from laughing.

"And," Donna said, "you need to think twice before you put your friends' needs ahead of the organization's needs."

A bolt of pain cracked a ragged diagonal down Jen's lower abdomen, and she hugged her waist and leaned forward, wincing. "Message received, Donna," she said to the carpet.

"What is *wrong* with you?" Donna asked.

"I'm fine," Jen gasped, surprised by pain.

"Well," Donna said, swallowing the word in hesitation, unsure whether or not she should press her advantage, "we can't use that footage. Of your friend. Total waste of time." Jen could sense Donna shifting on her feet, her bangles jostling one another in discomfort.

A hand stroked Jen's back. Daisy was standing beside her, holding a glass of water.

"I don't think she is feeling very good right now, Donna," Daisy said.

Jen, doubled over, heard Donna exhale through her nose. "You set a good example for us all, Daisy. We can learn from you. You can teach us. And I hope you feel better, Julie," Donna said as she clinked and clanged away.

Later, Jen remembered feeling happy for Daisy just then, that she had inspired such words of praise from the LIFt board chair. She made a mental note to remind Daisy to mention it in her six-month performance review. That happiness in turn produced a secondary happiness in Jen, that she was capable of considering the feelings of others even at a moment when she was bending and folding into herself, crumpling into a ball under the terrifying pressure of at least two types of pain, and she had no one but herself to blame for the pain, and no more space left in the pocket of time to put off the pain and its outrageous demands.

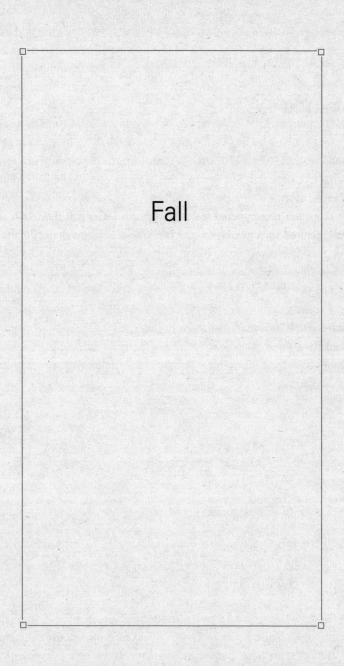

Fall

The Thing That Happened

Sometimes it was crying, sometimes it was sobbing, and sometimes it was something else. The something else felt as though there was too much oxygen inside her, too much air—*too much life,* Jen thought; *ha ha what a hilarious notion*—expanding and kicking against either side of her rib cage until it would crack, air pushing, pushing, air bottle-necked just below her sternum, air that could escape only in small gulps, a mouth wide open but so little coming out of it, a wet ripping sound producing nothing but more of itself.

Nothing will come of nothing
Speak again

Jen would squeeze her eyes shut and pound her fist on the duvet, on the sofa, on the edge of the obscene bathtub under the screaming bathroom lights, as she tried to push, push the air out, again and again.

So much effort and so much time and so much waste and for what? she thought, as water roared out of the tap.

The thing that happened started happening on a Friday evening. Jen didn't want Jim to see what was happening. She locked herself in their bathroom for hours, for an entire day. He went to the bar down the street to use the men's room. They called no one but the doctor's office. She went to the doctor's office alone, which was a mistake.

"I'm sorry, honey, I'm so sorry," she cried into Jim's chest after she came back from the doctor's office. "Who *does* that? Why did I *do* that? I'm sorry I'm sorry I'm sorry. I left us alone. I left us alone."

"No, you didn't," Jim said. "You never did. I'm here. We're here."

"I'm sorry," Jen said.

"You didn't do anything wrong," Jim said.

"I'm sorry," Jen said again, and after that she did not recognize the sounds spurting from her as her own.

The crying turned into sobbing and it turned into something else. Jim held Jen as she shook and shrieked with the effort of pushing, pushing the air.

"It's just—it's just air," Jen cried.

"It's okay," Jim whispered into her hair.

"It's just—panic—panic—"

"Shhh, you're okay. You're going to be okay."

Jen fell asleep crying and woke up crying. By the second day both of her eyes were swollen almost shut. She hurt already and the crying made the parts that hurt hurt even more. But she couldn't stop.

She dreamed that the blood in her veins turned to blackstrap molasses. A nurse with a giant needle struggled to tap a viable vein, then extracted four vials and offered her a taste. Jen refused, and the nurse shrugged and took a sip.

"I wasn't expecting it to be bitter," the nurse said, licking her lips.

Jen had other dreams, dreams that she tried to forget, dreams that made her think part of her mind had gone rotten and pestilent, that it should be cut away before it infected the rest.

They never called the thing that happened by its name. After it was over, Jim never asked about it, and Jen never brought it up. The thing that happened was a country unto itself. Its borders were permanently closed. It spoke for itself in the event of itself, once, and it brooked no further discussion.

Causation

Monday, 9.30 a.m.

The bell was ringing, and Jen was sprinting across a field toward it. Her heart thumped so hard it clapped the grit from her chest cavity and rib cage, kicking up a swirl of dust that made her cough and retch as she ran. She knew this and could feel it. She had to touch the door before the bell stopped ringing. She had to. That was the rule. But her legs were giving out. The sockets of her hips were oxidizing. Her sides cramped and seized. Twenty feet from the door she fell forward, and some force pulled her arms behind her, and just as her face slammed into the ground she opened her eyes and saw her cell phone in bed next to her, ringing.

"Hey, Jen," Karina was saying on her speaker phone. "Happy fall."

"Hey, Karina," Jen murmured.

"First day of autumn still feels just like summer."

"Mm-hmm."

"I got your husband's email and thought I'd call to check in." Karina's voice echoed and spun around in the air. "Feeling under the weather?"

"Um, yeah," Jen said, her tongue thick and filmy. She became aware of the ache in her lower abdomen, a pulling and shredding, and remembered.

"I'm sorry to hear that. Did I wake you?"

"Thanks, and no, it's okay," Jen lied, with a small, weak laugh. *Why do you always laugh?* she thought. *Why is everything you think and say laughable?*

"Should you be in the *hospital?*" Karina asked.

Jen regurgitated the same little laugh. *Stop stop doing that,* she thought. "I'm just home."

"So it's not a *life-threatening* situation, I take it," Karina said.

Jen pictured her: the eyes narrowed into Möbius strips of empathy and disappointment, the rhythmic encouraging nods.

"Oh, no, nothing like that," Jen said.

"Do you have the flu?"

"Uh, no. No."

Karina sighed. "I'm hearing a tone of evasion, Jen, and I want to understand. I'm calling out of concern for you and concern for your achievements. We have a lot of work to get done in the next few days ahead of the launch, and we're counting on you to be fully present. That's how much we value you."

"Sure, of course, but—"

"This is a time for all of us to come together, even if we're under the weather. We can make little sacrifices now, or we can make big sacrifices later. That's our choice to make. You're a key part of the team, Jen. What do you say? We'll give you all the support you need if you're not feeling one hundred percent. But we need the same support from you."

"Karina—" Jen's throat seized and clicked. She closed her eyes.

"Are you still there?"

"I can't come in today. I can't. I can't." Jen's voice bent and shuddered.

The line clattered as Karina picked up the phone. All at once her voice was inside Jen's head. "What's wrong?"

"I had—it's just—"

"What is it, sweetie? Take your time."

"I had a—I had a—"

"Oh, sweetheart," Karina said. "Are you—"

"No—"

"*Were* you—"

Jen began sobbing. For a second she felt relieved.

"Oh, darling," Karina said. "I'm so sorry. I thought that maybe you were—other women can always tell—and now—oh, sweet Jen. That is the hardest, hardest thing any woman can go through."

Karina's cooing voice, higher-pitched and unfamiliar, stroked Jen's relief into trepidation. "No, it's okay," Jen said, her voice still slushy.

Her teeth seemed in the way of her tongue. "This wasn't—it wasn't—I hadn't planned—"

She was about to say *I hadn't planned to tell you,* but then she remembered that she hadn't told Karina anything at all.

"I see," Karina said after a moment. "Still. It must be hard."

Jen had stopped paying attention. She breathed in through her nose and out through her mouth. "I'm going to go now. Okay, Karina? Is that okay?"

"Okay, sweetie. Feel better, take care."

Monday, 12.30 p.m.

Jen was dozing in bed when her cell phone rang. It was Jim.

"Hey, honey, just checking in. How are you feeling?"

"I'm okay. I'm glad to hear your voice."

"I'm glad to hear your voice, too, sweetheart."

Jen turned on her side and pulled her knees up, nestling the phone between her ear and her pillow, and listened to Jim not talking for a minute or two.

"Okay, well," Jim said, "I was just checking in."

"Stay a little while longer."

"Of course," Jim said. "Did you—by any chance did you talk to Pam?"

"No."

"I bet you could call her, honey. I mean, if you wanted to."

Jen said nothing.

"She would want to hear from you. If she knew. She would."

"Number one, she told me not to—"

"But that was before—"

"And number two, I don't—she has a right to be angry with me. She does."

"Okay, that's fair, but so what? Circumstances change."

"If I tell her what happened, it's like the scene in a bad movie when you find out that the unlikable antagonist watched her parents drown when she was a kid or something, and that explains why she's such an asshole, and doesn't everything seem so different now."

"No. It's not like that at all."

"Plus I don't want to draw a connection in her mind between the thing with her and *this* thing," Jen said.

"I don't think she would."

"I would, if I were her," Jen said. "She might even think I was blaming her—"

"That's irrational," Jim broke in, and caught himself. "No, I'm sorry, I shouldn't say *irrational*. I don't mean to invalidate anything you're feeling. But trust me, she would never think that."

"Why not? One thing happened and then another thing happened."

"Sure, honey, and I just ate a sandwich and now I'm going to teach my kids some Greek myths. That doesn't mean my sandwich wrote the Greek myths."

"I think she would connect the two things," Jen said. A theatrical singsong was creeping into her voice. She knew now that she was performing, saying things for effect, reveling in the novelty and miserable thrill of her predicament. "It certainly makes for a tidy narrative," she said, the words syncopated. *Tidy narrative* swooped up and down on the scale, hitting middle C on the first syllable of *narrative*. "Cause and effect."

"Okay, enough," Jim said. "This is absurd. This is not a fucking *narrative*, Jennifer. It's not an input-output model. What happened is not your fff—you know what, fuck this. Fuck your narrative."

Jen felt a guilty satisfaction, a bilious tickle of delight, at the controlled explosion she had detonated on the other end of the line. She wondered if the kick could overcome the shame sufficiently to produce its own modest endorphin rush.

"I'm sorry," she said.

"You don't have to be sorry," he said. "I'm sorry. You're going to be okay. I have to go to my next class, okay? I love you."

Jen could hear Jim hesitating before he hung up the phone. "You should get your artwork back from her," he said. "From Pam."

"There's a lot of things I should do," Jen said.

Tuesday, 9.30 a.m.

Jen and Franny were still asleep in bed when her cell phone rang.

"Hey, Jen, how are ya?" It was Sunny on speaker.

"Oh, hey, Sunny." Jen's lips stuck gummily together.

"Listen, hon, it's nine-thirty. When can we expect you?"

"Wait, what?" Jen wiped her mouth with the back of her hand and sat up. Franny sat up, too, arching her back. "I talked to Karina yesterday and told her I needed to take a sick day."

"Right, hon, but that was yesterday. What about today?" Sunny's voice was now muffled and small, balled up in paper, as if she'd turned away from the speaker to fish for something in her handbag.

"Sick *days*, plural," Jen said.

Sunny said nothing.

"I'm—I'm entitled to them?" Jen asked.

"Entitled, ha! Don't I know it," Sunny said, her voice big and clear again. "Jen, babe, we *neeeeed* you here. We're depending on you. Leora's gonna *fa-reek ow-oot* if she doesn't have her team intact, kiddo."

Jen's teeth began chattering against the phone. She held it slightly away from her. "I talked to Karina yesterday—"

"I *know*, hon, I'm so sorry. I can't even imagine what you're going through."

Jen dropped the phone on the bed and picked it up again. "So Karina told—and Karina said—"

"Jen, honey, Karina *asked* me to call you."

"Okay," Jen said. "Okay. Um, okay. What I was going to say was, I talked to her yesterday and thought we—we had an understanding."

"We *do* understand, honey, but we've got a launch! We can't afford to lose another day—"

"You *understand*?" Jen said. "That's funny, a second ago you said you couldn't possibly imagine."

"Hey, now, hold up, girl, don't take this out on me. Channel that sorrow, channel that womanly power and passion, but don't wield it against someone who's on your side. Use it for good."

Jen looked around the bedroom and logged the items in it. This was a technique taught in the mindfulness seminar that was compulsory for all new LIFt staffers. When feeling upset or impulsive, the instructor explained from her lotus-pose perch atop the conference-room table, you should take sixty to ninety seconds to take stock of the physical reality surrounding you. The goal, the teacher said, was to "hit a mental reset button," in order to make friendly everyday objects feel realer and more immediate than whatever source of anxiety might be flooding your frontal lobes at that instant.

The sun was shining. Jen watched the curtain drifting in the window—off-white on purchase, now a dusky yellow. She counted the watercolor-textured peacocks on the bedspread. She tugged absently at the fitted sheet, puckered in its perpetual slow-motion efforts to unpeel itself from the mattress. She cataloged the books on Jim's side of the bed—Astors, astrophysics, Aztecs—and the stacks of art catalogs and sketchbooks on her side. She logged Franny, purring on the bed beside her. Franny generally preferred not to be crowded, but she didn't wriggle as Jen pulled her close and pressed her face into her fur. The phone slipped from between Jen's ear and shoulder and dropped to the bed again.

"Jen? Are you there?"

Jen stroked Franny's fur where her tears had dampened it and picked up the phone. "Sunny," Jen said, "are you seriously telling me I have to come in today?"

"I'm not your keeper!" Sunny said. "I'm not the boss of you. *You're* the boss of you. I'm telling you what's what. I am *providing you with information.*"

Tuesday, 3.30 p.m.

"Jen!"

Slowly, methodically, Jen stood up from her desk and turned to see Karina across the floor of the LIFt offices. Karina made a tossing motion over her shoulder: a big beckoning arc. As Jen began to walk toward her, Karina turned her back and returned to her office.

Jen halted. She turned, walked back to her desk, and sat down, the chair wheezing under the impact. She held her fists in her lap and waited.

Her phone rang. Karina's extension. "Did you get lost?" Karina asked.

"No," Jen said.

"Well, then, get over here, kiddo, I'm dying to see you."

Jen slammed the phone down and stalked across the floor to Karina's office. Her limbs were stiff and heavy. Her face felt sunburned. Everything hurt.

"How *are* you?" Karina was asking.

"Fine, fine," Jen said. "So—"

"Sit, please, hon, and shut the door," Karina said.

Jen shut the door but remained standing. "So we have the first passes on the edits on the videos—"

"That's good. But I wasn't asking how are the edits. I was asking how are *you*?"

"I'm fine."

"Feeling okay physically?"

"Yup."

"And what about emotionally?"

"Yup."

"You're sure?"

"Yup. Yeah. Yes."

"Oh, honey, I wish I weren't out of tissues."

Jen swiped the back of her hand across one cheekbone, then the other. "No, I'm okay, I just—I don't want to talk about it, if that's—I don't want to talk about it."

"Well, you don't have to talk about it with little old me. But you shouldn't keep it bottled up. Forgive me for asking, but is there a licensed professional you've been in contact with?"

Jen could feel her tears hitting her blouse. She stared at the cluster of framed photographs on Karina's desk. Karina with Leora, blurred at a cocktail party, their eyes rabid red in the camera's pop. Karina with her tousle-haired, bespectacled husband on some beach. Karina with her son and daughter when they were babies, toddlers, preschoolers. "I'm okay," Jen said. "I appreciate your concern."

"What I can't—" Karina paused. She looked up toward the ceiling, as if for celestial counsel, and then spoke very slowly. "What I can't . . . put my finger on . . ." she said, "is why . . . well, given that this was unplanned . . . why you are so upset."

Jen kept looking at the photographs. Karina's son had his father's features and his mother's coloring; her daughter had the inverse. "I guess that is strange, isn't it," Jen said to the photographs. Her mind busied itself projecting their faces, tracing the projections, painting the traces.

"Strange? No, that's not the word I would use," Karina said. "I just don't understand, and I *want* to, because I care about you. We all do. We're all thinking about you right now."

The beachy highlights in Karina's daughter's hair might be tricky to mix—too much white would turn them to toothpaste, but too much yellow would bleach them chlorine green.

"I have the edits," Jen said to the photographs, "and I'd love to know if you want to watch them or if we can go ahead and finish up with them."

"Of course," Karina said. "You want all of this to be over with."

Jen kept her head down as she walked back to her desk, one cupped hand held faux-pensively to her philtrum to conceal any redness or swelling until she *flump*ed back into her chair. Daisy knocked gently on their shared cubicle wall, and Jen knocked reassuringly back.

whatDaisyknew: ARE YOU OK
jenski1848: No. But yes.

Daisy replied by attaching a .jpg file of a dachshund puppy enfolded in a hamburger bun.

jenski1848: Thanks, D. You're a good friend.

Daisy did not reply.

A Lot Going On

"Dad emailed to say how upset you were that I hadn't called in a while," Jen was saying to her mother. "I'm really sorry."

"What?" Jen's mom asked, twisting the word out to three syllables, phlegmy with incredulity. "I never said that. Your *father,* for goodness' sake!" Jen's mom sighed and regained her composure.

"Well, in any case, I'm sorry, Mom."

"You have a *lot* going on."

"No, it's not that—I just—haven't been feeling well."

"Oh? Are you eating right? Exercising?"

"I—no, I guess I haven't been doing those things as much as I should."

"You should see a doctor," Jen's mom said. "There's not a whole lot your old mom can do for you if you're not taking care of yourself. Go talk to a doctor."

"I hadn't thought of that," Jen said.

Dolly

Jen was at work, leaving a voicemail for Jim.

"In the dream, I'm in a simple Lutheran church, everything's wood; hard, cold pews; hard, cold everything, but lots of leg room. You're on the aisle and I'm sitting beside you. I know you're you, but you don't look like you; you look like Max von Sydow in *Through a Glass Darkly.* On my lap, sitting up like a regular person, is the embalmed and neatly dressed corpse of a middle-aged English woman named Dolly. Everyone else in the pews also has an embalmed corpse on their lap, except you. There's a small, shuffling group of mourners that stops by each pew to pay their respects to the deceased. One of them is Dolly's dad. Dolly's dad leans over to see his daughter, kind of awkwardly bent over you. He's wrecked, just totally destroyed by this whole ritual, but he's trying his best to put on a good face, and the result is that he's doing this kind of high-pitched, hooting-crying thing, and he keeps saying in his posh British accent, 'Goodbye, Dolly, goodbye, we love you, Dolly, bye-bye, now, Dolly, that's our girl, Dolly, goodbye.' Over and over. Dolly's mother stands by his side, silent, just watching Dolly with this fathomless expression. I keep apologizing to you for how difficult this is, and you are silent. As the mourners are dispersing, I notice that Dolly is picking at her face. I say 'No, no, Dolly, don't do that, sweetheart.' I turn her toward me—now I'm cradling her—and she's scratching and pulling really hard. Her skin is breaking and bleeding. I try to pull her hands away, but she's too strong for me. Then I think, *What does it matter if she picks her face? She's dead.* That was the end of the dream."

Jen pushed the button to listen to her message, then pushed the button to erase the voicemail from Jim's inbox, then hung up.

Who Speaks That Language?

The online launch of the Leora Infinitas Foundation and its "web channel," known as LIFe Lines, proceeded as scheduled. ("*Website* seems stale to me, and *blog* seems so limiting," Leora, or maybe Donna, wrote in Leora's Welcome Letter to readers. "*Web channel* feels like a network that is also a conduit—a sticky-sweet yet liberating web of endless possibilities.") Also publishing on schedule was LIFe Lines's flagship video suite, "Overcoming Adversity." (Six segments, edited down from seven.) LIFt's kickoff campaign, the interactive Total Transformation Challenge (TTC), likewise launched on time, and by the end of day one had attracted 1,137 entries—each of which contained seven vows toward improvement in the assigned areas of Mind, Body, Spirit, Space, Earth, Mission, and Heart. Altogether the launch was an unqualified success insofar as it was not a total disaster, a dichotomy captured on the morning of day one, when Sunny rushed over to Jen and asked her if they could unlaunch the site.

"That would be like un-born-ing a baby," Daisy said.

"Um, *inappropriate*, Daisy," Sunny said, looking at Jen.

"Un-birthing a baby, I guess," Daisy said.

"Daisy is right," Jen said. "But let's fix what we can."

Some of the rationales for an unlaunch were sound. For example, two of LIFt's newly announced grants, one to support teaching computer skills to girls in Colombia and one to support a girls' entrepreneurship program in Rio de Janeiro, hadn't actually been signed off by their underwriter, which was in both cases the Bluff Foundation.

Some of the rationales for the unlaunch seemed somewhat less sound, such as Leora's reported dissatisfaction with the background color of the logo.

"We're seeing *plum* when we're really going for *amethyst*," Sunny explained.

Part of the reason Leora may have been distracted from the finer details of her website launch was that she had spent much of September lining up off-the-record breakfast meetings in New York City and Los Angeles and Washington, D.C., with small groups of female journalists convened for maximum hybrid vigor, from veteran foreign bureau chiefs to young feminist bloggers, in the chambers of downtown cafés and brasseries more frequently reserved for upmarket baby-shower brunches. In some cases, the breakfasts—which, as far as the public was concerned, never actually happened—resulted in positive coverage of LIFt and TTC where otherwise there would have been none; in other cases, they turned what would have been snarky or withering coverage into positive coverage or, at the very least, peaceably ribbing coverage. Babette Exley, proprietor of the influentially cruel blog *Nastygram Ladyparts* and undisclosed invitee to one of Leora's undisclosed breakfasts, headlined her post on the launch I CAN'T TOTALLY HATE LEORA INFINITAS' WELL-MEANING NEW LADYVENTURE, AS MUCH AS I WANT TO.

In a bittersweet twist, a lone note of inadvertent critique of the LIFt launch and the TTC campaign came from Ruby Stevens-Meisel, whose effectively anonymous public status and undetermined off-the-grid location ensured that her name, or rather her pseudonym, would be left off the breakfast invitations. It was Ruby Stevens-Meisel who first publicly acknowledged the unfortunate double life of the TTC acronym.

"Is the rebranding of TTC—the mutation of the yearning admission 'Trying to Conceive' into the gauntlet-throwing 'Total Transformation Challenge'—a form of poetic license or fruitful coincidence?" Stevens-Meisel asked. "Even in launching an Internet venture, it is not Leora Infinitas's responsibility to learn every corner of Internet jargon and parlance. I doubt she knew about the dual meaning of TTC, which has become a rueful badge of belonging for the infertile community. But to acknowledge Leora's blissful ignorance—not only of any darker recesses of the online experience in general, but also, specifically, of the private agony, shame, and frustration of infertility—is not necessarily to discount the strange serendipity at play here. What she is asking of women with the TTC campaign is what she has constantly asked of herself: to nourish and incubate a better version of oneself. She is asking her audience to conceive who they are and give birth to that woman, bring her squalling triumphantly into the world. She is merely the midwife, the humble attendant. Leora Infinitas is the doula of the self."

TOTALLY TERRIBLY CONFUSED: LEEZA INFANZIA DOESN'T KNOW IT, BUT SHE JUST GOT EVERYBODY PREGNANT was Nastygram Ladyparts' subsequent headline.

"You know, I have to be honest with you, I *didn't* actually know about this coincidence," a benevolent Leora said during one morning-show appearance, inclining toward the question as if it offered a fond embrace. "One of the really exciting things about this new adventure is learning about all this stuff and really getting in touch with the online community. I have so much to learn. I've always been here as a student as well as a teacher. It's humbling. Luckily, it's also a *lot* of fun."

"It's just such a huge oversight," Sunny said at a staff meeting that same week.

"No, if we'd had proper oversight in place this wouldn't have happened," Donna corrected Sunny.

"That's exactly what I'm saying!" Sunny said.

Jen looked at her phone.

Pamela Radden <raddenpamela@gmail.com>
Thursday, Oct 8 11:24 AM
To: Jen <Jenski1848@gmail.com>
Subject: Re: Hi

Dear Jen

I got your note and I appreciate it. Look everyone fucks up once in a while including me. There will come a time when I'm not angry about this and we can be friends again It might not even take that long I'll get in touch with you then. I hope you can understand

All my love
Pam

"It feels to me as though we're *inhabiting* a space without first *learning the language* of that space," Leora was saying. "I can't do *everything*. I'm not interested in micromanagement. But how did this happen?"

Jen put aside her phone and stared openly at Karina. Chin in one hand and pen in the other, Karina looked up at Leora, ducked her head to take a few notes, and looked up again. Jen had never seen Karina take notes in a staff meeting before. Karina's expression was unreadable, save for a legible sympathy with Leora's predicament.

"It makes us seem out of touch with what our audience hungers for," Leora said.

Out of touch, Jen wrote in her notebook. She watched the letters, waiting in vain for them to reassemble themselves in her mind as flowers or animals or random strangers that she could coax out with her pen.

Sunny was headbanging. Jen resumed staring at Karina.

"It is so crucial that we understand the needs of our audience, perhaps even before *they* do," Leora said. "Is there someone on the staff who knows Internet jargon? One of us who speaks that language?"

"I would nominate Daisy," Karina said, putting down her pen and running her fingers through her hair. "She's always up on the latest trends."

Daisy—up on latest trends, Jen wrote in her notebook. The curved lines and crosses refused to turn or sprout or bloom.

"*Oversight* is a contronym," Daisy said, after Jen returned to their cubicles and delivered an abridged transcript of the meeting. "A contronym is a word that means its opposite. Like *cleave*. Or *garnish*."

"Like *sanction*," Jen said.

"Like *left*," Daisy said.

"Wait, how is *left* a contronym?" Jen asked.

"Like if I said *all I have left*, that could mean the stuff I still have or the stuff I don't have anymore," Daisy said.

"Ohhh, I thought you meant like *turn left at the stop sign*," Jen said.

"I have work left," Daisy announced to the overhead fluorescent lights. "I have left work."

Jen rummaged around in her handbag for her recently resumed semi-daily allowance of Animexa. At Sunny's request, Jen would be spending the rest of today and many todays in the future skimming Total Transformation Challenge essay submissions for what Sunny defined via email as "potentially defamatory or offensive language or any content that otherwise does not conform with the Total Transformation Challenge (TTC) project and/or LIFt's standards." The rolling task had seemed endless, monotonous, a vehicle of seething resentment. Whenever she was about to embark on another skimming session, Jen broke off half of an Animexa tablet, swallowed it with coffee from the Starbucks half a block away, and felt instantly soothed by the sheer anticipation of the mild tachycardia that would follow in fifteen to twenty minutes' time to confirm the completed blockade of her dopamine and norepinephrine transporters, which in turn booted up the same automaton-Jen that Animexa had so skillfully programmed to write LIFt memos.

This automaton-Jen could register neither disdain nor affection for the women who participated in TTC, although she suspected that, were she not presently located behind the glass partition of Animexa, she might be touched by their earnestness, by their apparent lack of acquaintance with irony or cool. These women kept vision boards and gratitude journals. They drew up and signed household-maintenance contracts replete with chore wheels and no-nagging clauses. They scheduled me-time and followed mindful-eating rules and wrote essays about how their own regular attendance at yoga classes was really a gift they gave to their kids and about the importance of feeling compassion for themselves even when they broke their mindful-eating rules.

Jen opened the Total Transformation Challenge submission page, containing empty text boxes for each of the seven TTC mission categories. She had drafted these herself, though the final template was the product of three subcommittee meetings and seven interminable rounds of revision. But Jen had never tested the template herself, because the TTC mission statements hewed too closely to the act of journal-keeping. Embarrassment had always thwarted Jen's attempts to keep any kind of journal. She was embarrassed by the mundane nature of the events she was recording in the moment, or she would happen upon an old notebook or computer file and feel embarrassed at the preoccupations and pretensions of her former self. This latter form of post-facto embarrassment was largely a function of style, as Jen's contemporary eye tended to scan her past entries as seesawing between prolix melodrama and an inadvertently comic affectlessness—the personal journal as grocery list. Jen knew that she had let embarrassment excuse her carelessness with the precious concrete and cognitive artifacts of her own life, entire months and years she could never retrace, and for this, too, she was embarrassed.

Pam, by contrast, was a master self-archivist, every smallest passage of her life logged and filed, and many of these passages repatterned and digested into art, which in Jen's view turned both Pam's work and Pam herself into case studies in disciplined self-respect. Just as Meg's self-respect was expressed in her careful and constant appraisal of time to come, Pam's self-respect was expressed in her careful and constant recording of time already spent. Yet Jen herself could not escape the conviction that there was an egotistical audacity to private record-keeping, albeit one that applied only to her own exceptional—that is to say, her own exceptionally unexceptional—case.

She considered the instructions for the first Total Transformation Challenge category and typed a response.

TTC CATEGORY 1: MIND

How can you challenge your mind to look hard at its own blind spots and push past negative thinking? How can you conjure new ways of sharing your own unique joy, outlook, and personhood with the world in order to help others?

Your response here:

I challenge my mind to help my brain figure out how Animexa modulates my levels of dopamine and norepinephrine and recalibrate itself accordingly so that I never want or need to take it again.

Jen stopped typing to shade her eyes with her fingers, because her bulging pupils were gulping and sucking at the fluorescent overhead lights.

Judy and the Really Fabulous Guy

"Maybe we should start a business just for Judy," Daisy said to Jen.

"We could work out of the guest quarters of Judy's guest quarters," Jen replied.

"Judy could pay us in spa coupons and bichon puppies," Daisy said.

Judy was Jen and Daisy's shorthand name for any and all Friends of Leora Infinitas, or F.O.L.I., which sounded out as Folly but quickly transmogrified into Fawley—in tribute to the comprehensively unfortunate Jude Fawley of one of Jen and Daisy's shared favorite novels, *Jude the Obscure*—and had then whittled itself down to Jude, and finally Judy. In the days and weeks after LIFt's official launch, Jen spent a plurality of her work hours talking on the phone with Judy, going to coffee or lunch with Judy, and, most important, editing Judy's contributions to the LIFe Lines web channel, which had originated as a blog of updates about programs around the world that LIFt supported but which increasingly devoted itself to Judy's own personal thoughts on women's education, entrepreneurship, and empowerment. Despite all these hours Jen logged with Judy, Judy did not occupy space or have mass (not with any constancy, at least), nor could she be said to be a discrete entity. She was instead an abstract and composite character, or rather a liquid set of characteristics—there was typically an artisanal flourish to her charitable interests, a vested interest in offsetting her carbon footprint, and a stated commitment to public schools that coexisted with her two to three children not being enrolled in them—and these characteristics took on the shape and volume of her assigned vessel, which was invariably and conspicuously and extremely thin, bespeaking a fragility, as well as a volatility, that in turn bespoke the vessel's value. Judy could be capricious and prickly; she could be stubborn about basic points of grammar; and her breadth and depth of everyday knowledge rose and fell according to no known scale. She could, Jen imagined, name-check a jeweler's cut or the season and year of a vintage handbag on sight, yet she seemed unsure if, for example, people who were not recipients of public assistance programs could access the city's public transportation system.

"I'm *not* lying," Jen told Daisy at the time. "My MetroCard fell out of my coat at the coat check, and as I picked it up, Judy kind of chucked me on the arm and said, 'So glad we still have a safety net in this society.'"

"That doesn't mean anything," Daisy said. "She could have meant the carpet was the safety net."

"I was *there*, man," Jen said.

This particular iteration of Judy—she would be forever after known as Safety Net Judy—had just filed a LIFe Lines essay to Jen about her volunteer work with a reading initiative for elementary-school girls and how it reminded Judy of the time her fourth-grade teacher had caught Judy cheating during the Great Lakes Read-a-Thon Contest by asking her about a crucial plot point in *Harriet the Spy* and thus teaching young Judy a lifelong lesson in the importance of authenticity. In order to avoid reading Safety Net Judy's essay, Jen tabbed to another Judy's essay that she was also avoiding reading and saw Daisy's muddy reflection on her screen.

"Who wrote this—Hedge Fund Judy?" Daisy asked, reading over Jen's shoulder.

"Hand-Sanitizer Heiress Judy," Jen said.

"Is the piece really called 'Learning to Lasso the Lingo of the Fertility Rodeo'?" Daisy asked, peering more closely.

"For now." After all the confusion over what TTC actually stood for, Leora had requested the commissioning of a suite of LIFe Lines essays about women's experiences with the decision to have children. Hand-Sanitizer Heiress Judy was the first to file her contribution.

"It's jargon-y," Daisy said.

"For real. I've been spending all this time on infertility websites— you know, just to figure out all the nomenclature in this piece—and it's truly a whole dialect unto itself," Jen said. "For instance, what do you think BFP stands for?"

Daisy considered. "Baby for Purchase."

"Nope, Big Fat Positive. That means you've got a positive pregnancy test. Oh, this one comes up a lot, too—OPK. What do you think OPK stands for?"

"Ovary Place Kicker."

"Close—Ovulation Predictor Kit. You buy a kit, you pee on a stick, and it tells you when to have sex."

"And there are lots of numbers here, too," Daisy said.

"Some of those tell you the diameter of a follicle before it ruptures," Jen said.

"Ruptures to release an egg?"

"Not necessarily—you can test to see when the follicle is going to rupture, but you don't necessarily know whether or not there's an egg in there."

"So it's like the bullpen gate swings open, but maybe there's no bull in there," Daisy said.

"You know," Jen said, "I'm all for printing whatever is on Judy's mind, but I'm wondering if there's a mixed message here. In one section of the site, we're writing about projects LIFt is funding to help women not get pregnant, and in another, we're writing about how we can't get pregnant."

"Maybe we could fund a grant to cover the shipping costs of mailing all the surplus babies to the Judys," Daisy said.

"*Is* fertility a rodeo?" Jen asked.

"Maybe a mixed message requires mixed metaphors," Daisy said.

"With fertilization I think of salmon swimming upstream," Jen said. "I guess that's clichéd."

"But in a rodeo you're in, like, a dusty arena, and you're trying to lasso—it *is* a bull, right?" Daisy asked. "Or sometimes it's a pig?"

"A steer, maybe?"

"So is the lasso the sperm and the steer is the egg? Where are the salmon? What's the vagina?"

"It's hard to find a vagina at the rodeo," Jen said.

"So this Judy was thirty-three when she decided to go to a fertility doctor," Daisy said. "That's not so old."

"It's not all about age," Jen said. "It can be so many different things."

Daisy picked up her ringing phone. Jen, intending to wander back to Safety Net Judy's essay, instead lingered over the Total Transformation Challenge submission page.

"They're asking us to do a head count of all the people whose lives were transformed by the program, then divide the organization's budget by that number of people served," Daisy was saying into the phone. "This is not humanities—this is math. Are you an *addition* sign or a *subtraction* sign?"

Jen considered the instructions for the second category and typed a response.

TTC CATEGORY 2: BODY

How can you challenge yourself to love your body, to treat it as a temple? How can you find ways to express your gratitude for all the amazing things your body can do?

Your response here:

I challenge my body to love itself enough to harvest from the Garden of Earthly Delights.

"That's because he thinks of his foundation as a vending machine," Daisy was saying into the phone. "You put your money in the top slot and structural change comes out of the bottom slot with your Diet Coke."

Jen's inbox pinged.

Karina—LIFt
Thursday, Oct 22 5:54 PM
To: Jen—LIFt
Subject: Come to Belize with me

Hi Jen

I have a delicious proposition for you. I'm traveling to Belize in December with one of our new board members. Really fabulous guy who—well, I'll tell you all about it in person. I'm going to have a lot of ground to cover while I'm there, and I'm afraid I just won't be able to do it all by myself. And that's where you come in, dear girl!

And look, not to get into this too much, but you should have a break. You deserve one!

Say yes,
K.

Just then Jen identified the physiological components of pleasure, satisfaction, and joyful anticipation whirling into kaleidoscopic coordination with one another before just as quickly spinning away, their limbic messaging scrambled by a sharp retort from Jen's prefrontal lobes affirming that Jen's entire stimulus-response network, in order to maintain a gray and anxious homeostasis, was catastrophically dependent on the reactions and approval of indiscriminately selected third parties.

Jen stared at Karina's "Say yes" long enough that the letters began to twist away from their semiotic attachments, evoking nothing but their own shapes, then switched back to the Total Transformation Challenge submission page. She considered the instructions for the third category and typed a response.

TTC CATEGORY 3: SPIRIT

How can you challenge your spirit to come into full flower and experience maximum connection with the people and values you cherish most?

Your response here:

I challenge my spirit to locate itself and announce itself to me, because I don't know what it looks like, or what it does, or if I have one.

Particularizing

The really fabulous guy, as Karina later explained, turned out to be Travis Paddock, aka "the Healthy Huntsman," CEO and cofounder of the fitness company BodMod™ International and face of the BodMod Nutritionals™ line of shakes, smoothie blends, snack bars, and sports gels, all of which used a proprietary blend of ingredients that Paddock sourced from indigenous communities around the world.

"His area of expertise is known as 'particularizing,'" explained Karina, grabbing a BodMod Green Goodness Stack-a-Maca Bang!™ Bar from a box under her desk and handing it to Jen.

To unwrap a BodMod Green Goodness Stack-a-Maca Bang!™ Bar was also to unwrap the weathered Anglo-Saxon terrain of Travis Paddock's grinning face, which adorned all of his products and which Karina had inevitably described as "ruggedly handsome" and which, to Jen's eyes, bumped awkwardly against the Malibu-bleached locks that flopped onto his deep-lined forehead from a hairline of uncertain geographic coordinates. But Jen understood that, to BodMod™'s intended audience, Paddock's decapitated head atop a one-pound canister of BodMod Pro-Team Protein Pow!Der™ instantly signified rude health and complicatedly clean living, and presented a useful stand-in for the intricately managed physique that was showcased in BodMod™'s promotional videos, in which Paddock, in tight-fitting T-shirts and cargo pants, might be glimpsed gripping the husk of a pedicab in Quito to create a bas-relief of his triceps or dashing across the Peruvian highland at twilight, hauling a backpack full of maca in order to illustrate its invigorating qualities.

"A Quechua wife would feed her groom maca on the eve of battle, ensuring that her man would return from the front lines triumphant and unscathed, to greet a bride proudly pregnant with his warrior son," Paddock explained in voice-over as his silhouette jogged into the sunset.

"He's just old-school man's man's *man*, you know?" Karina asked Jen. "The surfer as hunter-gatherer, board over one shoulder and a clean-shot wildebeest over the other."

"This is really exciting," Jen said, "but didn't Leora say recently that she wanted to stick with an all-female board?"

"Quite the contrary," Karina said, biting her lip flirtatiously. "Leora has been saying that she wants more men, plural, on the board, to send the message that women's issues are *everybody's* issues. You know, that word *integration*—she said it was important to her, and Leora doesn't say anything she doesn't mean."

"Wow, cool-guy casting alert," Jen said, nodding emphatically.

"For every single nourishment that we choose to put inside our body," Paddock intoned to the camera in another promotional video, standing alongside a startled-looking Bolivian farmer whose shoulder tensed in Paddock's manful grip, "you have to ask yourself one question: *What are the medicinals?*" Then the camera cut to Paddock at an unidentified farmers' market, in a different country and a different shade of tight-fitting T-shirt, peering up from a close inspection of a batch of *yacón* roots to tell the camera: "BodMod answers that question. Think of it as Superfoods, Simplified."

"It's all natural, totally pure, untouched by anything but the hand of God," Karina said. "What this dude is doing, it's like fair trade on steroids. No, what am I saying—it's like fair trade on medicinal cacao and *sacha inchi*!"

"Right, because steroids aren't natural," Jen said. "I mean, they *are* natural in that they're organic compounds, but anabolic steroids are kind of definitively unnatural . . ."

"You're exactly right," Karina said, staring into space.

Paddock's plan in Belize, Karina explained, was to research and develop a line of herbal teas derived from the nation's diverse ecosystem, particularly its trees: the bark of the bay cedar ("to aid digestion") and the Billy Webb ("to boost immunity") and the copal ("to restore the body's pH balance"), the pulp of the calabash tree ("to increase the red blood cell count"), the leaves of the *Senna alata* ("to detoxify the liver and kidneys"), and the seed pods of the stinking toe tree ("to relieve fatigue and the symptoms of diabetes").

"Can you imagine?" Karina asked Jen. "You've got this guy who looks like a Norse god, who does the Nevada Silverman every year and plays water polo with weights on his ankles just to spice things up, and he's going to market a line of *herbal teas*? It's just so wild!"

"Totally," Jen said. "Well, I am so grateful for this opportunity, and really psyched that you asked me along. I've never been to Belize—I don't even know much about it. My husband will be so jealous."

"You know, I don't think I've ever asked you before—what does your husband do?" Karina asked, resting her elbow on her desk and her chin on her fist and squinting, as if about to squeeze all of her powers of attention into an orange juice–like concentrate composed solely of binary data on Jen's husband's occupation.

"He teaches fifth grade in a public school in Flatbush," Jen said.

Karina shimmed her chin back and forth atop her fist in wonderment. "That's God's work right there," she said. "You've got a keeper. And where's he from, what about his parents?"

"He's from Erie, Pennsylvania; only child," Jen said. "His mom was a waitress. She died a few years ago. Cancer."

Karina furrowed her brow and mashed her lips together. "I'm sorry to hear that."

"Yeah, she was awesome," Jen said. "And—and what about your husband, Karina?"

"He's in advertising," Karina said, rolling her eyes and flopping backward against her chair. "Raw deal."

"Oh! Why is that a raw deal?" Jen asked.

"When people have less money to spend, the first thing they spend less money on is advertising. Been a tough time for him. I feel for the guy."

Jen tried to imagine a scenario in which she would say "I feel for the guy" in regard to Jim, and then refocused. "Oh, no, Karina, did he—well, it's none of my business, but was he affected by the financial apocalypse?"

Karina tossed her head and laughed. "Oh, man, the *apocalypse*," she said. "I'll have to remember that. That's a good one. He's fine. He didn't lose his job, if that's what you're trying to ask me, although sometimes I think that would have been the softer blow. But he did have to be part of a lot of tough decisions about cost-cutting, restructuring staff, the usual brutal calculus of keeping the lights on when there's a storm outside lashing your power lines." Karina sighed. "Whatever. He's obviously not dashing around the foothills of the Andes trying to save the world, one exotic herb at a time. *Anyway*. What else?"

"So, what is our agenda for the trip?" Jen asked. "Other than hanging out with this awesome guy, which is agenda enough, obviously!"

"Ha, *agenda*—that is *such* a Jen question, such a Jen *word*," Karina said. "I love it. I do. I love you! But to be honest, we're off to a subtropical paradise with a board member who's sourcing foods that can cure everything from procrastination to cancer, and he's helping entire communities of subsistence farmers while he does it. Really, how much of an *agenda* do we need?"

"Sure, sure," Jen said. "And so, many of these subsistence farmers are—women?"

"Yes, of course," Karina said. "It's a real by-women-for-women kind of deal. For a project affiliated with LIFt, I think that goes without saying."

"Travis Paddock's eye-watering macho masculine manliness notwithstanding," Jen said, and cushion-laughed.

"I don't follow," Karina said.

"Just so I understand," Jen said, "we're tagging along on one of his research trips, right? And I'm guessing that we could meet with some local farmers or collectives—women farmers, women's collectives—that could benefit from a LIFt grant? Is that the general idea? And my role—the communications role here would be—documentation? Photos, interviews . . ."

"Mmm," Karina said.

"And so, this might sound like a weird question, but is there a way in which this becomes a kind of promotional opportunity for Travis's company—it's called BodMod, right?" Jen asked.

"Promotional opportunity, huh. I mean, if you want to be cynical about it, sure, you can put it that way," Karina said, twisting her mouth into a constipated smile. "If that's your *agenda*."

"No, that's not what I meant," Jen said, resisting the urge to cushion-laugh again. "Like I said, I think you've just been in deeper with this project, and I'm clumsily trying to catch up!"

"Catch up when you land in Belize," Karina said, swiveling her body toward her computer and laying her fingers on her keyboard while keeping her eyes locked with Jen's, her head poised at a 90-degree angle from the rest of her body. "Be in the moment and just open yourself up to the journey. Who knows what we'll discover there, right?"

"I just—I know you're busy, I just want to make sure that there isn't anything we need to keep in mind in terms of—of any kind of collaboration we're making between LIFt as a charitable entity and BodMod as a for-profit business."

Karina frowned. "Good to know," she said, drumming her fingers lightly on her keyboard and turning her head toward her computer screen.

"Maybe we could loop Daisy in?" Jen asked. "She would have all the intel on programs we could consider funding in Belize."

"We'll certainly keep it in mind," Karina said to her monitor.

"Well, we can discuss it now if you want?" Jen said. She was still resisting the urge to cushion-laugh, but just then a little puff of concil-iatory air escaped.

"Look, Jen," Karina said to her computer, "if this opportunity just isn't calling your name—if you just can't *hear* it—I understand com-pletely. There're plenty of other people on the LIFt team who might be able to strike that harmony the moment they hear the tune, so to speak." Karina clicked her mouse to open an email.

"No, no, I'm really excited to go—I can hear the harmony!" said Jen, finally succumbing again to the lure of the cushion-laugh. "I can't wait. Apologies for giving off a different impression."

"Like I said, just open yourself up to the journey," Karina said to her email.

"Absolutely," Jen said, rising to go. "Door open or closed?"

"Closed. Also, can you see if Donna is in her office?"

Jen peered next door. "Nope, not at her desk."

"Can you just take a spin around the building and round her up for me?" Karina asked, her eyes fixed glassily on her screen and her fingers already typing. "Thanks."

Financially Is the Easiest Part

"I just don't know that I'm up for this," Jen said. It was her monthly check-in at Dr. Lee's private office, which was tucked away in a quieter back corridor of the henhouse, perhaps forty paces away from the Garden of Earthly Delights. "Physically or emotionally or financially."

"Financially is the easiest part," Dr. Lee said.

"Oh, really?" Jen said with ironic glee.

Dr. Lee squeezed her eyes shut and shook her head. "Forgive me, you must understand, our clientele is—"

"It's okay," Jen said. "Even with WellnessSolutions not covering the—the procedure, there are still payment plans, installment plans, income-based sliding scales, all that. It's not as formidable as it is at other clinics. I did the research, and—"

Jen exhaled and looked out the window. Dr. Lee's office overlooked a Grecian-phallus monument perched in the center of a tiny patch of walled grass in a busy intersection. Jen had been jaywalking past the phallus for more than a year on her trips to the henhouse, and she had never once stopped to read the plaque. She had no idea what the phallus commemorated. For all she knew it honored not past mayors or congressmen or land-grabbers but served instead as a totem of power and fecundity meant to embolden all visitors to the Garden of Earthly Delights.

"Well," Dr. Lee said, placing her palms on her desk in a pose of adjournment. "Let me know what you decide."

They stood and shook hands. "I have some work travel coming up, and it's the holidays soon—I'll come to a decision after that," Jen said. "In the New Year."

She went to open the door, hesitated, and turned back. "I don't know why I keep saying *I*. I'm not the only one doing this. It's Jim and me. It's you. Your colleagues."

"It's still isolating," Dr. Lee said. "Patients talk about that. You know, the clinic offers a support group—"

"I went to one; I got up and left after ten minutes like a jerk," Jen said. "It reinforced the feeling that I'm getting at—it's almost like the more people get involved with this, the more isolated I feel. Whereas if we could have done this alone in a bedroom or a broom closet or the backseat of a car like normal people, I never would have felt isolated at all."

"Well," Dr. Lee said again.

That night, Jen dreamed that she received a certified letter from a collection agency, and Jim explained, remorsefully, that he had been using their shared WellnessSolutions health-insurance card as a credit card for the past year under the mistaken impression that their household expenses would be covered by their premium and copay.

"I'm so sorry," Jim kept saying in the dream. "I tried to guess how it worked, and I guessed wrong."

In Fact

MARGARETHE!: Sorry I'm not calling you back; Millie is sick and gross and I just got her down and if she wakes up again I know we'll be up all night.

jenski1848: Aw, poor little lady.

MARGARETHE!: Oh, man, I just found more barf in my hair, hang on <Muzak plays>

MARGARETHE!: Back! You're leaving first thing in the morning, right?

jenski1848: Theoretically, although I can't find my passport.

MARGARETHE!: I want to hear about the trip, but first—and I wanted to ask you about this in person, but—what happened? With you and Pam?

MARGARETHE!: And full disclosure, I asked Pam this question already, and I didn't really get anything out of her.

jenski1848: It was my fault.

MARGARETHE!: OK . . .

MARGARETHE!: I'm not interested in taking sides, I just wish one of you could tell me what happened.

jenski1848: I asked her to do something—pressured her to do something, really—and I shouldn't have, and she's angry.

MARGARETHE!: Pam said it was an interview? That's basically all I got out of her.

MARGARETHE!: Sorry if I'm being pushy! It's just so sad that you guys aren't talking.

jenski1848: An interview, yes.

MARGARETHE!: OK, well, so what? It couldn't have been that bad, and she could have said no.

jenski1848: And what do you say to her about it when I'm not around?

MARGARETHE!: I say, "It couldn't have been that bad, and you could have said no." Jesus. I said that to her yesterday, in fact. You can ask her.

jenski1848: No, I can't, "in fact."

MARGARETHE!: Don't be awful. I know I'm pushing too hard on this, and I apologize, and I'll stop, but don't be awful.

jenski1848: I'm sorry, too, Meg. I'm really sorry. It will all be OK. We just need to give her some space. I think sometimes I lose sight of all she's been through. She deserves some slack.

jenski1848: I hope that doesn't sound like I'm condescending to her.

MARGARETHE!: Ooh, now I get to ask a Jen question: Are you saying all that for my benefit or are you saying that because you think it's true?

jenski1848: <Status set to: Unavailable>

Asleep

When Jen finally came to bed, bags packed and passport located, Jim was lying still, but she couldn't hear him breathing, and because she couldn't yet make out his familiar rhythm of inhale and exhale, she knew he wasn't asleep but only lingering on the threshold of sleep, ready to turn back, and insofar as there was space for thought, she thought about why she would ever think about anything else but this, to want such relief so badly and to be filled with it more or less whenever she chose, and afterward as she thought she was fading into sleep, she couldn't remember the last time they had convened an all-hands meeting without it having been in some sense scheduled in advance or at least without her knowing where it landed in the calendar, and therefore whether or not it might theoretically serve a larger purpose, and above them what sounded like an armoire crashed to the floor, and he gasped and turned again to wrap his arms around his wife, and his wife realized that her husband still wasn't asleep, and as he pressed against her again his wife pushed her fists hard against her husband's shoulder blades, hoping to release the ecstatic pressure of desperately wanting what she already had.

Gotta Run with the Plebes

Jen watched Karina waiting just outside the gate at the Belize City airport, clasping and rubbing her hands together. It was bizarre, Jen thought, to glimpse Karina—however briefly—in a public place as if she were alone, unguarded, amid her excitement and her private thoughts. Virtually everything Jen knew of Karina amounted to an interpretation of a performance, consciously acted out in front of an audience. Jen thought of the tactic that Pam said she sometimes used on her more ill-at-ease photographic subjects, when, after twenty or so minutes of holding themselves stiffly before her camera, they would hear Pam call out, "That's it, we've got the shot," and the subject would either crack a grin of merry reprieve or sink and sigh into pensive relief—and *that* would be the moment when Pam squeezed off a few more frames, when she *really* got the shot. It was a trick, yes, but one that the subject almost always instinctively understood. The trick, of course, was to forget yourself for just a few seconds, to allow yourself to be safely alone before a documenting eye.

"He's just in the gents'," Karina informed Jen by way of greeting. "Usually Travis would charter his own flight, obviously," she added, "but this time around, you know, he's gotta run with the plebes."

Jen wondered if running with the plebes meant that LIFt was footing the bill for Travis Paddock's trip as well as hers and Karina's. Jen had wondered about the financial arrangements behind their itinerary as she and her fellow coach passengers had inched past the first-class cabin, one of its rows occupied by Karina and an unidentified man, presumably Travis Paddock, their faces obscured by copies of *Grazia* and *Men's Health*, respectively, elbows pressed together across armrests.

Now a bronzed figure emerged from the men's room closest to their exit gate, his wide-legged carriage seesawing like a cowboy's. In person, Travis Paddock was smaller and wirier than the image of him that Jen had extrapolated from the homunculus staring out from the box-top of his smoothie starter kit. His stride accelerated as he grew closer to Karina, who called out, "Mr. Paddock, I presume!" in a pre-emptive tone as she glanced anxiously in Jen's direction. He stopped a few feet short of Karina, pivoted 30 degrees toward Jen, and reached out to grip her hand with all the power invested in him by BodMod Nutritionals™.

"Travis Paddock, BodMod Nutritionals," Travis Paddock intoned, pumping Jen's arm like a cable pulley in a weight room.

"So Travis has an SUV waiting for us," Karina said. A custardy sing-song lapped around her voice. "Out here, most people would hire a driver, but not Travis," Karina added. "He is pure-cut DIY."

Jen realized that her mouth was hanging open. "Yeah," she said. "I bet you *built* that SUV, Travis."

Outside, the air hung like damp wool, a chilly undertow kicking at a steady breeze. A sooty cloud cover was dissolving the pale blue sky, as if the day were aging in time-lapse, its pigments drained by pollutants, tomorrow's colors already muted by today's subtle epigenetic changes. The city's specific sleepiness felt almost suburban to Jen, as if the rows of nineteenth-century colonial structures, tin-roofed and weatherproofed and raised on stilts, hosted an absent bedroom community of daily travelers to some mysterious island location, accessible only via passport and password.

"Look at the huge line outside that—is that a shopping mall?" Jen said inanely from the backseat. Travis and Karina had kept an eerie silence since pickup.

Travis, behind the wheel, glanced out the window. "That's a sort of security checkpoint for the cruise ships that dock here," he said. "Way to keep out the riffraff."

"Capitalism, huh?" Karina said from the front passenger seat.

They headed southeast along the coast, the gray haze obscuring the shoreline, then cut straight west toward their hotel in Cayo District, near the Guatemalan border. As they passed through the outskirts of Belize City, the landscape turned both greener and more desolate. The houses on their rickety stilts became fewer and farther between. Discarded auto parts languished in the yards. Chickens rooted in piles of garbage. A rooster and a pelican happened past. Dogs and coconut palms everywhere. They passed a graveyard of golf carts ("Did you see that graveyard of golf carts?" Jen asked, to no reply), an abandoned school bus, and three little girls stacked on one purple bicycle: one whose legs dangled from the front basket, one perched precariously on the edge of the seat, and the biggest girl in the center, pedaling steadily. Jen leaned out her window to snap a photograph of the girls—two of whom looked up in stoic accusation—and she immediately regretted it. She turned her camera's attentions instead to the region's residential aesthetics: The houses were bubblegum pink or spearmint or baby's-room blue, salmon and racing green and magenta.

"They paint them that color so they can watch them fade," Travis said.

"I can see what attracted you to this place, Travis," Karina said. "It's a paradise, and yet there is so much *good* to be done."

"Paradise in progress," Travis said.

"Very well put," Karina said.

"So, uh, you've got your work cut out for you the next day or so, huh, Jen," Travis said over his shoulder.

"Oh, ha, yeah, tell me about it," Jen said. "Hiking through paradise-in-progress, in search of nature's next great elixir. Under these conditions, we should unionize." She caught herself. "Not that what you do isn't really hard work, Travis. I'd love to hear *more* about what you do—everything about what you do, actually!" She giggled without knowing why.

Travis caught Jen's eye in the rearview mirror and peered at her curiously, nose tilted upward, as if he'd caught the elusive scent of a precious particularizable herb at the exact second that a breeze across the highland scrambled the direction from which it came.

"You're not—coming with us?" Travis asked.

"Oh! Sorry," Jen said. "I didn't mean to make any assumptions."

Jen felt oddly allied with Travis as they both glanced over at Karina. Karina looked out the window serenely, even though the route was growing bumpier all the time, the road at turns rutted and beach-soft. Then she stirred in her seat in an overdetermined way, as if she were robotically playing out the eightieth take of a movie scene for a demanding director. "Oh, goodness," Karina said, making a diphthong out of *good*, "I was lost in a world of my own." They had just passed a mile of marshland, and now they were coming up on a soccer field, empty save for plastic bottles, its midfield buckled under several inches of stagnant, milky water.

Karina turned her head halfway toward Jen with some effort, as if she were wearing a neck brace. Her movement expressed not physical discomfort but the psychic pain of relocating from the flow state.

"So, Jen, I've been thinking," Karina said. "If you do the cost-benefit analysis of our little adventure, it really doesn't make a whole lot of sense for the two of us to double up with Travis—I mean, one of us can take notes and observe the action just as well as the other can. But it just so happens that, in this tiny little country, there's another amazing opportunity for LIFt just waiting to be fulfilled, if one of us will be so bold as to accept the mission."

"What are the odds," Jen said.

"I *know*, right?" Karina said. "So, remember when we were talking about integrating our board, being more inclusive of everyone in our mission to empower women?"

"Mm-hm," Jen said.

"Have you heard of a friend of Leora's named Baz Angler?"

"Let me think," Jen said. "Software fortune? Video games?"

"See, Jen," Karina said, "you're always one step ahead of me."

The Garinagu Eco Lodge

A half-hour later, Travis was steering onto a narrow, winding path that seemed to vanish ahead beneath a thickening canopy of dark trees, as the road shifted and sifted under the tires. After a half-mile of snaking and weaving, the terrain flattened into a crackle of graveled lot, and the wooden gates of the Garinagu Eco Lodge sidled into Jen's frame of vision. As the three of them exited the truck into surprisingly bright sunlight—the Garinagu Eco Lodge, Jen immediately intuited, occupied an independent ecosystem unto itself, with its own flora, fauna, and climate patterns—a slight, shyly smiling young woman, clad in a flight attendant's ensemble of close-fitting white blouse, gray pencil skirt, and blue-and-white paisley cravat, wordlessly handed Jen a snifter glass of mango juice festooned with a matching paisley parasol, while a corresponding pair of slight, shyly smiling young men in their corresponding white-gray paisley uniforms began wordlessly removing the luggage from the back of the SUV.

"The luggage is—separate—" Karina called out over the hood. "Labeled." Without another word, she and Travis started slowly on one of the cobbled walkways that crisscrossed the grassy main grounds of the lodge, each path shaded by palm fronds and dotted with citronella lanterns, and leading to an evenly spaced line of thatched-roof cabanas.

The young woman, whose name, Eva, was embossed on a dainty brass brooch pinned to her lapel, administered pleasantries confirming the adequacy of each leg of Jen's journey and outlining the overall geography, amenities, and administrative formalities native to the Garinagu Eco Lodge, then handed Jen her key, attached to a leather-stitched emblem of a coatimundi. Jen thanked Eva profusely, then rummaged around in her handbag pointlessly for a few minutes in order to put more space between her movements and those of Karina and Travis, who appeared to share an appointed destination.

Jen's luggage awaited her just inside the door to her bungalow, which was roughly the size of her apartment, a breezy, pine-scented embrace of mahogany and cherry-stained cedar swathed in nubby multicolored textiles, bright reds and greens and yellows. Next to an enormous canopy bed, a wood-carved humanoid dragon grinned gummily up at Jen from the indigo-wood bedside table, his lower back doubling as a compartment of ginger mints and a complimentary bottle of champagne between his paws. Jen walked out to the porch, where wooden stairs led to an orchid trail and then a narrower, steeper pathway through crowded assemblies of cedars, palms, and flowering plants down to the stone shores of a sapphire stream. Jen could just glimpse a waterfall. She looked at the deck chairs and the swaying hammock and stood swaying in time with the trees.

Jen placed her palm on the handrail to the stairs, one foot poised over the top step. The breeze caressed her face, and the shadows on the orchid trail seemed to lengthen in real time.

She drew back her foot, turned, and hurried out of the bungalow, shoved onward by the same feeling that had punched and jabbed at her daily for as long as she could remember—the feeling that she had squandered time, so much time, obscenities of time, and yet some finite amount of time still miraculously remained, still within her reach, if only she could ever be clever and resourceful enough to know in which direction to sprint for it.

Standing at the palm-fronded front desk, Jen scanned the day's itinerary. The Garinagu Eco Lodge offered a full range of scheduled activities, itemized on a four-page letterpress menu, including late-afternoon canoeing and horseback riding, twilight birding expeditions, moonlight jaguar-spotting missions, semi-hourly cooking demos, and walk-in spa experiences. Jen smiled wistfully at Eva.

"I'm going to need your help," Jen said, setting the itinerary aside. "I need to book a car rental for early tomorrow morning. I'll need some maps, and I'll need to talk to someone who has driven around Belize a lot. And then I'm going to need a computer with an Internet connection."

"So a working vacation, then?" Eva asked.

Jen stared over Eva's shoulder. You could see the waterfall from the front desk, too. "Looks like it."

Experience the Experience

That night, Jen dreamed that she was a tiny person living alone in a tiny square room, surrounded on all sides by identical tiny square rooms, in a giant matrix of tiny square rooms, each of them occupied by pairs of tiny people. Her room was large enough for a bed, a sink, and a toilet. She knew in the dream that all of her earthly possessions were stored under the bed. She also knew that she was the only single-occupancy tenant in the entire giant matrix of tiny square rooms. She lay flat on her back on her bed and listened to a polyphonic surge of vocalizations, so dense and varied that they took on gaseous weight, like a rapidly moving storm front, heaving at the walls, unfurling over her tiny ceiling, bumping against the tiny square window above the tiny sink. Layer upon skein of moaning, cooing, sighing, grunting, slurping. It was the sound of a thousand tangled limbs and arching backs and scrunching faces. An irregular *thomp* and *wümp* punched the tiny ceiling directly above Jen's head and the tiny floor beneath Jen's bed amid the muffled cacophony, again and again, until she woke up.

She sat up in the enormous canopy bed and looked out the screened porch to the first purplish light winking through the trees. Somewhere a giant coffee machine, vast enough to stir and hydrate every eco-tourist in Central America, was moaning and cooing and sighing. Jen padded to the porch to see if she could make out the waterfall yet. She could hear the coffee machines in a terrifying mechanized chorus, grinding and harrumphing from all the surrounding bungalows, *ehhrrrrr*ing and *uhhuugghh*ing in service of an invisible army of caffeine-starved predawn risers. She inhaled and smelled only pine.

What she'd been hearing all the time were the howler monkeys, high in the treetops. No one was awake but her and them.

Jen showered and dressed and—just to help wake up, she told herself, just for that extra *oomph* she needed to navigate a unique and unexpected situation—she broke off half an Animexa tablet, palming it into her mouth with tap water from the sink after brushing her teeth. She slipped the other half into her wallet for later, just in case. As she was putting on her shoes, she fished the other half of the Animexa out of her wallet and swallowed it dry. She walked into the *ehhrrrrr*ing and *uhhuugghh*ing predawn mist and up the citronella-lit path to the Garinagu Eco Lodge main house, which housed a dusty tangerine-colored iMac G3 with a dial-up modem connection.

First, Jen scrolled her email to make sure that one of the Judys hadn't had any urgent late-night brainstorms on one of the trickier transitional sentences in her essay on the question of whether Restylane injections were a symptom of self-love or self-loathing. Then, Jen would squeeze in another hour or two of research on her mysterious quarry, Baz Angler, whose Internet footprint Jen had attempted to trace the previous day.

"So I'm super-excited to meet this guy," Jen had said from the backseat of Travis Paddock's SUV. "But what do we *want* from Mr. Angler, exactly?"

"You know—and don't take this the wrong way—but I wonder if you'll do yourself and this experience a disservice by approaching it from, well, from a *transactional* place," Karina had said. "If you focus too much of what *you're* getting from *him* and what *he's* getting from *you*, you miss out on—well, you won't even know *what* you're missing out on. In terms of the experience, I mean."

"Who—who even set this up?" Jen had asked. "Is he expecting us? Me?"

"Just try to let go," Travis had said. "Experience the experience."

But Jen had no clue as to what she was being asked to let go of, given the obscurity of the origins and cause of her appointment with Baz Angler and the ominous haze that hung around Angler himself, an eccentric recluse and certified genius with a stated interest in MDMA-aided time travel and a net worth estimated in the mid-to-high nine figures.

Chewing a thumbnail in the beneficent glow of the iMac G3, Jen skimmed the latest batch of Total Transformation Challenge essay submissions. She considered the instructions for the fourth category and typed a response.

TTC CATEGORY 4: EARTH

How can you challenge yourself to strengthen your pact with Mother Earth and commit to leaving the natural world a better place for our children?

Your response here:

I challenge myself to experience the experience of paradise-in-progress.

Jen reckoned that the best way to prepare to experience the experience of her journey to Belize was to look things up about Baz Angler on the Internet, or at least on the past-imperfect tense of the Internet available in the breakfast room of the Garinagu Eco Lodge.

baz angler software fortune
baz angler fortune 500
baz angler fantasy role play
baz angler narco-trafficking
baz angler sorcery
baz angler harem
baz angler vegan satanism

There were numerous undisputed facts about Richard Benedict "Baz" Angler available online. One of three sons of a computer science professor father and a librarian mother, he spent his early childhood outside Sydney and thereafter grew up in Massachusetts. He dropped out of MIT after three semesters, and at age twenty-two founded the video-game developer Gembryo Systems Inc., best known for the late-1980s blockbuster *Furthermost,* a free-roaming fantasy role-play video game set in a mystical dystopia, and its equally successful sequels *Farthermore* and *Everending,* the last of which featured the voice-acting talents of one Leora Infinitas as both the Dawn Queen Angharad, Defender of the Cloak of Athanasia, and the Twilight Queen Blodeuwedd, Protector of the Crown of Impregnability. A decade later, the software behemoth Vidente Corporation acquired Gembryo in a landmark deal in which Angler personally netted at least $100 million. He earned at least that again through savvy early investments in various enterprise software and antivirus software upstarts, as well as in Seagate and Microsoft. Meanwhile, royalties and licensing fees from the various *Furthermore* movie franchises, TV-cartoon franchises, comic books, merchandise, and increasingly degraded and desiccated video-game sequels, prequels, and spinoffs had flowed forth for years after Vidente had swallowed Gembryo whole.

There were equally numerous disputed facts about Baz Angler available online. One rumor was that the financial apocalypse had devastated his investments, forcing him to sell numerous properties around the world—a cattle ranch in Australia's Northern Territory, a horse ranch in Montana, a beachfront estate in Hawaii—and driving him to far more modest quarters in unglamorous Belize. One largely unsourced report, which Jen found on a reputable gaming blog, had him developing antibiotic plants on the New River with a pair of comely Big Pharma refugees; another, almost entirely unsourced report from a different, less reputable gaming blog claimed that the antibiotic-plant project was a front for a drug-smuggling operation. The most stubbornly viral rumor suggested that Angler's longtime immersion in the universe of the *Furthermost* trilogy, paired with his equally longtime immersion in cutting-edge hallucinogens, had severed the line he'd always walked, both in his life and so profitably in his work, between fantasy and reality.

In *Everending,* the raven-haired and brooding wizard-in-training Trahaearn has acquired both the Cloak of Athanasia and the Crown of

Impregnability in his questing across the postapocalyptic greenscapes of the once and future kingdom Apologia, where he is accompanied by the loyal druid Maredudd and the wily genetically engineered dragon Wmffre; for his efforts, Trahaearn is honored by his Leora Infinitas–voiced twin warrior queens with the title of Earl of Cockney, which was the nickname bestowed upon the pubescent Baz Angler by his classmates in Cambridge, Massachusetts, who mistook his Australian tones for those of East End London. By the time of *Everending IX: The Enlargement*, the Earl of Cockney né Trahaearn's countenance and form had shape-shifted into a hologram of Angler himself: flapping dark tresses now rusty tufts, tanned and buffed hide now all sharp, freckled-pale angles. Baz Angler's own creation had become Baz Angler.

"And thus Trahaearn, Earl of Cockney, becomes himself!" proclaimed the Dawn Queen Angharad and the Twilight Queen Blodeuwedd in unison.

As Jen scribbled down Maredudd's genealogy in her notebook, she knew the exact moment both halves of the Animexa tablet began to take effect, because of the subtlest tremor that stirred her hand as she wrote, and the equally subtle euphoria that animated the tremor—euphoria miniaturized into a pinprick, a coruscating grain of sand, the slenderest threading thrill zigzagging up her throat, clutching her jaw, and starbursting behind her eyes so that her entire field of vision both brightened and narrowed, whiting out any signal or noise outside her skull and screen. It was the same subtle and tightly focused euphoria that had fueled the writing and rewriting of a hundred unread LIFt memos—only stronger now, as Jen's tolerance had slipped during her months of abstinence.

Last, Jen found, there were numerous previously disputed facts about Baz Angler available online—that is, they were disputed until Jen was able to report them firsthand. One of these, given glancing notice in an alt-medicine blogger's mostly amiable post on the antibiotic-plant project, was that Baz Angler was a connoisseur of the sharp arts: a student of knife making, a historian of ironmongery, a somewhat profligate collector of ancient swords.

Jen silently confirmed this later the same morning, as she shut the door of Eva's dented Corolla behind her and moved through the over-grown grass toward Baz Angler's clapboard house-on-stilts, imagining that the roseate apparition at the top of the front steps, who gripped a rocks glass in one hand and a machete in the other, held the machete toward her as a totem not of warning but of welcome, like a plate of fresh-baked brownies, she thought, or a cool glass of lemonade, or a simple outstretched hand.

That's Your Reality

"It's just *real life* out here, you know?" Baz Angler was saying.

Baz Angler had already given Jen a brief tour of his "compound," as he referred to it, situated on several acres of cleared forest, with a two-thousand-square-foot main house ringed in the rear by a semicircle of smaller, crookeder bungalows, a vegetable garden, and a greenhouse nearly the size of the central residence. Accompanying Baz Angler was a lanky aide-de-camp who looked not yet out of his teens, who introduced himself as Ram and who radiated a grinning, gushing, anything-to-accommodate energy of a kind that always stiffened Jen's neck and shoulder muscles and set a vein in her forehead pulsing—a tension born of recognition of the same energy in herself, a response to stimuli akin to flinching away from a mirror. Baz Angler seemed immediately more at ease once they were back in the sparsely fur-nished front room of his primary residence, where the air was cooler and the smell of sewage wasn't as strong as it was outdoors, and where Ram excused himself to the kitchen with an exaggerated wave and a doggy grin. A young woman in cutoffs and a white tank top, whom Baz Angler introduced as Star, slumped mutely on a sunken, faded red couch, painting her toenails, a mangy German shepherd napping at her feet. Star's apparent doppelgänger, who wore cutoffs and a blue tank top, whom Baz Angler introduced as Unity, slumped mutely in the doorway to the kitchen and sullenly watched from a few feet away as Baz Angler stood and held court for his audience of three, the sash of his grape-and-lemon-yellow dressing gown coming dangerously loose at his lower abdomen, his lectern a deeply scarred slab of picnic table that he tapped and slapped and occasionally pounded with his glinting jade-handled machete.

Confusingly, Unity, not Star, was the doppelgänger with the giant red star on one bicep and an interlocking gold chain of stars winding around one leg. Given the electrical charge of competition that sparked and hummed between the two young women, Jen wondered if Unity had gotten the tattoos to undermine Star's chosen name, or if Star had chosen her name to undermine Unity's tattoos.

"If it's hot here in this country, you *feel* that it's hot," Baz Angler was saying. After decades abroad, his strong Australian accent sounded emphatic, well practiced. "You don't hide from it. The bodily waste that we produce every day, well, if the sewage system breaks down—and things are always breaking down around here, fact of life—there it is, you face it. Out there in the world—in that *other* world, your world of cities and suburbs and skyscrapers and highways—we literally shield ourselves *from* ourselves, every minute of every day. All that infrastructure is one big hiding place. Here, that's not possible. Your five senses are totally engaged. No room for denial. Maybe it's not always pretty." He locked eyes meaningfully with Unity as he drove and twisted the machete into the table's battered surface. "I admit, it's often *very* pretty. But it's always real."

"Right, right," Jen said. Star glared at Jen ferociously. "So, Baz, how do you know Leora?" Jen asked.

"Yeah, Leora and me, we go way back," Baz Angler said. *Why bake*. "We used to have the best conversations. Leora and I used to talk about the power of the speech act—the *abracadabra*. The practice of making a resolution and then sticking to that vow so closely that saying it makes it so. Imagine being that honest, that true with yourself."

"Oh, yeah, like a marriage vow," Jen said. "'I do' makes it true."

Baz Angler chortled and spun the blade around on its tip. "Yeah, you only have to look at the divorce rates to know how well *that* works," he said.

"Well, it's like anything else—depends on the resolve of the people making the resolution," Jen said, rocking slightly in her seat to help convey cheery agreeability.

"Marriage, monogamy—just more of those truisms where we deny reality, thinking that we're keeping ourselves safe, hidden from harm, when we overlook the greatest danger of them all, which would be to deny ourselves the right to conjure our own best and brightest reality. Monogamy is a lie. I look at Star. I love Star. I look at Unity. I love Unity. I look at a woman I haven't met yet. I love that woman I haven't met yet. What could be more dangerous than denying ourselves love? What could be more harmful than to blind ourselves to life?"

Baz Angler was carving notches into the table, almost sawing at it.

"You're curious about this here beautiful blade, aren't you?" he asked Jen. "You can't stop staring at it."

"I sure can't!" Jen said.

"It belonged to Carlos Manuel de Céspedes," he said. "I bet you don't know who Carlos Manuel de Céspedes was, do ya?"

"He—let's see, he was the sugar plantation owner in Cuba who freed his slaves, which led to the Cuban wars of independence against Spain?" Jen said. "Did I get that right?"

"Ho-ho-*ho*, whoa, we've got a live one here," Baz Angler said, pantomiming a round of applause and rearing around to look at Star, who sucked her teeth and rolled her eyes. "Okay, Ms. Historian," he said as he turned back to Jen, the blade puncturing and spinning, puncturing and spinning, "in that case, why don't *you* tell *me* about this here beautiful blade?"

Jen blushed and cushion-laughed. "Oh, now, that I couldn't help you with."

Baz Angler pulsed his head slowly up and down, allowing Jen's admission of ignorance to hang in the air, to spread and settle. "The *criollos* had two things in their favor against the *peninsulares*," he said after a judicious silence. His tongue danced wantonly around the unfamiliar Spanish *l*'s and *r*'s. "One of the things in their favor, of course, was yellow fever. And two was the machete charge." The blade *thunk*ed and spun, *thunk*ed and spun.

"The *peninsulares*, they had superior forces, superior resources, the infrastructure, the riches," he said. The blade went *pock pock pock pock* against the table to underline each item on the list. "But you know what they didn't have? They didn't have that sense of *real life*. That's why their bodies betrayed them. That's why they couldn't handle hand-to-hand combat, the flesh against flesh, the blade against bone—the *intimacy* of the *real*, they couldn't take it." The spinning machete slipped partway from Baz Angler's grasp and sliced a fresh arc into the battered table before he regained a firm grasp on its brilliant green handle. He gazed at it much as he'd gazed at Unity.

"I can see why it's so meaningful to you," Jen said.

"Got it at auction in Havana years ago," Baz Angler said. "Don't think they knew what they had here."

"Do you know what you have? I mean, is it verified—do you know for sure that it's really real?" Jen asked. The Animexa had catapulted the question out of her mouth. Animexa always lowered Jen's threshold of inhibition, which sometimes had the double-negative effect of rendering Jen mute: Aware that Animexa compromised her ability to judge the appropriateness of any given comment, she often erred on the side of silence.

"Verified?" Baz asked. "Do I know what I have? I know what I have. It's in my hand. Here it is." *Pock pock pock.*

"You should take the machete to the guys on *Pawn Stars*," Jen said. "Or *Antiques Roadshow*." Her time away from full-dose Animexa left her fumbling to find the mute button.

Baz balanced the blade on his teeth and lifted his palms toward the heavens. "What do we need TV for when we've got real life?" he asked, the machete blocking and gagging his consonants.

"We've got TV here," Star broke in. "He doesn't let us have it in his house," she added, pouting, "but we have a satellite hookup out back."

"What I can *verify,*" Baz said over Star, palming the machete again, "is that this here beautiful blade isn't just a beautiful blade. It's a message, from Céspedes to me. Maybe he didn't write the message down. Maybe he didn't telegraph it to me in 1870 for me to receive here in 2009. But I can interpret the message all the same. I can *verify* it."

"What is the message of the machete?" Jen asked.

"Who *cares,*" Unity whined from the couch, not looking up from her toes.

"Maybe the message is a secret between him and me," Baz Angler said. His smirk revealed that the pleasure of disclosure couldn't snuff out the corresponding pleasure of withholding—that he could enjoy them both, if only he silently twirled the machete on the table for just a few more revolutions before he continued.

"Céspedes was betrayed," Baz finally said. "Booted. A bloody coup. The Cubans wouldn't let him leave and wouldn't give him security. He was a sitting duck for the Spaniards. Never had a chance. His death is a cautionary tale for any leader, any visionary, anybody with *balls,* and this"—*pock pock pock pock*—"this is the warning and the salvation."

"Darn, I don't have balls," Jen said. The Animexa continued to surprise her with its japes and pranks.

"Anybody can have balls," Baz said.

"So I'm conjuring a best and brightest reality in which I have testicles and your machete is a metaphor," Jen said, laughing. "Cool!"

"Metaphor—okay, if you want to get fancy-highfalutin about it."

"To be honest," Jen said, "it doesn't *look* like a metaphor."

"What, this?" Baz asked, waggling the machete. "Makin' you nervous?"

Jen sigh-laughed. "A little!" She smiled while raising her furrowed eyebrows to telegraph apologetic anxiety, as if to ask pardon on behalf of her own neuroses for any implied criticism of Angler's hosting skills.

"So you see this and you sense—fear? You see a threat?"

"It's a machete," Jen said.

"That's just a word," Baz Angler said. "What *is* the thing you're obscuring with language? What does it consist of? What does it possess? How does it act upon the world?"

"I mean, yes, it's threatening," Jen said.

"But a threat to what? Your safety? Your flesh? Or just your sense of decorum?"

"Lunch is ready!" said Ram brightly, emerging from the kitchen with a cooler. "For our trip, I mean. We'll have it later."

"Our trip?" Jen asked.

"But *why* do you see a threat?" Baz was asking. "If that's in fact what you see. Because you could choose to see so many things. You could choose to see history. You could choose to see a practical implement for clearing undergrowth—the very kind used to create the clearing for this very compound where you are sitting right now. You could choose to see it as a simple and reliable tool for any number of agricultural tasks, like cutting sugarcane."

"I *could* choose!" Jen said. "Are we going somewhere?"

"You are proceeding on a conjecture. A presumption. A hypothesis, at best. In doing so, you believe yourself to be in control of your reality. But in fact, I'm controlling your reality—and what you *think* is your reality doesn't account for that. You granted me the right to control your reality the instant you started projecting a false reality onto an inanimate object."

"I'm *bored*," Unity keened. "Let's go already."

"To be continued," Baz said. He smiled, Jen thought, like a wolf.

"Where are we going?" Jen asked.

"In so many ways, that's up to you," Baz Angler said over his shoulder as he loped toward the front door. "When you come face-to-face with reality, with *real life,* that's the first step toward conjuring your own reality, your best and brightest reality, which is really what we're talking about when we're talking about making a life for ourselves, achieving our dreams, making a difference in this world."

"I can see how you and Leora would have hit it off," Jen said to the retreating figure. She looked at Ram, who gave her a double thumbs-up.

"We're going to a desert island!" Ram exclaimed, and Jen put up her hand to return his high-five.

Furthermost, Farthermore, Everending

"I think I can get LIFt to pay for this call," Jen stammered into her hotel-room phone, comforter thrown over her head, her lips numb and trembling.

"Are you okay?" Jim was asking.

Jen wriggled beneath a phantom prickling sensation that dotted her entire sheath of skin. "It started out fine," she said. "It started out *fine*."

"What started?" Jim asked.

"I followed Baz in Eva's car to the coast—"

"Who is Baz?" Jim asked.

"—and then we were going to take the ferry. We were going to take the ferry to Caye Caulker. From Caye Caulker they said we were going to the quote-unquote 'island.'"

"Who is 'they'?" Jim asked.

"There was a graveyard of golf carts," Jen said. "I remember this. I passed them driving Eva's car. There was an empty yellow bus, abandoned by the roadside. There was a tin shack, all on its own, painted orange and blue, with a handwritten sign out front that said SILVER FOX GUEST HOUSE. There were whitish-gray pools of water in the roads. The roads were sandy and uneven. Nowhere for the water on the ground to go. Poofy white-gray clouds shrouding everything."

"What is the island?" Jim asked. "Let's go back to the island."

"On the ferry, Ram was having trouble sitting still. Star and Unity were like a big tangle of limbs, all wrapped up in each other, but—resentfully so."

"This is Baz's entourage?" Jim asked. "Where is Eva?"

"When we reached Caye Caulker, the pier was covered in garbage and missing chunks of wood. There was a big hunk of concrete, half submerged, next to the pier, and it looked like maybe an earlier attempt at a pier. There was broken glass and bottle caps bobbing in the turtle grass. The water was shallow and smelled of garbage. A few tourists were trying to snorkel in it. We all climbed into a small boat with two men who—I didn't catch their names. As we get in, Baz thumps his chest with both fists and he yells, 'These sacs are big and clean, thanks to the same air that bears the quetzal's wings!'"

"I'm suddenly feeling better about this story," Jim said.

"There are no life jackets."

"Oh," Jim said.

"The next thing I remember is—we're speedboating into a storm cell. The sea is rising under a deep, dark cloud cover. The rain starts. There are buckets of salt water, stinging, flying into the boat and into our faces. The wind is like a knife and the water is zigzagging around it. We are freezing and, for some reason, we are laughing."

"Ha, ha!" Jim said.

"It's like this for a long time. Maybe it was hours. And then we arrive at 'the island.' The winds seem to be reaching gale force. The island looks like leftover shards from Bikini Atoll. We huddle under what looks like a bus shelter made of bamboo. Star is saying things like, "I think it might be one degree warmer over here." Unity is saying things like, "Look, that might be a patch of blue sky coming out." Ram gets restless and goes out to try to snorkel in the water, which is only ankle-deep. Even far away from shore, it's only ankle-deep. Ram comes back with a bleeding gouge in his knee. He is laughing and Star and Unity are laughing."

"It *is* funny when you think about it," Jim said.

"And Baz says something like, 'Shallow water so far out means a surge is coming. The pressure is sucking all the water out.' Then the two men whose names I haven't caught serve us fish and grilled onions and white bread. The fish still have the heads and eyes attached. We drink lots and lots of rum punch and Belikin beer. I drink two enormous rum punches and don't feel a thing. Ram has two big rum punches and four beers and doesn't feel a thing. Ram says, 'I don't feel a thing,' and he laughs and then I laugh, too. We are shivering violently and don't feel a thing. Star and Unity are chugging from flasks. I don't know if they feel anything. Later on, Star and Unity disappear for a while on the other side of the bus shelter with Baz, and Ram tries to snorkel again."

"Ram has gumption," Jim said. "Ram should write memos for LIFt."

"So then after we enjoy the island for a while, we climb back into the boat. Baz and Star and Unity are back and everyone is laughing. Time starts to get very weird here. I don't know how long we were on the island. I don't know how long we were in the boat. There is no sense of time because the storm cover—it wipes away the shadows and you can't track the movement of the sun. On the way back to Caye Caulker, we are sure that every caye we see is Caulker, but it never is, and then every time it becomes clear that the caye is not Caulker, we laugh more. Caye Caulker is no longer a place—like, we've been there, but it doesn't exist anymore—"

"Wait, are you still alive?" Jim asked. "At this point in the story?"

"—it doesn't exist anymore except as a horizon line, or like an asymptote, and that is funny, and it is progressively funnier. It gets darker and colder and rainier all the time. The wind bawls and the wind gets bigger. The wind has arms and hands."

Jim growled in pity and terror.

"It's like we're boating into a cold jet engine. The sea is swelling and dropping, swelling and dropping. The boat lurches *veryveryfast* over the waves, and then the waves recede in a trough, and the boat lands with a massive *thump* each time. With every *thump*, a huge pail of salt water lands *splat* in our faces. With every *thump*, I clear six inches of air between the boat seat and my butt."

"Did anybody get *boinged* out of the boat?" Jim asked.

"Sometimes I think to look around, and everyone in the boat looks like castaways who are resisting rescue. The laughter is getting bigger and *more*, and it starts to sound like hysteria. Or maybe the hysteria set in before that and we were too hysterical to notice. It only settles down once darkness falls entirely. Then it gets very quiet. We are heading straight into another squall. The other cayes and islands around us— they just disappear."

"So it's total darkness now?"

"We have two hundred meters of visibility at most—it's probably much less. The red blinking light of Caye Caulker is vanishing and flickering and vanishing again. It keeps falling away behind the palm trees. Our boat has just a tiny port-and-starboard light on it. Maybe no one is seeing us. As we're moving into the parking zone for boats, a huge luxury yacht looms up out of the darkness. The pilot yells at his copilot and the boat steers hard to the right and lurches up on its side and it nearly tips over. The pilots relax and laugh because they're so relieved the danger has passed. But then they notice that a dinghy is attached to the yacht, and again, they steer hard, lurch to the right, and laugh. Everyone is laughing again now except me."

"Killjoy," Jim said.

"I ask them what is so funny, and Unity is laughing and says, 'We almost died, and then we almost died again.'"

"It's the refrain that's funny," Jim said.

"And then Ram says if we had hit that boat we would either have been impaled on pulverized fiberglass or knocked unconscious and drowned, and he starts to say something else, but he's laughing too hard to continue. As we approach the dock, there's a small crowd assembled, watching us as the two men whose names I haven't caught begin roping the boat. Baz is taunting the crowd, yelling, 'You were gonna call the Coast Guard, weren't ya! Admit it!'"

"Sick burn," Jim said.

"And Ram is talking about what a great adventure we've had and Baz is yelling about primal joy and there's an officer of some type, in a badge and official hat and jacket, who grabs my hand and helps me onto the dock. My legs are shaking uncontrollably, and I'm kneeling down on the planks, waiting for my thigh and calf muscles to stop spasming, and I'm watching Star and Unity already strolling hand in hand up the dock toward the blinking Christmas lights strung around the back deck of a nightclub that's built on stilts. Baz says that I need to get up, and Ram asks me if I am quote-unquote 'ready to sample some Caye Caulker nightlife.'"

"Please, please, tell me you are calling from the club right now," Jim said.

Jen cradled the receiver against her collarbone, wrapped up the comforter around her more tightly, and fell sideways into a fetal position on the bed. "No," she said, "but—but I did—I went out with them."

"You did?" Jim asked, his voice tilting upward.

"Yeah," Jen said. "It was fun. Fun night. Showed them I was a trouper." Her breath was hot against a flapping fold of the blanket.

"Honey," Jim said. "That is great. I'm proud of you."

She tried to remember a time she had ever lied to Jim before, and couldn't.

"I am not barring—boring far—going to a bar," Jen had actually said, her eyes fixed on the planks, her legs scrabbling around beneath her on the wet dock. "Not bar now, right now."

"Back to the mainland, then?" Baz Angler asked. "Ram can make sure you get home safe."

"I need," she said, placing the bottom of one foot carefully on the dock and testing her weight. "I *need*."

"Hooh, boy," Ram said. "We really did a number on you."

"I need a number, I mean a minute," Jen said, stumbling backward and placing one hand down for balance. "A minute. What—what am I doing here?"

Baz Angler clapped his hands, beat his chest, and bayed at the full, shrouded moon.

"Why do I need to be here? Why am I here?" Jen asked, pushing down on her hand and flailing upward into a furtive hunched-warrior pose.

Baz cawed like a crow thrice and punched himself in the head.

"I mean not to—I don't mean existentially," Jen said.

Baz Angler mirrored Jen's low-riding warrior pose. "I think Leora wants me to join her board of directors," he said from his crouched position, then cartwheeled into a one-armed handstand on the dock's dark slimy surface.

"Okay," Jen said, sinking into a cross-legged heap. She stared out at the moon. "Would you like to join Leora's board of directors?" she asked the moon.

That was when everything started to go black, but Jen was fairly certain that Baz Angler said yes.

When Ram returned Jen to the lodge a couple of hours later, Karina and Travis sat closely together on the back patio of the main house. They pulled apart at the sight of Jen and asked her questions about her day. When Jen opened her mouth to speak, nothing came out. She walked through the patio on her rubber legs and on to her bungalow.

Flaming Tonnage

The next morning, Jen's eyes opened slowly, with excruciating care, encased as they were in a drying full-body mold of papier-mâché. Charred flat on her back, she was positive that if she didn't move quickly, the adhesive would solidify completely and bury her alive in her bed, but at the same time, if she *did* move quickly, the adhesive would tear her skin from her bones in clumps.

Jen lifted her hands to her face, pressing the pads of her fingers to her cheeks. Some diabolical prosthetics-maker or deranged plastic surgeon had experimented on her in the night, razoring off her flesh and applying some leathery graft in its place. She rolled, grunting, onto her side onto the hot metal of an iron and bolted upright, the flesh of one shoulder searing red. In the bathroom she flipped on the overhead light. What she saw, briefly, was crustaceous, dull red, a blistering exoskeleton. She twisted around to peer at her back and cried aloud, and flipped off the light.

She found a bottle of aloe and a water pitcher, filled the water pitcher with lukewarm water from the tap. She spent the next twenty-four hours sitting on the edge of the enormous canopy bed, naked, watching sitcoms in syndication and *Judge Judy*, eating salted nuts and M&M's from the minibar, drinking from and refilling the pitcher, and rubbing the aloe into all the crustaceous regions. Two angry patches on the backs of her calves. An enraged red line that parted her hair.

When she ran out of aloe, she put on first a pair of cutoffs and then a T-shirt, stifling a screech when the flaming tonnage of the T-shirt fabric slammed into one bright-red shoulder, and pushed and slapped the flaming tonnage back over her head, her mouth mewling through the cotton. She took an elastic-banded short skirt and pulled it up over her hips and under her armpits as an ad-hoc halter top. Her hand on the doorknob, she turned back to fish out her bottle of Animexa from her bag.

"For courage!" she said aloud to herself, breaking off half a tablet and popping it between her chapped lips.

Outside the bungalow, the clouds had diffused and parted company and the sun had traveled closer to the earth in the night and now took up the whole sky. She started to jog to the main house, but the jostling further tenderized her skin. She walked rapidly on her toes instead, until she reached Eva at the front desk. She showed wide-eyed Eva the empty bottle of aloe and asked for more.

"Oh, no, no, you're cooking yourself alive in this," Eva said. Thirty minutes later, Jen had in her hands a prescription tube of shiny translucent goo and a larger store-bought tube of thick white cream, which she was to alternate applying every two hours.

On Jen's last day in Belize, she tearfully pulled on her swimsuit and a long-sleeved T-shirt that sawed at her ground-beef flesh, popped half an Animexa tablet, took the ferry back to Caye Caulker, and, still teary under her wide straw hat, purchased a spot on a group snorkeling tour of the nearby reef. Manning the boat were two men whose names she didn't catch.

The rest of the group in their snorkel gear kicked and splashed near the surface, peering down on the reef. Jen, her shirt still on and her thick, wet hair splayed protectively over her neck, plunged in as deep as her lungs and cumbersome snorkel mask would allow. The lumpy ocean floor stirred and heaved upward, mutating into a manta ray. Brain coral pulsed. Rainbow formations of fish fanned and feinted. The mask cut and bit into her scorched face like a machete on a pic-nic table. After a while she tossed her gear into the boat. She filled her lungs and dived down to the shallow ocean floor again, eyes wide open, hugging her knees, watching a turtle float by. She laughed, and watched and listened to her breath turn into bubbles until she ran out of breath.

Vacation from Your Vacation

Jen and Karina waited to put their bags through security at the Belize City airport.

"You poor thing," Karina said from behind her big-fly sunglasses as she combed her fingers through her ponytail. "You look like you need a vacation from your vacation."

"Yeah," Jen said. It hurt to smile. "It was so overcast and rainy the whole day I was out with Baz Angler—so *dark*—I just completely for-got to put sunscreen on."

"Out an entire day in the Caribbean and no sunblock," Karina said, shaking her head. "Jen, what are we going to *do* with you?"

"I know, I know," Jen said, nodding, her usual cushion-laugh squeaking out as a pained *heh*. "Heavy cloud cover is no substitute for UV protection. I learned the hard way. But as you probably know, Baz is really into *reality*, and I sure did get a dose of reality."

Karina continued to shake her head, and Jen continued to nod.

"So," Jen said, "is Travis on our flight?"

"You know, I didn't want to say, but that brother didn't just leave the U.S. of A.—he might have left planet earth," Karina said, tapping her sunglasses and raising her eyebrows.

Jen's rolling suitcase clattered onto its side, and as she leaned over, grimacing, to pull it upright, her tote bag slipped to the floor, too, tossing lip gloss and car keys onto the linoleum and setting Jen's shoulder alight again. An eidetic image, unbidden and undeniable, burned into Jen's mind—a gauzy silhouette of Karina atop Travis in an enormous canopy bed, her back arched, her hands scraping compulsively at her tossing hair, Travis beneath her wearing nothing but a polo shirt, counting down a multitasking round of tricep lifts on the colorful bedspread as Karina writhed above.

"I see," Jen said, gripping the handle of her suitcase harder.

"A few irons missing in his golf bag, know what I mean?" Karina said, tongue nestled between her teeth.

Jen's mouth was hanging open. "Wait, who are we talking about?"

Karina's expression behind her big-fly sunglasses was inscrutable. "Your new BFF and our likely new board member," she said. "Baz. He's *nuts*. Am I right?"

"Oh, yeah, well," Jen said, looking down at the floor. "The thing is, Karina, if that was the case—if we knew Baz was a handful—it would have been good for me to know that about him ahead of time." Jen was talking to the floor. Her synapses ejaculated three more pumps of Karina's hips atop Travis *ungh ungh ungh* before she could blink them away. "Good for LIFt, I mean," Jen continued. "Just in terms of being able to plan ahead, to strategize—I just—I wish I'd known more ahead of time. That's all. No harm done, of course." She feared that she was coming across as pouty, bratty, so she wrested her features into an amiable alignment and looked up at Karina.

Twinges of pleasure played at Karina's lips. This was who she was, Jen remembered, not for the first time. When Karina had information to disclose that could be helpful, she wouldn't disclose, and yet when it might have conferred favor on Karina to withhold information—to appear ignorant and therefore innocent—she freely disclosed, because the clear and present benefits of demonstrable informational superiority were more palpable, more valuable to her, than the less immediately tangible benefits of trust or goodwill she might have salvaged by withholding. This was something Karina had in common with Baz Angler, Jen thought. An iron missing in their respective golf bags.

Not a Perfect System

"I just don't understand how a disagreement about whether or not Congress votes to extend unemployment benefits somehow turns into people threatening to leave before the pumpkin pie is even served," Jen was saying to her mother on the phone.

Jen had in truth been happy for her brothers' argument to erupt over her parents' Thanksgiving dinner table, as the yelling and gesticulating and slamming of fists on table had drowned out her sisters-in-law's tag-team queries about when they could expect Jen and Jim to "start a family" (in Sharon's straightforward terms) and/or "get going already!" (Betsy's more insouciant wording).

"Well, I admire your brothers' passion," Jen's mom said. "They feel strongly about things, and that's what they have in common, never mind politics. Their passion is their common ground."

"It's ridiculous, childish behavior," Jen said.

"What are your plans for Christmas?" Jen's mom asked.

"I still need to book the tickets," Jen said.

"Okay, well," Jen's mom said, sighing heavily, "you know, I *hate* to bring this up, and before I do, I need you to know that I *certainly* don't care about this, and your *father* certainly doesn't care—I mean, he doesn't care all that much—but I would be terribly remiss if I didn't say *something*, so—"

"What? What is it?" Jen asked.

"It has been noted," Jen's mom said, her staccato inflection introducing a contractual formality to her speech, "that you did not spend the assigned family budget on gifts last Christmas."

"What? Noted by who?"

"That is unimportant to the moral of the story, and—"

"What is the moral of the story?" Jen asked.

"—and it is of course *completely* up to you what you spend, but I *would* ask the two of you to try to keep the family budget in mind."

"I thought we were supposed to spend one hundred fifty dollars per person," Jen said.

"Right, so you and Jim should be spending three hundred dollars *per recipient*, because there are *two* of you," Jen's mom replied. "God, I hate this. It's only to keep it fair, please understand that."

Jen laughed. "I don't even have three hundred dollars to spend on *anyone*, and I'm supposed to figure out how to spend three hundred dollars on *Dad*?" she asked. "All he ever wants is a power tool or a biography of a president."

"Look, I know it's not a perfect system," Jen's mom said. Jen could already hear her fading out, her mother's slender fingers slowly turning the volume dial on this particular conversation from low to off, her eyes sliding away toward the closest table in need of retidying or the closest glowing television screen. "This is *truly* the best way your father knows to keep it equitable. Okay, hon? I'll let ya go now."

Magic Carpet Ride

Jim and Millie were sweeping the perimeter of Meg and Marc's loft playing Magic Carpet Ride while Jen and Meg sat at the glass-and-oak dining table, shelling pistachios. Magic Carpet Ride involved placing Millie atop any soft, smooth-bottomed object—a rag rug, a bathroom mat, Buzz the golden retriever's dog basket—and Jim pulling Millie and the smooth-bottomed object as far and rapidly as possible until the smooth-bottomed object had wrested itself free of Millie or Millie had collapsed over on her side squeeing with laughter, whichever came first.

Magic Carpet Ride also had a vocal component.

"Magic carpet ride! Magic carpet ride!" Jim called out.

"Magi cop rye! Magi cop rye!" Millie called out.

Meg was asking Jen about her Thanksgiving. Meg had spent Thanksgiving at the home of her maternal aunt, who was a countess by marriage, or maybe a baroness, and who, in a move inexplicable to the rest of her exceedingly discreet family, had just assented to a glossy magazine feature about the top floor of her town house, which consisted entirely of a bathroom carved out of gold Calacatta marble imported from Italy. "We have the equivalent of a Roman aqueduct flowing beneath the floors—no more cold feet after a warm bath," Meg's aunt had explained to the magazine writer.

"It was stupid," Jen said. "Thanksgiving was stupid. It wasn't as stupid as the trip to Belize."

"You look fine, by the way," Meg said now. "You look beautiful. A bit pink, but healthy pink. I thought you would look like something I forgot on the stove."

"You can't see my back, though—it's covered in cobwebs, only the cobwebs are *sautéed flesh*," Jen said.

Millie ran hollering past with Buzz's dog basket over her head, with Jim crab-walking a few paces behind her.

"So far as I can tell," Jen continued, "Leora wanted someone to go to Belize to talk with Baz Angler about joining her board, and Karina espied an opportunity to finagle a romantic Caribbean getaway with the Indiana Jones of nutrition bars, so long as she could loop me in to handle the actual work. But that's just an educated guess. Is this what people do?"

At the periphery of Jen's vision, Millie flew through the air hooting and *floomph*ed onto the sofa, Magic Carpet Ride having readily segued into the Hammock Game.

"No," Meg said. "This is not what people do."

Jen chomped a pistachio. "At least the fact that they sent me does bespeak a confidence in my abilities."

Floomph

"Do you actually want Leora Infinitas's confidence in your abilities?" Meg asked. "Is that an ambition of yours?"

"I have never even made eye contact with Leora Infinitas," Jen said. "I don't think she knows my name or what I do. I'm not even entirely sure she knows I went on this ridiculous trip or that she paid for it."

Floomph

Jen snapped another pistachio. "You know," she said, "speaking of meeting people, I never met a single Belizean there who wasn't serving me in some way. Handing me a drink. Taking my bags. Boating my boat to nowhere. I never had a single conversation with someone with whom my organization was nominally connecting."

Floomph

Meg shrugged. "But that was up to you," she said, not unkindly. "What was stopping you?"

"You're right," Jen said, as a screeching Millie skidded into her lap and climbed atop her. "Nothing was stopping me," she said, hugging the little girl to her chest and looking up at Jim, who was panting with Buzz's red bandanna kerchief clenched between his teeth.

Metaphors

The train was all messed up again. Jen was bundled for the cold, but per usual it took Jim a month or so to habituate to dressing for wintry weather, and so he had equipped himself for the long walk home from the last stop in merely a light jacket, no scarf or gloves or hat. This seasonal sartorial pattern never varied, and neither did Jen's annoyance with it. Jen would have testified under oath that her irritation was an expression of empathy for her partner's comfort and of concern for any undue stress on his immune system at the start of flu season. She guessed that Jim would have testified under oath that his partner's irritation was in fact a form of judgment—a judgment that he lacked in basic adult competencies, that he was short on commonsensical foresight, that he could not project himself into a predictable future, such as, for example, the cold, windy future located just outside their chronically overheated apartment whenever he left it to report to work or visit friends, and that this shortcoming was somehow symbolic— microcosmic—of Jen's Jen-like grasp of Jim's Jim-ness.

"Aren't you cold?" Jen asked.

"I'm fine," Jim said.

Jen rubbed one mittened hand against Jim's hunched back and hustled to keep up with his brisk pace.

"I love watching you with Millie," Jen said.

"I love watching *you* with Millie," Jim replied, blowing air into his cupped palms and then covering his red ears with his hands. "You're awesome with her."

"Do you want my scarf? You could kind of wrap it around your ears."

"No," Jim said quickly, taking his hands away from his ears.

Jen linked her arm in his and they walked silently for a while.

"You know, this is going to sound weird, but—you know that I love Millie for herself, right?" Jen asked.

"Of course you do."

"But do you know what I mean?"

"Not really."

"Then why did you say you know something when you don't know?"

"Why don't you just tell me what you mean?"

"I mean that I love her not as—not as a metaphor for something I want for myself. She's not a symbol of what I long for and don't have."

"You don't have to convince me of that," Jim said.

"She's not a substitution," Jen said, more insistently. "Millie is Millie."

"Honey, don't take this the wrong way," Jim said, "but when you're trying to talk yourself into something, or out of something, you don't have to pretend like you're really having a conversation with me. You can just talk to yourself. I don't need to be involved."

"It's like she's not *useful*," Jen said.

"What?" Jim asked.

"Nothing," Jen said. "I'm just blathering."

"No, you're not," Jim said, and pulled one arm tightly around her. They walked past the uncharacteristically mellow dogs of Brancato's Grocery, shoulder pressed to shoulder.

What Jen tried and failed to articulate was that her relationship with Millie stood as the purest one in her life, because Millie had no precise or measurable utility. For the first years that Jen and Jim were together, Jen could not have said that Jim had a precise or measurable utility, either. In more recent years, though, and especially since their marriage, she had assigned to Jim empirical values: the numerical amount of his contribution to their shared rent and household expenses and his projected monetary contribution in years to come; his contributions to household chores as measured in time; his ability to provide speed-trial results of regularly assessed and reliably consistent high quality in the Garden of Earthly Delights; etc. Conversely, Jen was painfully aware of her lack of any precise, measurable utility to Meg: Jen would never find herself in a position to line up gainful employment for Meg if she needed it, or a cost-free vacation rental house for Meg if she so desired it.

Ironically, if anyone could have placed a high value on Jen's precise and measurable utility at the moment, it might have been Pam, for the hours and hours that Jen couldn't bear to calculate, the spine-wrenching, muscle-torching weeks that Jen had sunk into those paintings—in a spirit of friendship, in a spirit of creative collaboration for the pure sake of it, but not, as Jen knew now, in a spirit that could be reciprocated by deploying Pam as a means to a different, arguably more mercenary end.

"Hey, did you ever get your paintings back from Pam?" Jim asked.

"I was just sort of thinking about that," Jen replied.

That night, Jen opened the Total Transformation Challenge submission page on her laptop. She considered the instructions for the fifth category and typed a response.

TTC CATEGORY 5: SPACE

How can you challenge yourself to make sure that your home is a reflection of your best self—your creativity, your capacity for forging loving relationships, your inner peace?

Your response here:

I challenge myself to finally find some nice frames for Millie's drawings and hang them up.

We Are Doing Good Here

Jen, Karina, and Sunny stood around Donna's desk looking at photographs. Jen had commissioned an award-winning young photographer and current Agence France-Presse stringer to take no-fee pictures of the teenaged recipients of a higher-education scholarship program in

Nigeria that LIFt had helped to fund. Jen had been delighted with the photographs of the five Nigerian scholars, who would be featured in a print and brochure campaign and on the LIFt website; the girls looked at ease in front of Françoise's camera, smiling in almost every shot—carefree smiles and shy smiles and breaking-into-laughter smiles—against a matte black background.

"Why are they wearing these Western mall clothes?" Donna had asked. "Did we put them in these clothes?"

"No, of course not," Jen had replied. "They are wearing their own clothes."

"Who are they laughing at?" Sunny had asked.

"Have these been, uh, airbrushed yet?" Karina had asked.

"Oof, orthodontics, am I right, Karina?" Sunny had asked.

"Françoise can definitely touch them up, but the vibe we're going for is newsy, casual—a flattering but representative snapshot," Jen had said. She had anticipated some version of this very conversation, and had rehearsed for it.

"I just can't get past the jeans and T-shirts," Donna had said. "It's confusing."

"Look, I know it's awkward, but it just keeps on coming up, so I'll just keep on saying it—with all of our communications efforts, we always need to think about *optics*, Jen," Karina had said, tapping the image of the scholar with the highest body mass index.

Since then, Jules the social-media intern had pointed the team toward a fashion photographer's black-and-white studio portraits of teenaged girls from Cameroon, uniformly smooth-skinned and high-cheekboned and dressed in traditional garb, and all of whom held the camera with bottomlessly somber, unsmiling expressions. Petra mocked up new print and web pages using these pictures, with inspirational quotes in an italicized script overlaying the edges of the images. Printouts of the pictures from Cameroon now lay side by side with the pictures from Nigeria, fanned across Donna's desk.

"God, these are just gorgeous," Karina said.

"Mmmm," Sunny groaned. Jen imagined Sunny in a terry-cloth

robe and towel turban, draping the printouts over her face like a hot, fragrant towel.

"This isn't even worth discussing," Donna said.

"Wait, but this quote, 'I have known since I was a little girl that my future was in my education'—I'd have to check the transcript, but I'm pretty sure that Promise said that," Jen said, pointing to a quotation overlaying a close-up of a Cameroonian girl, her hands clasped and pressed to her jawline, her giant startled eyes piercing the lens. "Promise, the Nigerian scholar. That's not Promise."

"Which one is Promise?" Karina asked. "The one in the Beyoncé crop top?"

"They're wearing *jeans*," Donna reiterated, her bangles clattering in shared frustration. "Have we forgotten this?"

"Françoise is in Lagos for a few more days—we could ask her for something in a more low-key style, if that's what we're going for," Jen said.

"I would hardly call these images low-key," Sunny said. "They are *arresting. Stunning.* You can't tear your eyes away from them."

"If anything, they're *high*-key," Donna said.

"No, sorry," Jen said, "what I meant is that *low-key* is the technical term for this style of portraiture—that kind of high-contrast, moody, shadowy, brooding effect that you all are responding to so strongly—"

"I know you're an artist, Jen, but this isn't a studio visit," Karina said.

"Don't get me wrong, the photos from Cameroon *are* absolutely stunning, and they were a good choice," Jen said. Jen knew this to be false. Instead of properly lighting the set, the photographer responsible for the Cameroon shoot had illuminated it after the fact using the dodging tool in Photoshop. In one profile shot, a girl's jawline was lost in darkness, yet somehow light pooled in her collarbone. "It would be *so great* if we could use these photos, honestly, and I'm grateful to Jules for finding them," Jen continued. "She has an eye! But the fact of the matter is that we *can't* use them, because they don't represent the story we're telling, which is about our Nigerian scholars. These girls from Cameroon aren't the girls from Nigeria. It's simple?"

Donna stared at her phone. Karina shrugged. "I just don't see the problem here," Karina said, glancing around at Donna and Sunny with eyebrows raised. "We've never wrung our hands and gnashed our teeth about stock photos in any other cases."

"And they'll never know," Donna and her bangles said to her phone.

"They have the Internet in Nigeria," Jen said.

"Well, we'll use these just in the print brochures, then," Donna said, her voice cresting with frustration. "What is the harm?"

"But to Karina's point, these aren't stock photos," Jen said. "We use stock photos to illustrate ideas, concepts. These girls, these scholars, aren't ideas or concepts. The image should represent the—the thing it's supposed to represent."

"The *thing*?" Sunny asked.

"These are all *beeeyooooteeeful* girls," Donna intoned.

"They are not things!" Sunny said.

"I'm not disputing any of that," Jen said.

"We are doing *good* here," said Sunny, tearing up.

Jen returned to her desk.

jenski1848: I imagine you can guess how that went.
whatDaisyknew: ON IT

Jen heard Daisy's grammatically perfect but comically American-accented French over the cubicle wall. "Françoise, do you remember if any of the girls was wearing a head wrap or anything?" Daisy was inquiring. "Something in, like, I don't know, a batik print or something? Why do you ask? Oh, just because here at LIFt we ascribe a philanthropic value to prejudice and stereotypes about the 'deserving' poor and they're bound up in a specific kind of aesthetics. Which involves head wraps. And flowy garments." *Des vêtements fluides.*

Jen opened the Total Transformation Challenge submission page on her computer. She considered the instructions for the sixth category and typed a response.

TTC CATEGORY 6: MISSION

How can you challenge yourself in your career to make sure that your work squares with your values and is in harmonic balance with the rest of your life?

Your response here:

WE ARE DOING GOOD HERE WE ARE DOING GOOD HERE WE ARE DOING GOOD HERE WE ARE DOING

Jen's phone was ringing. The caller ID seemed familiar—a Judy, most likely.

"Hello, my name is Dakota, and I'm calling on behalf of Mrs. Flossie Durbin," said the sweet crystalline voice on the other line. "Mrs. Durbin would like to set up a meeting with you at your earliest convenience to discuss her portrait."

Winter

Christmas Eve

Jen excused herself and Jim from the usual Christmas festivities at her parents' house in Youngstown, and the attendant $300-per-head surcharge on said festivities, by informing her mother that she had taken "a last-minute house-sitting gig for a friend." This statement was, at least in legalistic terms, true. The alternative arrangement could be fairly labeled as "last-minute," as it had presented itself one week before the purported date of Jen and Jim's flight to Ohio and would have required Jen to cancel said flight, had she ever booked the flight in the first place, which she had not. The alternative arrangement could be likewise accurately described as a "house-sitting gig," as Jen had indeed repeatedly assumed seated positions in the house as part of completing the terms of her brief employment there, and, much to her shock, had been given free rein of the house while its occupant was abroad for the holidays, though Jen had no plans to sleep or eat in the house or otherwise use it as a short-term residence.

"Who is this friend?" her mother asked on the phone, after Jen had fended off her queries about the prospects of Jen receiving a refund for the canceled flight that she had not booked. "Is it that Meg?"

"No," Jen said. "It's an older lady—I met her recently through work—who's helping me with some of my art stuff."

"Oh. Well," Jen's mother replied, in the mock-sobbing tone she used when she wished both to display disappointment and to make a deflective joke about her own ostentatious display of disappointment, "we sure will miss you at Christmas." *Kruss-muss.* Jen's mother laughed nervously.

Jen's mother made it easy for Jen to lie to her, or to lie by omission.

But it was never easy for Jen to deduce if her mother knew she was lying, by omission or otherwise.

The omission, in this case, took partial form as Mrs. Flossie Durbin's limestone Renaissance Revival town house. Via her assistant Dakota, Mrs. Durbin had invited Jen and Jim to stay in the town house over the holidays while Jen finished the portrait of Mrs. Durbin, which she was mapping out and modifying from a candid snapshot she'd found on *New York Social Diary*, even though Mrs. Durbin had gently insisted on two traditional and serenely pointless "sittings." In her previous visits to this particular Durbin residence, Jen had simply edited out her surroundings for fear of gawping at them, as if she could pretend that she and Mrs. Durbin were performing in front of a green screen for a hybrid animation/live-action film. Now there was no one but Jim to look at Jen looking, yet she was still afraid to peer too closely at any of Mrs. Durbin's furnishings or possessions, much less touch, use, discuss, or apply her body weight to any of Mrs. Durbin's furnishings or possessions. If Jen's eyes rested on any single sconce or vase or rock-crystal candleholder too long, her brain would transmit grisly flash-point images of clattering disaster. A violent muscle spasm chucking her arm across the *faux-marbre* Florentine chimneypiece, smashing a terra-cotta vase to the floor. A blot of chocolate or grease or dog feces achieving self-awareness and smuggling itself in from the outside world on Jen's coat sleeve, dive-bombing the herringbone-tweed linen sofa or accenting cotton *toile de jouy* and trompe l'oeil *boiserie*. A sleep-walking spell ending in the bloody caterwauling death of a Regency convex mirror.

"I feel like we should lay down towels before we sit anywhere," Jen said. Jim was taking a book down from a polished walnut bookcase in what Jen's mother would have called Mrs. Durbin's "living room" and what Jim had decided to call the "ballroom," and Jen reflexively raised both hands, fingers fluttering, as if Jim were about to lock into a trance by which unseen forces would seize control of his body and command his arms to lob the book squarely at the chandelier overhead.

"You're going about this all wrong," Jim said. "If there were ever a time to have towel-free sex in somebody else's bed, and then to sleep in that bed and maybe even sit down on that bed, it is now."

"Can you put the book back?" Jen asked, chewing on her left thumbnail.

Jim put the book back. "That's a Sterling Ruby in the gym, you know," he said, lowering himself carefully into what Jen guessed was a hand-marbleized leather armchair.

"And that's a John Currin right behind you," Jen said, switching to her right thumbnail. Jim reared around to see, too quickly.

Jen would have preferred it if she and Jim had confined themselves to what Mrs. Durbin called her "study," which was presently empty on the eve of being redecorated and thus contained little that could be maimed or destroyed by an errant footfall or direct eye contact or the onset of a previously undiagnosed seizure disorder, save perhaps for the fireplace and the ebonized oak flooring and the glass of the double casement window looking out onto the park, and, of course, Jen's work-in-progress canvas. The study was where Mrs. Durbin had sat, in a since-disappeared button-backed fauteuil covered in gold silk jacquard, on two successive Sunday afternoons while Jen sketched her, backlit by the winter sunshine angling low and feeble through the window. Mrs. Durbin's hair was the color of white wine. Her eyes had the alert and well-rested result of the most advanced and subtle blepharoplasty. For their first "sitting," Mrs. Durbin was upholstered in what Jen guessed to be a Chanel suit; on the second, a Givenchy brocade jacket and cigarette pants. Mrs. Durbin said very little. She would have been the oldest and serenest and richest of the Judys, satiny in her stillness and so astonishingly thin that her thinness seemed less the product of frenzied Judy-esque willpower and more as if Mrs. Durbin had hired a team of experts to hack into her mainframe and recalibrate it to run smoothly and silently on 30 to 35 percent less energy than other, less optimized Judys.

"What speaks to Mrs. Durbin about your work is that it is unabashedly upbeat, literally in-your-face, which goes against the grain of how we've been feeling as a culture lately, in what have been difficult and—

frankly—depressing times," Dakota had explained to Jen over the phone. "She says it's like you've taken the temperature of the culture, shrugged, and just thrown the thermometer away. And now that the economy is starting to turn a corner, it's like you were ahead of the curve all along. Two thousand ten is going to be your year!"

Jen tentatively positioned her ass on the edge of a cane-back chair near Jim, then stood again. "I still feel uncomfortable that Mrs. Durbin fundamentally misunderstands what I was trying to do," she said to Jim. "I wasn't presenting joy. It's more about the fake ways we present ourselves to the world, the masks we put on. I was trying to dramatize that, or satirize that. The idea of the portraits in Pam's show was pretty straightforward—it was creating a maniacally happy stock-photo counterpoint to the bureaucratic horror and sadism of our health-care system."

"Are you dictating a grant proposal?" Jim asked.

"I didn't even know that at the time, but Pam did," Jen said. She tried again to lower herself into the cane-back chair.

"You could look at it this way: It's not really your business whether Mrs. Flossie Durbin gets it or not," Jim said. "Arguably it's not even your business to define what there is for Mrs. Flossie Durbin to get."

"Do you think there are surveillance cameras in here?" Jen asked.

"Your job is to make the stuff, and then it belongs to the world and it's out of your hands," Jim said.

"You're right," Jen said. "And it's not like Mrs. Durbin's portrait is going to have that same feeling of—"

"—of delirious happiness that you've been impaled on an electric fence," Jim said.

"This will be a pleasant and benign portrait of a benign and pleasant woman. It's just weird to think that a happy false façade was just what we needed after the financial apocalypse. If we're all openly unhappy, then at least we know what we're dealing with."

"That part of your grant proposal might hold up if we weren't all pretty openly unhappy already," Jim said. "Also, Jen."

"What?"

"Look around you for a second."

Jen laughed again and shaded her eyes with her hand. "I know."

"No, seriously. Look around you."

Jen lowered her hand, rolled her eyes, then rolled them around the room.

"Look at where you are. Look at what you're doing, and who you're doing it for."

"I know. I don't understand how this happened," Jen said.

"Let's go have some towel sex," Jim said.

"Okay," Jen said. "But not here."

Jim bolted up from the armchair and Jen winced. As she grabbed her things, she saw a new email on her phone.

Pam <raddenpamela@gmail.com>
Thursday, Dec 24 6:31 PM
To: Jen <Jenski1848@gmail.com>
Subject: Please fwd to Franny

Dear Jen,

Do you want to get lunch sometime after the holidays? Paulo and I are back from Colombia on the 2nd. Also, I'm attaching a photo of a new friend for Franny. She should arrive in the spring.

Love,
Pam

Jen opened the attached image and at first she thought she was looking at the sonar footage of the wreckage of the flight that had disappeared without a trace the previous summer. Then she realized her mistake, and she yelped with honest and unguarded delight even as a narrow seam of dread began to open up inside her.

A Tousled, Effortless Cool

"Have you looked at our website today?" Daisy asked Jen over the cubicle wall in lieu of a morning salutation. It was their second day back at work after the New Year.

"Let me guess," Jen said, peeling off her coat. "Donna wasn't happy with the pictures of the girls from the São Paulo self-defense project, so we ran a slide show of Gisele Bündchen-Brady's workout regimen instead."

"I turned your computer on already so that you could waste no time looking at our website today," Daisy said.

Jen nudged her mouse to wake up her monitor. "Did Leora commission her makeup artist from *Father of Invention* to give the Nigerian scholars Seven-Minute Magic Makeovers featuring the LeoraDiance skin-care line?" Jen asked as she typed in her password.

"I think you're giving your immediate future short shrift," Daisy said. "Your immediate future is bright and full of possibility and available to you on our website today."

Jen opened the LIFt home page. She blinked hard, once, then rapidly in succession.

"Take all the time you need," Daisy said. "Live in the moment."

Jen clicked on the top-right link, which took her to a page topped with a full-column horizon shot of a man in a baseball cap and tight polo shirt, standing knee-deep in a lush field of greens against a verdant backdrop and grinning hard at some rhapsodic vision just past the camera's sight line.

Meet Our New Board Member: Travis Paddock

Travis Paddock is the entrepreneur behind the barnstorming fitness and nutrition startup BodMod™ International, and he smiles a lot, as if to offset the deep, dark recesses of pure concentration he brings to every endeavor. He'd be intimidating—if it weren't for that mischievous flash in his eyes.

Right now, those striking eyes—as cerulean blue as the brilliant Belizean sky creating a picture-postcard backdrop behind Paddock—are trained on, of all things, a mealy clump of whiteish pulp from a calabash tree. He has traveled thousands of miles to Belize's Cayo District for what might seem like a sad and soggy reward, until you remember that this is the man who also answers to the name "the Healthy Huntsman," who searches high and low for the purest, most nutritiously dense "superfoods" the world has to offer. Whether he's on or off the field of discovery, Paddock radiates a tousled, effortless cool—a "Look Ma, No Hands" persona that has jazzed his business from the get-go.

He palms the pulp from hand to hand and laughs, his perfect piano-key teeth flashing . . .

"Are you looking at our website today?" Daisy asked from behind the cubicle wall.

Jen half-stood up and craned her neck around to make sure Karina wasn't in the vicinity.

"His body parts sure do flash a lot," Daisy said. "Good communications work there, Jen."

Jen sat down again.

jenski1848: Switching to chat. This is like an infomercial.
whatDaisyknew: LOOK MA NO HANDS
jenski1848: How is this in service of "empowering women"?? Honestly, is this where we are in this organization right now?
whatDaisyknew: I THINK OF IT AS A PLACE WHERE I CAN DEVELOP MY TOUSLED, EFFORTLESS COOL

Jen closed the instant-message window and broke off half an Animexa tablet that she'd stashed in her wallet. Three hours had to elapse before she could leave the office to meet Pam for lunch, and if she didn't assign a powerful central-nervous-system stimulant to monitor her thoughts and actions vigilantly during those three hours, she risked dissipating each of the 180 minutes with righteous IMing, idle brooding, and mindless Internet browsing, when in fact the best and most efficient available use of her time would be to line-edit Hedge Fund Judy 2's newly filed essay for LIFe Lines on resolving not to make New Year's resolutions:

> The word resolution. It's a funny one. My thesaurus offers synonyms such as firmness, immovability, and staunchness. And yet my dictionary tells me, paradoxically, that the word itself is pliable. Flexible. Resolution could mean "a firm decision to do or not do something," of course. That's the way we mean it when we make New Year's resolutions. It could mean "the action of solving a problem," which also sounds like a New Year's resolution to me. It could mean "the degree of detail visible in a photographic or television image." That likewise feels of a piece with our New Year's resolutions, since the beginning of a New Year prompts us to look at ourselves in finer detail and helps bring our lives into sharper focus.
>
> But my favorite version of resolution is "in music, the passing of a discord into a concord during the course of changing harmony." Now, that's exactly the kind of New Year's Resolution I resolve to make this year. Not necessarily the firm, immovable, or staunch kind of resolution. Instead, I urge us all to make resolutions that acknowledge the push-and-pull messiness of everyday life. Resolutions that find pliable, flexible solutions to problems we face all the time. Resolutions that honor and cherish the fact that every single day represents "a passing of a discord into a concord." A search not for one resolved melody, but an ever-changing harmony.

Jen scrolled down on the file to confirm that the essay continued for about 1,100 more words on this theme. She then pasted Hedge Fund Judy 2's untouched text into the content management system, found and uploaded a stock image of revelers at a New Year's Eve party, published the essay to the LIFe Lines blog, and sent a congratulatory email to Hedge Fund Judy 2. Then Jen spent the next two hours and forty-five minutes reading the *Nastygram Ladyparts* archives and trying not to eavesdrop on Daisy.

"I dream of the day that this board hears the parable of the sex worker and the cow," Daisy was saying into the phone. "You know that one? There's a sex worker in a developing country, and some well-intentioned charitable organization comes along and gives her a cow. 'Hey, look, aren't you excited about your cow, now you don't have to be a sex worker anymore!' Right? But it turns out she has to take on double the number of clients as she did before, because she needs more money to support the cow." Daisy paused, listening to her caller. "No, I don't know that this actually happened. The story may be apocryphal. The sex worker may or may not exist, and she may or may not have acquired a cow. But I do know for a fact that we are the cow."

The Sperm That Got Away

As Pam entered the vestibule of the Chinese restaurant where she and Jen were meeting for lunch, she pulled Jen into a full-body, hands-vigorously-rubbing-shoulder-blades hug. Jen felt the taut curve of Pam's belly against her.

"Congratulations," Jen said into Pam's hair. "I'm sorry."

"I'm sorry, too," Pam said into Jen's hair.

"I missed you," Jen said.

"Me, too," Pam said.

Pam stepped back from Jen, and they gripped the crooks of each other's arms. Pam beamed for a long moment at Jen. She blinked languidly, as if punctuating the final sentence of a silent conversation that had settled once and for all the reasons why they were sorry and the causes for their having missed each other.

"So I'm doing this group show with Taige Hammerback," Pam was saying after they'd sat down and ordered their food. "I'll do a scaled-down version of *Break in Case of Emergency,* or whatever fits. He also let me know—regarding any inevitable press coverage of the exhibition—that he never smiles in pictures, ever, and that he strongly prefers that people not smile in pictures taken with him, if they can help it, because—he says—it's physiologically impossible to smile during orgasm."

"Ordinarily," Jen said, "Taige Hammerback's orgasms would be our main topic of conversation, but first we need to have a serious talk about that picture you emailed me."

"Okay, but wait—I'm not stalling—I just wanted to make sure it was all right with you if I use some of your paintings again for the show," Pam said.

"Of course it is," Jen said, "and of course you are stalling."

"Oh, good. Well. I haven't even really told anyone yet—I can still get away with hiding her, all wrapped up for the winter," Pam said, pulling absently at the midsection of her loose sweater.

"I'm so happy for you, Pam."

"We told my dad and my stepmom," Pam said, "and we told Paulo's parents, and now I've told you." Pam was turning her water glass in 30-degree rotations. She looked up at Jen. "I wanted you to be the first to know, along with immediate family, and Meg."

"Thank you," Jen said. They waited silently as the waiter set down their plates. Pam held her gaze until Jen looked away, blushing.

"So was this—something that had been on your mind for a while?" Jen asked, once their waiter had moved to another table.

"No. Completely unplanned. The sperm that got away."

Jen smiled and nodded and opened her mouth to speak, but did not speak.

"But we knew we wanted to eventually," Pam said, "and everyone says you're never really ready anyway . . ."

"That's wonderful," Jen said. "I'm so, so happy for you."

"Part of the reason I wanted to tell you as soon as I could was because you always trusted me with everything you were going through with— with this stuff," Pam said. "That always meant a lot to me."

"I don't have any news on that front," Jen said preemptively, smiling. "I kind of needed not to think about it for a while. Now I have to decide on next steps."

Jen would tell Pam someday about the Thing That Happened. Not now.

"I want to hear more about the sperm that got away!" Jen said. "Seriously. I really do. It's okay. I'm okay. I want to talk about it with you. If you want to."

"Well, so," Pam said, taking a deep breath, "you skip over one little bit of planning and suddenly you have a mountain of planning to do, and there's a nonnegotiable deadline attached to all of it. There's the show, of course. We have to move apartments, obviously."

"You should move to Flatbush!" Jen said. "Or Not Ditmas Park. Big and biggish spaces for cheap. But I've given you and Paulo this speech before."

"Yeah, that's a good thought," Pam said. "Right now we've got our eye on this place on, uh, it's just a block or so from Meg, actually."

The seam of dread began to open up inside Jen again, just below her breastplate.

"I mean, it's not set in stone yet," Pam said. "And, I guess this is the other piece of news—Paulo and I are getting married."

"Oh my God! A baby and a new place and a wedding! This is insane, Pam! This is your year!"

The seam of dread was notching apart, tooth by tooth, like a zipper. Jen gripped her unused chopsticks in a fist, her nails digging into her palm.

"Well, the wedding is whatever. It's mostly to please Paulo's parents. They're traditional that way. Luckily, they're fine with waiting until after the baby is born, or at least they're pretending to be okay with the baby being a bastard for a little while. We'll probably do it in Bogotá next winter."

"Oh, cool, a destination wedding! I haven't been to one of those since Meg and Marc's rendezvous in Paris."

The seam of dread was tearing itself open as Jen's throat was closing shut.

"Who has The Dress, you or Meg?" Pam asked.

Jen swigged her hot tea. "I do." "Vacuum-sealed in my bedroom closet. Although Meg probably should have received sole custody of The Dress. With Meg it probably would've gotten its own cryogenic chamber and rotating team of attendants."

The Dress was the exquisitely simple off-white silk gown—bias-cut, slender straps, what Jim called "the enchanted nightgown of the faerie world"—that Meg's mother had worn to elope with Meg's father nearly four decades previously. Jen had worn it to her own City Hall wedding, accessorized with strappy sandals, flea-market bangles, and honeysuckle twisted into a loose French knot, devised by Pam's hands. Meg had worn The Dress to her own wedding, of course, barefoot, bare-necked, and bare-armed, face and nails unpainted, uncombed hair grazing her collarbone. No one—not Meg's mother, not Jen or Pam—saw Meg in The Dress until minutes before she took her vows. Meg's beauty on that day was flabbergasting, not least for its naked-ness, and yet also for its aura of privacy maintained even in front of hundreds of people. Only a girl with unlimited resources for embel-lishment could decide to forgo all adornments with such transcen-dent results, Jen thought. That refusal was instrumental to the overall effect—but only if it were a true refusal, borne out of choice, not of necessity.

"It's very important to me that I wear The Dress," Pam was saying. "Paulo's mother is already trying to talk us into this venue that's just bananas and a wedding party the size of an armada, and I'm going to let her have her way on pretty much everything because they're paying for it—I'm already getting emails about the bridal registry—but The Dress is not up for discussion."

"You know," Jen said, "I feel silly that I don't know anything about Paulo's family. I knew they were in Colombia, but not much more than that. What are they like?"

"They're nice," Pam said, twisting her napkin. "They're *nice*. Paulo doesn't like to talk about them much—I mean, he talks about them with me, but even that took a long time."

"Why?"

"Because . . ." Pam trailed off. "He doesn't want people to get any preconceived notions about him because of who his parents are."

"Why? They're in real estate or something?"

"Paulo's father is a property developer. I guess you could call him a—a tycoon. A *real estate baron*. Paulo's brother and sister are very much embedded in the family business, and meanwhile Paulo just flounced off to the States and started throwing pails of paint on things, or at least that's how his father sees it."

Jen piled an entire frond of sautéed spicy soy bok choy between her teeth, folding it in half with an artful curl of her tongue—two tiny droplets of sauce swan-diving out of her mouth and onto the tablecloth as the frond flipped back—and pulsing her head rhythmically as she chomped.

"His parents aren't judgmental so much as they're just—confused. About Paulo's choices, what he wants out of life. Meanwhile, Paulo is concerned about being seen as some rich-kid dilettante. And he's honestly never taken much—if anything—from them, at least not since he left school. He always wanted to prove that he could make it on his own—and that is something he does have in common with his father, that work ethic. But now that there's a third party involved, and she is currently taking up the priceless and heretofore undeveloped North American real estate that is my womb . . ."

Pam trailed off again, looking startled.

Jen shoveled more bok choy and gulped from her water glass. The Animexa tablet had increased the wattage on the restaurant's surgery-ward lights. Her fingers were numb. She hoped all the food-shoveling had opened the vessels in her face and prevented the blood from draining from her cheeks.

"I never would have guessed that about Paulo," Jen said. "Not that any of what you've told me is some guilty secret. But he seems so down-to-earth."

"He is," Pam said, staring at her plate.

"And you never—you guys never—"

"We've never lived in anything but shithole apartments?" Pam asked her plate, deadpan.

"And you even split the rent on those shitholes with others!" Jen said.

Pam laughed. "I'm sorry if it's weird that we never talked about this," she said. "I mean, like you said before—it's not like it was a secret; it's not like it was something to hide or disclose. But he's so private, while you and I are so open with each other, and I love you both so much, and—it created this weird contradiction sometimes."

"It's okay," Jen said. "It's resolved now."

Summer Camp

Jen parted from Pam with a promise to visit the work-in-progress space for the scaled-down *Break in Case of Emergency* ahead of its opening, then turned in the direction of the LIFt offices. Outside, every surface, whether material or atmospheric, seemed frozen in sooty gray stone, letting in little light and less heat. Jen turned back toward the restaurant, realizing she'd forgotten to tell Pam about her appointments with Mrs. Flossie Durbin, but Pam had already disappeared down the stairway of the closest subway entrance. Jen turned back again, corkscrewed around by dizziness. Disoriented as she was, her internal navigator pivoted her three blocks in LIFt's opposite direction instead, toward Jen's favorite library branch in the city: a modest, under-patronized brick square of Beaux Arts aspirations, its quiet courtyard garden ringed with benches.

To reach the courtyard, you first walked through the cozy, happily overstocked children's reading room and its monthly rotation of art projects. January marked a collaboration between a high-school art class and preschoolers learning the alphabet. First the preschoolers had marked bright, bold letters on oversized construction paper. Then the high-school students had interpreted each letter as a representation of an animal. One sloping leg of an *A* shape-shifted into the scaly back of a grinning alligator. The humps of a *B* revealed themselves as the ample belly and thighs of an affable bear. The attenuated bottom curve of a *C* morphed into the flicking tail of a rotund, imperious tabby cat.

The tabby began to wiggle and shimmer, and Jen continued into the courtyard. Then she turned back, because she wanted to know which animal they'd chosen to represent *X—Xerus inauris,* a giant African squirrel wearing a boa and a monocle—and then she spun around again toward the courtyard. She was dizzy again, or maybe she'd been dizzy since lunch, her peripheral vision streaming with muddy waters, her lower back filmed in a clammy sweat.

When Jen was in preschool, her teacher had handed out booklets intended for a week-to-week alphabet project that students could complete at home with their parents: drawing the letters of the alphabet and cutting pictures out of magazines that corresponded to each letter. Jen misunderstood the assignment, which she had taken up privately with a dull pencil in a visual language that was self-evident to her four-year-old perceptions, though she as yet lacked the fine motor skills to translate those perceptions onto the page: the wobbly pencil asterisk that meant *A for Ant,* the densely tangled pencil blob that meant *B for Bee.* At some point, though, there must have been a clarifying parent-teacher consultation at preschool drop-off or pickup, and somewhere around the *F*'s or *G*'s the largely interchangeable graphite splotches were supplanted by neatly scissored color photographs from the likes of *Ladies' Home Journal* and *Good Housekeeping,* which Jen's mother, sitting at their kitchen table, carefully cut and glued onto each page as Jen sat quietly beside her.

"There ya go," Jen's mother said, handing the booklet to Jen, having finished filling it in one hurried and mostly silent afternoon session, skipping without comment over X.

So many of Jen's childhood memories—so many of her memories, period—possessed this quality of hazy misapprehension followed by hard correction, a kind of dipping in and out of cognizance and then a stiff-legged flailing to catch up, to fill in redacted sentences and patch over skipped communications, a state of consciousness that could be measured fairly accurately in unsigned permission slips and half-finished homework assignments and hour upon hour of accumulated tardiness. Jen knew that she could have defined herself against this template, had she ever asserted the willpower to do so. But instead she had fitted herself to the template.

There would always be a room in the house, she thought, where people were gathered, murmuring pleasantly to one another, and Jen would be sure to stumble on it mere minutes before the festivities broke up, and the people inside the room would welcome her, not with hesitation but with mild regret, with kind but uncomfortable smiles, a compassion in their eyes.

Jen sat down on one of the empty benches in the empty courtyard. On her collar she could almost smell the sour breath of her own self-pity. Her self-pity subsisted in part on simple carbohydrates and on the salt mined from the sodium-rich instant soups of a drafty childhood, but it was mostly self-sustaining, feeding on itself, an apparently inescapable genetic susceptibility to self-pity being one of the major reasons Jen pitied herself. She closed her eyes against the yellowish orbital streaks ringing around her head and submitted to self-pity's embrace, tilting her face toward the slanting winter sun, inhaling and exhaling slowly.

She and her self-pity knew now, as the pleasant people gathered in the secret-seeming room must have known all along, that early adulthood for most of her college peers was a kind of summer camp, a character-building exercise in make-believe, a hope chest of nostalgia, a lakeside idyll that marked the shimmering threshold before real life began. The cramped, subsidized housing where Meg and Marc had lived for nearly two years during law school, throwing monthly four-course dinner parties at which half the guests ate in the tiny kitchen and the other half ate in the tiny bedroom, rotating guest by guest at regular intervals to hybridize conversation and interaction—that was summer camp. When Lauren Reilly, daughter of another partner at Meg's father's law firm, moved into her boyfriend's one-window studio to paper over the year between when she finished law school and her boyfriend started medical school—that was summer camp. Pam and Paulo's mildewy, transient-filled studio space was summer camp. Meg's semiannual clothing swaps were summer camp. Pam's Champion sweatshirts were summer camp.

Paulo's working-class artist's uniform—the overalls, the boots, the grooming—was not summer camp, Jen decided, nor was it a costume or a smoke screen. It wasn't even a disavowal of his inheritance. It instead bespoke a rich man who could work with his hands and knew the language of tools and machinery, who had not allowed wealth to insulate him from the mechanical or chemical world. Like Meg in The Dress, Paulo appeared more aristocratic in his proletariat garb because the uniform was a choice made possible by privilege, and by the confidence borne of privilege.

Meg's wedding—Chapelle Expiatoire, Hôtel de Crillon, Prada bridesmaid's dress that Jen had sometimes worn around the house during her enforced sabbatical—was the end of summer camp. Pam's wedding would be the end of summer camp.

Meeting your best friends in college was dangerous, if only because college was the great leveler. Everyone in college lives like a college student. Nobody necessarily knows who's on financial aid and who's not and how much. Nobody would ever ask such things. The stratifications are hidden so well as to be forgotten. Marriage and childbearing and the ceremonies attendant upon them also commemorated the reemergence of those stratifications for those who'd ignored or discounted them.

Sometimes all Jen wanted was a record of accounts. A ledger. A schedule of incomings and outgoings. Receipts. She wanted to know what her and Jim's combined salary would be as expressed as a percentage of Meg and Marc's total income (salary + bonus if applicable + income from inter vivos trust + return on investments + incidental monetizable gifts from family). She wanted to know the difference between the gross and the net. She wanted to know how many months (years?) she and Jim would have to work to earn the money that Meg and Marc spent in a month. She wanted to attach a number to what Meg would define as a "splurge," and then calculate her own definition of a "splurge" as a percentage of a Meg splurge, and then calculate the respective impacts of their splurges on their respective monthly outgoings. She wanted to know how much Meg's wedding and apartment and apartment renovation had cost and how much Pam's wedding and apartment and apartment renovation would cost, every last line item, and the source of funds for each line item, and if the source was interest or a dividend, she wanted to know the source of that interest or dividend.

She wanted to know, once and for all, how the math broke down on what Baz Angler would call *real life*.

Meg, Pam, and Jen used to know everything about Meg, Pam, and Jen. The three of them used to know each day the other bled. They used to know—it was possible they still remembered—the exact anatomical proportions and halitosis risk factors of each of the other's pantheon of sexual partners. Two of them had once assisted in the removal of the third's sanitary product, temporarily misplaced inside her body cavity during finals week. And yet the statement of accounts was full of clean pages, bright and blank as the faces awaiting entry to the Garden of Earthly Delights. The statement of accounts was in a ledger kept in an unlocked drawer in the secret-seeming room. If you were already in the room, you had no cause to ask to see it.

Jen hadn't looked at her phone in hours.

Karina—LIFt
Tuesday, Jan 5 2:35 PM

To: Jen—LIFt
Subject: WHERE ARE YOU?
Priority: High!

And where is Daisy?!? You've both been gone forEVER—we have an emergency here!

Knight on a White Steed

Karina generally took a minimalist approach to her toilette, but today telltale streaks of foundation and concealer swiped around her eyes and mascara mottled under her pinkish lower lashes. The tip of Karina's nose burned bright red, as if the inflammation had singed the concealer. She smiled at Jen with her teeth bared, unusually. Jen's mind automatically mapped a large-scale portrait of Karina, ready to be added to the walls of *Break in Case of Emergency*.

"My allergies are kicking in ridiculously early this year," Karina said, sniffling. "The nerve, huh?" She touched the back of one finger to her nose.

"Oh, man, that's tough," Jen said. "I'm so sorry I was gone so long; I had back-to-back meetings, and then—"

"It's just one order of business," Karina interrupted, "but it *is* quite urgent—we *are* going to have to take that Travis Paddock introduction down."

"Pardon?"

Karina cocked her head to one side and shrugged. "Yeah, afraid so."

"I don't understand."

Karina made the face Jen had seen before: bottom lip pulling away from clenched teeth, bugged-out sidelong glance appealing to a sympathetic invisible authority. "What can I say?" Karina asked. "One of those things."

"Hmm, well, we've already shared it with all of LIFt's followers on social media, all the BodMod, um, affiliates have already been linking to the introduction and quoting from it—"

"It's a—a pyramid scheme." Karina flinched at the phrase, as if she were trying to fling her mouth off her face. Her eyes shone. "BodMod Nutritionals is a pyramid scheme. Mr. Paddock is"—Karina rubbed her nose again—"not the knight on a white steed that you and I thought he was."

You and I

"But—"

"Live and learn, right? Let's not be afraid to admit our mistakes, and learn from them."

Our mistakes

"Of course, but we can't just take it down," Jen said.

Karina's face tightened; the faint swelling around her eyes and nose made it more difficult for her to keep a poker face. "Look, nobody's more pained by this than I am," Karina said. "I mean, I hate to see all our work—"

Our work

"—go down the drain. But it's for the best. Let's not give this guy's sleazy little scheme any more oxygen, and we can just move on."

"Travis is still on the board, right?"

Though sitting still at her desk, Karina seemed breathless.

"We are taking it down," Karina said evenly.

"But he's still a board member—right?—and anyway, that's not how the Internet works." Jen's mouth set itself in a hooting formation, as if she could suck the words back from the air.

Karina's nose was now red from bridge to tip. "Oh, is that so?" she said. "How *does* the Internet work? Educate this old-timer."

"I don't mean to be condescending, but it lives in cache forever. The train has left the station."

"Be that as it may," Karina said, "let's get the train back into the station. Thanks." Karina turned back to her computer.

"We *can't*," Jen said.

"Leora made this request herself," Karina said, too quickly. "She asked that we take it down." Karina's eyes darted around before regaining steady, angry eye contact with Jen.

Her eyes flashed

"And last I checked," Karina said, "this is Leora's foundation, not mine, not yours." Karina turned back to her computer again and began composing an email, or pretended to. "That's all, thanks." She drawled the *thanks* ironically as she typed.

Jen walked back to her cubicle, where Daisy was unsnapping her puffer coat.

whatDaisyknew: I GOT BORED SO I WENT TO SEE AVATAR HOPE THAT'S
OK
jenski1848: Good work today, D.

Jen logged out of her computer and logged back in under the generic logon that LIFt interns used. She opened Karina's Travis Paddock summary in a browser, took screenshots, and exported the entire file as a PDF, then attached the file as a draft in a disused Hotmail account that she had opened under Franny's name years ago. She wiped the browser history, cleared the cache, and logged back in as herself.

whatDaisyknew: WHAT DID I MISS
jenski1848: I just took down the Travis Paddock advertisement per
Karina and Leora's request. It never happened.

Daisy Kilroyed over the cubicle wall, watching as Jen pulled on her coat.

"They know that's not how the Internet works, right?" Daisy asked Jen's desk surface.

Jen silently buttoned her coat.

"And that you can't treat a board member like that?" Daisy asked.

Jen swung her tote bag over her shoulder.

"Did Karina get dumped?" Daisy asked. "She looks like somebody who just got dumped."

Out of the corner of her eye, Jen could make out Jules the social-media intern's head rotating 90 degrees right, one ear trained on Daisy like a motion-sensor camera.

"She has the puffy eyes and shell-shocked comportment of a textbook dumpee," Daisy said.

"I'll be back in an hour or so," Jen said.

"The smell of the dump site still clings to her, though she may have crawled from its wreckage hours ago," Daisy said. "Evidence remains. A candy wrapper stuck to her shoe. A foam packing peanut clinging tenderly to her hair."

"I have an appointment with Judy Smith," Jen added, invoking the code Daisy and Jen used whenever they had to leave the office and didn't wish to explain why they were leaving.

Jen returned to the library, heading straight for the nearest open cubby in the computer cluster. She forwarded the PDF to a newly made account, which she opened under a user name borrowed from the top item on the library's nearby "New and Hot Titles!" kiosk. She attached the PDF to a new message and began to type.

FROM: DanBrownsTheLostSymbol@yahoo.com
TO: info@dopenhauer; tips@nastygramladyparts

How does a certain much-publicized foundation and its infinity streams of family money "work tirelessly to empower women, here at home and in the developing world," according to its mission statement? Well, one way to do that is to spend thousands of dollars on advertorials for some rich white American guy's snake-oil pyramid scheme. Screenshots attached. Enjoy!

She hit send. She logged out of the two accounts, cleared the browser, emptied the cache, and switched off the computer.

She folded her hands on the desk. She was comfortably seated in a still pocket of time, no turbulence, 70 degrees Fahrenheit, pH balance of seven. She had no idea when this pocket of time would expire.

As Jen reached the bottom of the steps to the library, the corkscrew of dizziness spun her around again, and she vomited into a conveniently positioned trash basket. She did so almost casually, as if she were tossing an empty soda can. She fished a camouflaging stick of gum out of her tote bag as sparks of light trailed around the cold stone embankments of her peripheral vision.

Like a Newborn

Karina slouched against the empty filing cabinets, one thumb hooked jauntily in a belt loop. "You guys are stretched pretty thin today, huh?" she asked Jen and Daisy's backs. "A lot of meetings, I hear?" The arc of her voice placed the word *meetings* between quotation marks.

Jen turned around to face Karina. Daisy did not. "Yes, always busy after a holiday break," Jen said.

"See, the problem is, if both of you are out and about, who is minding the shop?" Karina asked. "This is such a critical time in the growth and development of LIFt. Think of it, if you need to, like a newborn—helpless and hungry and a little messy, even—no fault of her own—and in need of constant attention."

"Yes, absolutely," Jen said. "I think we're still getting back into the post-holiday groove and catching up with lots of stuff that got postponed until after the New Year. Right, Daisy?" she asked, raising her voice slightly to ensure that Daisy could hear through her headphones.

Daisy took off her headphones but did not turn around. "I went to see *Avatar*," she said to her monitor.

Karina shrugged merrily. "Can't argue with a woman's priorities!" she said.

"We'll be more vigilant in the future," Jen said.

"All right, ladies, let's get right back on track tomorrow, okay?" She punched the air in a spirit of convivial competition, a gesture somewhere between a clubby chuck on the shoulder and a right jab.

"And by the way, *fabulous* bouquet, Daisy," Karina added over her shoulder as she walked away. "You girls happen to know if Daisy has a secret suitor out there somewhere?" Karina asked the cubicle maze of indeterminately occupied assistants and interns as she passed by, not pausing for an answer.

"Oh, yeah, these came for you while you were out," Daisy said to Jen, passing an enormous crystal vase of flowers over the cubicle wall: hellebores, vanda orchids, hydrangeas, baby roses. The note affixed to the vase was from Dakota, conveying Mrs. Flossie Durbin's praise and thanks for her finished portrait.

Mrs. Durbin wanted you to know that her portrait will hang in her newly redecorated and restored study—a place of meditation and reflection, where it will remind her always to aspire to be a better version of herself. P.S. Don't forget to look for Mrs. Durbin's latest blog post—should be up by the time you receive this!

"Have you looked for Mrs. Durbin's latest blog post?" Daisy asked over the wall.

"Read it to me," Jen said, caressing her index finger over one of the hydrangeas.

"The coolly expert technical proficiency is warmed by a sunny presentation, an antidote to trying times," Daisy recited. "The portraits risk being unfashionable, which is exactly what makes them à la mode. Recommend."

Jen dipped her face into the bouquet, nuzzling it with closed eyes. "Daisy," she said into the petals, "I never really got here, but I am leaving now."

What Is Charity?

Nastygram Ladyparts had their editorial up the next morning.

Terrible Rich-Person Scheme Remains Terrible

Human alimony-collection agency <u>Leeza Infanzia</u> has lately been looking for fresh new orifices that can stash her <u>Mobro 4000</u> barges full of cash. She seems to have found her ideal landfill in the form of the <u>Leora Infinitas Foundation</u>, a hallucinatory potluck where the fusion menu of philanthropic contributions has ranged from <u>Nigerian educational grants for Cameroonian supermodels</u> to domain space for the <u>half-transcribed Klonopin fantasias</u> of miscellaneous second-string Brides of Finance. Lately, it seems, Leeza has been stacking surplus bills in the shape of a pyramid scheme: One of her minions posted—and just as quickly deleted—a breathless advertorial for a board member's company, something called BodMod Nutritionals™ (screenshots below), which we assume is the kind of ashes-and-gelatin "miracle weight-loss supplement" you might spot amid the cocaine and syringes at the margins of a Soloflex shoot. Nice that the report's writer (who is also Leeza's <u>"executive director"</u>) took a fancy Caribbean holiday to provide gripping on-the-scene reportage on BodMod, when all she really had to do was stay up for the 4:10 a.m. infomercial slot between the ad for the <u>wearable towel</u> and the ad for the <u>spray-on toupee</u> . . .

Ruby Stevens-Meisel's response appeared in *DOPENHAUER* a day later.

What is charity? In simplest terms, it is the act of helping those in need. It is not necessarily unreasonable to imagine that an inspiring portrait of good health and a globe-trotting entrepreneurial lifestyle might be an act of helping others to imagine themselves beyond themselves. We could call it a gift of possibility, a gift of motivation. Or we might imagine the odds that the adventurers themselves were in need of charity—perhaps the formidable Travis Paddock, the Healthy Huntsman, had somehow become the hunted, financially or emotionally or spiritually? Perhaps his enthralled observer was herself in thrall to some unseen crisis of health or judgment or vocation? Or a crisis of love, of devotion? This is pure speculation, of course—and if charity begins at home, so privacy needs to be preserved there as well. And perhaps the one who needs our charity the most right now is Leora Infinitas herself: Our gift to her can be the benefit of the doubt.

For Jen, the act of hitting send on the incriminating message should have broken the trance of reckless spiteful petty impulse—the trance of self-pity—that had created the message in the first place. And yet in the days and weeks that followed, Jen had remained safely inside the still pocket of time that had formed around her the instant that DanBrownsTheLostSymbol had logged off his local library computer terminal.

Part of the sustained calm may have been attributed to the neurochemical effects of the recent withdrawal of Sermoxal and equally sudden reintroduction of Animexa, the combination of which manufactured a soundproofing foam around Jen's central-nervous-system neurotransmitters and added a metallic sheen to her self-presentation as subtly but surely as it dilated her pupils.

Part of the sustained calm may have been attributed to the radio silence of the media at large—no other sites or publications picked up on the substance of *Nastygram Ladyparts*'s umbrage or *DOPENHAUER*'s muted disappointment—and of the LIFt executive braintrust, who remained hunkered down in the semi-isolated southern corridor in Leora's increasingly normalized absence. Jen and Daisy went nearly a week without sustaining a silent Karina ambush, nearly a week without serving as the audience for one of Sunny's impromptu rounds of jollity, which were always edged with Sunny's indignation at a perceived lack of jolly reciprocation—although Jen did recognize, even in her post-Sermoxal and High Animexa period of stainless-steel serenity, that the radio silence in itself could be cause for alarm.

And part of the sustained calm was induced by mere distraction: Following the publication of Mrs. Durbin's "Recommend," Jen's inbox had absorbed a steadily rising tide of requests for commissions via her website.

Re: Contact Jen!

Can you paint my baby in a kind of late-Renoir style? He's kind of rosy and lumpy like a late Renoir, like a living, drooling, pooping rejection of Impressionism (jpg attached).

Re: Contact Jen!

My boyfriend and I are pre-engaged and we're trying to take a "whimsical," "irreverent" approach to this whole wedding-industrial-complex thing. So we were thinking: Instead of doing the usual boring engagement-photo session, wouldn't it be awesome to have our portraits painted instead? We liked how you paint people to look PSYCHO because PSYCHO is how we feel when we think about all the wedding planning and mother-in-law managing we'll have to do over the next 14 months LOL!

Re: Contact Jen!

Do you do pet portraits? I would like you to paint my greyhound, Camelot. He is a happy soul, but he lacks the artistry to externalize it. However, I do not wish to anthropomorphize him.

"Jen?"

Jen looked up from a photograph of Camelot lounging in the Hall of Mirrors at Versailles to see Jules the social-media intern standing in front of her.

"I'm sorry to bother you, but we were all just wondering—is there anything we can do? To help out?"

Jules was wearing a baby-pink woolen dickey over a herringbone sixties-style woolen minidress. Pinned to her dickey was a gigantic brooch made of multicolored semiprecious stones in the shape of a peacock.

"Help?" Jen asked.

"We just got the impression that morale is kind of low around here, and nobody's really talking about how they're feeling," Jules said.

Jen kept staring at the peacock. The peacock's tail feathers contained yet concealed the image of a ballerina, slender arms raised over her head, each delicate hand cupping one of the peacock's eye-spots.

"And you know, maybe there's something we all can do," Jules said. "Or we can all just make a time to talk to one another, clear the air."

"I'm sorry, Jules," Jen said, clearing her throat primly, "but I'm not sure what we're talking about."

"The gossip online about—this—us," Jules said. "The rumors. Just the *vibe*."

"There's going to be a party," Daisy said over the cubicle wall. "A morale-boosting party. Or a benefit or something. At Leora's apartment. Sunny was talking about having a gift suite, but they ramped it back to party favors."

Jen smiled at Jules. "Hey, a party!" Jen said.

"Do you guys want to see?" Daisy asked. Without waiting for an answer, she rose and walked toward Leora's ad-hoc dressing room–slash–Petra's breast-milk-pumping room, Jen and Jules following uncertainly after her.

Daisy opened the door just as Petra was hastily exiting, her head ducked in bashful exasperation, clutching to her chest the anonymous black handbag with miscellaneous tubes and clamps popping out of its unzipped top. Behind the door stood Leora, Donna, Karina, and Sunny around a conference table covered in a bewilderingly colorful array of handicrafts, accessories, and artfully packaged baked goods. One chair was stacked with pinhole cameras constructed from recycled sari cloth and vintage fashion magazines. Another chair almost spilled over with handwoven wallets, purses, and a single lopsided tote from a Guatemalan weavers' collective that had recently received a LIFt grant.

Leora and Donna barely looked up at the intruders as Karina dug one hand around a clattering box full of hand-blown glass statement rings. Sunny strode toward the newcomers, fists pumping at her sides with aerobic enthusiasm, wearing an electrocuted smile.

"Thank *God* you guys are here," Sunny exclaimed. "I have *no idea* how we're going to narrow all this down to four or five party favors, so you *have* to help us."

"So, we're throwing a party!" Jen said inanely. "That's really cool!"

"Hells yeah!" Sunny said, waggling a beaded-and-feathered keychain to the side of her face as if it were an earring. "Because why should all the great parties happen during the holiday season? When people *really* need a pick-me-up in the dead of freakin'-frackin' *winter*—am I right or am I right? I know it's what *I* need—what a *week* we've had."

"Come closer, ladies, please," Leora said, staring at a potted white orchid. "We were just talking about how we *launched* the site, but we never *celebrated* it."

"Which creates a paradox," Donna said. "If we don't celebrate our launch, have we truly launched?"

"And we need some counterprogramming to combat all that trash on the Internet," Sunny said.

Donna made a moist disgusted sound with which her bangles agreed. "Don't even oxygenate it, Sunny," she said. "Let it wither and die of inattention. Make choices about the kinds of influences you let into your life."

"So true," Sunny said.

"It's just static," Karina said. "All you have to do is change the channel."

"Which is *precisely* what Jules and her team are out there doing every day," Leora said, still staring at the orchid.

"It's like a secret cave of treasures in here," Jules said.

"Is that orchid—a *cake*?" Leora asked, stepping closer to the pot and brushing the Guatemalan tote bag with her hip.

"These *are* treasures, Jen," Donna said to Jules, fingering a color-block cashmere scarf, "but it's all about *message*. By choosing these gifts for our invitees, what message are we sending about LIFt's mission, about our grantees?"

"I'm Jules," Jules said.

"I'm going into insulin shock just looking at this orchid," Leora said.

"The things that we find beautiful reflect our values," said Karina, fluffing her hair over the scarf she'd arranged in an intricate knot. "They aren't just a, you know, *material* thing."

The tote bag shrugged, slumped, and, in three slow, deathly flops, drifted and fell off the chair onto the carpet.

"We can't deny the material, the corporeal," Donna said, sniffing the cashmere. "But we can make it speak to our spirit."

Leora looked down at the crumpled tote bag, its nubby woven handle splayed over one toe of her heels.

"People should look into their gift bag at the end of a beautiful night and not only be delighted but also know—feel—*exactly* what LIFt stands for," Karina said.

Leora daintily extracted her foot from under the tote bag's handle, her mouth twisted in confusion.

"No one can take our message away from us, our mission," Donna said. "Certainly not some nameless online nobody."

"Stop oxygenating, will ya!" Sunny said.

Leora, still staring at the tote bag, limply kicked at it, once. Soundlessly, Sunny materialized at her side, plucked the tote bag off the floor, and sequestered the tote bag on its own chair across the room, as if the tote bag were to be quarantined for an unnamed contagion.

Envy

"I can't figure out if we're going for a bonsai or a synecdoche," Pam was saying over the ambient blare of the cement mixer parked across the street from her studio. As Jen arrived, Pam had just marked off three-eighths of the studio's square footage with electrical tape and stood at one corner with hands on hips, trying to visualize how to cram in some representative cross-section of the original *Break in Case of Emergency*. From the floor, Nick Cave seethed tinnily from mason jar–sized speakers attached to a Sony Discman that Pam had rescued off a Greenpoint stoop the previous day, *Murder Ballads* still inside.

Her backpack still slung over one arm and a plastic dry-cleaning bag folded over the other, Jen chewed one thumbnail. "What if it almost became like a living sound installation?" she asked. "The Wellness Solutions operators would be milling around, talking into their headsets, but then you'd also have the parody commercials, the sounds of breaking glass—"

"The sound of Jim popping bubble wrap," Pam interjected, her eyes still on the empty space. She wore a tight little smile.

"Oh, yeah, he loved that part," Jen said.

"You know," Pam said, "people asked me if Jim was part of the installation. Did I ever tell you that?"

Pam's tone was needling, but Jen couldn't discern where the sharp points were aiming. The cement mixer revved and groaned.

"No, you didn't," Jen said, following Pam's eyes down to a scuffed floorboard. "He'll be happy to hear it."

"I wish everyone had been as into it as Jim was," Pam said.

"Yeah," Jen said.

"Too bad Mrs. Flossie Durbin wasn't so into it," Pam said.

Jen exhaled and sank down to the floor, hugging her knees with her forearms, backpack and dry cleaning bunched in her lap. "Okay, since you brought it up—"

Pam drew herself up to her full height and squinted with renewed intensity at the empty space. "Since I brought what up?"

"I didn't know," Jen said, "if it would be weirder to bring it up or weirder to not bring it up, so let's just do it: I'm sorry that Mrs. Durbin came to see your work and—and whatever—got distracted by mine."

Pam brayed, a short, sharp expulsion of laughter. "Oh, *come the fuck on*, Jen," she said.

"I'm sorry if it made things awkward—I don't—I don't know how to do this or what to say," Jen said. She felt abject down on the floor, but getting up would only reinforce what a bad decision it had been to assume a supplicant's pose. "I'm sorry."

"Stop saying sorry," Pam said.

"I'm glad it happened, of course," Jen said, "only I wish it had happened differently."

"Meaning what?" Pam asked.

Jen tried to smooth the plastic sheet across her legs. "You are making this harder than it needs to be," she said.

"And you are making this a thing when it's not a thing," Pam said.

Things aren't things unless they happen to Pam, Jen thought, and shook her head to shake the thought away.

"I'm sss—I shouldn't have brought it up," Jen said, although Pam had brought it up.

"What do you want me to say, though?" Pam asked. "Do you want me to say that I'm envious?"

Jen closed her eyes. "You have no cause to be envious of me," Jen said. "No cause."

Jen rested inside her head for a moment. When she opened her eyes, Pam had sunk to the floor, too, arms wrapped around her knees. They stared together at the same floorboard.

The blare of the cement mixer halted, and the dirge of Nick Cave's baritone rose all alone through the empty air.

And with a little pen-knife held in her hand
She plugged him through and through

Jen and Pam laughed, exactly at the same time. Each dropped her head back, chin in the air, open smile as if to catch raindrops on her tongue. It was a gesture that Pam had picked up from Jen, or maybe that Jen had picked up from Pam, or maybe both of them had picked it up from Meg, but it belonged to all of them now.

"Is that what I think it is?" Pam asked, her finger making tiny circles in the air in the direction of Jen's lap.

Jen stood up and held the dry-cleaning bag aloft by the hanger. "We should put this somewhere safe."

Pam stood up, stepped out of her leggings, and yanked off her tunic. She walked toward Jen in only her underwear. She was still so thin, Jen thought. The curves of either side of her waist had flattened out. Her breasts were lower and heavier, her round belly hard and taut. Pam ripped open the plastic bag in Jen's arms and pulled The Dress over her head.

"I am a bride in white," Pam murmured, looking down at herself. "So it has come to this."

"You are going to be a wife and a mother," Jen said.

Silently, Pam fingered the fabric pulling at her hip as Jen smoothed one of the straps against her shoulder. Nick Cave was leering at Pam from the floor.

There she stands, this lovely creature

"This is so fucking corny—let's turn this off," Pam said matter-of-factly, her head still bowed.

"Don't worry," Jen said, as she leaned over to inspect a loose thread on the hemline. "He's not singing about you." Jen stepped back to look at Pam in The Dress from head to toe, and she smiled. "The lovely creature doesn't make it to the end of the song. But we will. Just wait."

Paid in Exposure

"I think it will be great for Pam in terms of exposure," said Jen. "But I think *Break in Case of Emergency* in its original form is the stronger statement."

On the night of the LIFt party, the train was all messed up again. On the long, blustery-cold walk to the closest working station in her highest heels and translucent hose, Jen tried to talk enough to drown out her own discomfort.

"Twice as strong," Jim replied, "because it had twice as many of your paintings."

Jen rubbed Jim's arm rapidly, as if to file down the edge in his voice. "Pam will be there tonight, by the way," she said brightly.

"Even though doing an interview with your boss destroyed her reputation?" Jim asked.

"No, it turns out that Paulo's mom knows Leora somehow, overlapping social circles—anyway, Pam could not have been nicer about Mrs. Durbin's, um, endorsement of me," Jen said.

"You were in some suspense about that?"

"Well, it was Pam's show, but I—I ended up with some of the attention. That could have been awkward for both of us."

Jim *pffted*.

"She was really sweet about it, seriously. And sweet doesn't come easily to Pam. It was funny—Taige Hammerback told Pam that a Flossie Durbin endorsement is actually a kiss of death, and Pam told him no, it's the jaws of life, and then Taige said—"

"Pam will have to get in line and become a paying customer now," Jim interrupted. "You're going to get so many commissions. By the way, how much did you get for the Flossie Durbin painting? I want to get Franny a new Cat Scratch Mountain and I'm hoping Mrs. Durbin can foot the bill."

Jen was quiet.

"This is suspenseful," Jim said. "It's a number so large that we need a new language to express it."

"I didn't—there wasn't—nothing," Jen stammered.

Jim was quiet.

"Nothing will come of nothing, child, speak again," he said evenly.

"I never negotiated a fee with Mrs. Durbin," Jen said, almost defiantly.

Jim was quiet.

"I *meant* to," Jen plowed on, her defiance receding as abruptly as it had broken in, as if she were speaking over Jim's protests. "But it just never came up, and she never asked, and it seemed so awkward to broach it, and—"

Jen swallowed some air, and Jim still said nothing.

"And you know, I'll get paid in exposure, you know? Like you said, I'm already getting so many commissions, word of mouth—"

"You are unbelievable," Jim said into his collar, as Jen pulled her arm away from his. "The way you let people take advantage of you."

"That's not fair—"

"Why was it *her* show?" Jim asked.

"What do you mean?"

"Why was it billed just as Pam's show?"

"Honey, I can't even keep track of what we're talking about from moment to moment—"

"Seriously, listen to me. You did a bunch of fucking giant paintings for her show. At least one of which Taige Hammerback is probably masturbating on right now. You worked forever on those fucking things, and they were awesome, and they were the only evidence of *any technical aptitude whatsoever* in her entire fucking show, and your name was in tiny fine print in the program."

"It wasn't *tiny* and I don't *care,* honestly."

"And now it's going to happen again. Are you even mentioned in the new show? *Do you exist?*"

"I don't care."

"It's stupid that you don't care."

Jim's voice was spiking in volume as they neared the block of the

Deli of Death. Hundreds of feet away, Jen could already hear the dogs barking halfheartedly.

"Don't call me stupid," Jen said.

"I did not call you stupid. I do not think you are stupid. I *do* think it's stupid not to care that a rich woman steals your work."

"Pam did not steal my work," Jen murmured. Then she realized that Jim was referring to Mrs. Durbin. She hadn't told Jim about Paulo's family yet. Pam's family, now.

"And I *do* think it's stupid not to care that Pam took credit for your shit."

"She did not! It was work-for-hire, or—"

"It was hundreds of hours of work *not* for hire. She didn't pay you a fucking penny. And need I remind you, you were unemployed at the time."

"Right! It's not like I had anything else going on. Jesus! She's my friend."

"And need I remind you that at the time you were—you were—"

"Don't, don't—"

"Surrounded by paint fumes, inhaling that stuff, for all you know that could have caused you to—"

"*Stop it,*" Jen said, halting in her tracks and clapping her hands over her temples. "Stop it, please, stop it. I can't talk about this. I can't."

"She could have *helped* you." Jim was pacing in a semicircle in front of Jen. His eyes were round and dark. "Your *friend.* And you ask her for one fucking favor and she puts you in friend jail and you're supposed to be so grateful that you've been pardoned for your crimes. After all you did for her *for free.*"

Jen lowered her hands and began walking again, faster. "So this is all about money," she said, as Jim fell into step next to her.

"No!" Jim said. "You've totally missed the fucking point as usual! This isn't about money. This is about you having some self-respect and not letting people walk all over you, whether it's your friends or people at work or Flossie fucking Durbin."

"So if I had taken money from my friends that would mean I have self-respect," Jen said. Walking faster, faster. "It's all so simple!"

"No," Jim said, "what would mean having real self-respect was if you stopped laying yourself at people's feet all the time, trying to earn their approval. It's like, if you could write somebody a check to like you, you would."

Jen stopped again, a dead stop, arms hanging limp at her sides, mouth agape. Jim walked a few more steps and then stopped, too, covering his face with his hands. Now the dogs had spotted them approaching, whereupon they began barking with renewed vigor, purpose, and focus.

"I'm sorry," Jim said into his palms, then turned to look at Jen, one hand reaching for her. "I'm sorry, I didn't mean—"

"Don't touch me," Jen said. His face back in his palms.

Jen watched him and waited.

She saw herself at the edge of a diving board hanging over an empty pool. She could feel the tingle in her toes, the last effervescent vertiginous moment before her feet pushed off, the board rippling.

"It's all about money," Jen said. "We can pretend like it's not, but it is. Always. And it always will be."

Jim said nothing.

"Maybe if I had real self-respect," Jen said slowly, champagne burbling inside her stomach, "I wouldn't have married a man who doesn't earn a decent living."

Jim put his hands behind his head and stared at the pavement.

"Maybe if I had real self-respect," Jen said, "I wouldn't have married a man who makes nothing nine months a year and then sits on his ass all summer."

Jim smiled grimly at the pavement.

The vertiginous feeling was gone. All Jen could see was the concrete bottom hurtling toward her. The champagne bubbles distended and popped.

"Maybe if I had real self-respect," Jen said, her voice choking, "I would have been more pragmatic. I wouldn't have married someone just because I loved him."

Jim's head laughed mirthlessly, loud and yawping. "Nice try," he said. "I'm going home." He turned and loped back in the direction of their apartment, the dogs now behind him.

Jen walked quickly after him, struggling to keep up, her heels almost slipping out from beneath her footfalls. "No, no, you can't—you have to come with me."

"Fuck you, Jennifer," he said, one middle finger raised in salute over his shoulder, his strides growing longer and quicker.

Jen stopped and watched him for half a block. She turned and looked at the snarling dogs, and at two tall men who had emerged from Brancato's to watch the show, and turned back again to Jim's retreating figure. What happened next happened without her permission.

"You can't just leave me here!" she screamed. Her voice shattered. An animal sound, primal and desperate, naked. *"You can't just leave me here!"*

She watched as Jim turned 180 degrees and speed-walked toward her. Rage contorted his face. He stalked past her toward the train station. She tried to keep up, her heels scratching and scrabbling after him; the side of her right foot touched the ground just as her left foot caught her fall with a hard momentary plant. Jim and then Jen passed the men and the dogs, who were baying and snarling, leashes taut, choking on their own aggression. Hurrying along behind her husband, toes scuffing and heels listing, Jen didn't feel frightened of the dogs anymore. The dogs were choosing sides in a playground battle. If not for their leashes, they still wouldn't have attacked. They would have formed a circle around the couple, rooting on the combatant of their choice.

Cheese Break

Leora's penthouse loft was miserably packed, the trebley din of hundreds of overlapping conversations pinging and echoing off the parquet floors and the Wedgwood-dome false ceiling to create gnarled gibberish waves of disorienting sound that roared around Jen and Jim as soon as they stepped off the private elevator, as if Leora's guests had been marshaled to replicate the debilitating effects of a long-range acoustic device.

"I've been here thirty seconds and I've already contracted an inner-ear infection from these people," Jim shouted. These were the first words he'd spoken to Jen since the Deli of Death. He still hadn't made eye contact with her. On the train ride over, he'd hustled to the opposite end of the carriage with his headphones jacked up all the way. On the walk from the train stop, he'd kept ahead of her.

It took them more than ten minutes to squeeze and nudge a path toward the drinks table. The only person Jen recognized on the slow, sweaty twenty-foot surge was Karina, who, upon seeing Jen, set her features in their familiar preemptive mode—eyes bugged out and side-long, bottom lip pulling away from clenched teeth—and held out the palm of one hand as an additional deterrent, her arm window-wiping back and forth in a deflective parody of *hello*.

"Oh, hey, Karina, this is my husb—okay, hope to see you later," Jen shouted as Karina turned away.

Toppling glass finally in hand, Jen intended to sidle back into the crowd to track down any friendly faces, but Jim had already retreated to a window at one corner of the loft, a glass of red in one hand and a glass of white in the other. Beside the window, in a heavy and intricately carved mahogany frame—plaster filigree and gold-leaf burnishing—hung a giant oil painting of Leora flanked by her daughters in a clothed reenactment of Raphael's *Three Graces*. The figure of the older daughter smirked at her apple beneath Leora's maternal beam, while the younger daughter ensorcelled her onlooker with round, dead doll eyes.

"You're just going to stand in a corner?" Jen yelled.

"You do whatever you want," Jim yelled, staring out the window and glugging from his glass of white. "I'm not going back in that."

"You're here!" Meg and Pam were by Jen's side, and Meg had some-how located a sound frequency at which she could pitch her voice and be heard without shouting. "Mrs. Durbin was here for exactly twelve and a half minutes and she asked after you, Jen," Meg said.

Pam's mouth moved, but Jen couldn't discern any of the words.

"I have some questions for Mrs. Durbin," Jim shouted, turning away from the window toward Meg.

"I'll have to continue communicating with Mrs. Durbin through the magic of the Internet," Jen shouted over Jim's shouting.

"There's a Bluff Foundation board member here who is literally ninety-four years old," Meg said, deftly switching subjects, "and it was so loud he started to cry, so we had to create a sort of satellite party in a back bedroom just for him."

Pam's mouth moved some more.

"I want to go to that party!" Jim shouted. Meg's detection of an audible but discreet pitch made Jim's shouting more embarrassing to Jen.

"Another issue is that both of his ex-wives are here tonight," Meg continued in the same miraculously low confidential tone, "so what we really need are a couple of satellite parties. I have to keep rotating between them to make sure that proper distances are kept and further tears are not shed."

"Oh, man," Jim yelled. "Sounds like you're really taking Tiger Canyon."

Meg sipped from her wine, impassive. "What?"

Jen rolled her eyes and sighed. "It's an inside joke," she said. "It's this thing about when things are difficult at work, or not going your way, you—never mind, it doesn't matter."

"What was it?" Meg asked. "Tiger Caravan?"

Pam's mouth moved some more.

"Forget it," Jim yelled, addressing Meg, his eyes on Jen. Two empty glasses stood on the windowsill behind him. "It's just a stupid joke. Stupid me and my stupid fucking jokes." He was hollering loudly enough that a few people turned to look at Jim as he shoved back into the crowd.

"I'm sorry," Jen said to Meg and Pam. "We are having a rough night."

"Do what you need to do," Meg said.

Jen pushed for ages toward points east, then north, then west through the crowd, finally locating Jim at a table of canapés and cheese. He was draining a third glass of wine—a fourth at the ready on the table beside him—and cramming cubes of cheddar into his mouth.

"Honey, that's enough."

"Enough what?" Jim was yelling louder than he needed to.

"You were rude to Meg and Pam."

"So what?" Jim asked, popping another cube of cheese into his mouth.

"So *stop*."

"Stop what?"

"Stop shoving the entire cheese plate into your mouth, for starters."

"We're at a rich people's party, Jen," Jim said, teething another cube of cheese and sliding it off its toothpick. "They'll have more cheese in the fridge. They have a special number they can call and *wham*, look at all that new cheese spilling out of the fridge."

"Can you just stop? Please."

"Did you see the coffee table made out of broken china?" Jim asked through a mouthful of cheese. "Wouldn't it be so empowering to women if we broke the broken-china table and found a fair-trade women's cooperative and gave them a microloan to build a new one? Maybe you could build one for Pam's next show? Or could that be an anchoring metaphor in one of those essays you publish? Something about destroying domesticity in order to reclaim it?"

"Honey—"

"Or something about broken cups and 'reading the tea leaves'? *From Breakdown to Breakthrough in the Time It Takes to Steep My Tea*?" Jim picked up his fourth glass of wine and chugged.

"Maybe we should go."

"*How Decoupage Helped Heal My Shattered Heart*?" Jim said. "*How Smashing China Gave Me the Courage to Smash My Marriage*?"

Sunny and her husband were a few feet away, staring at the shouting cheese-eater. Jen turned her back to them and pretended to deliberate over the cracker selection.

Jim stabbed another cube of cheese with the used toothpick and ate it. "You know, I'm doing these people a favor, eating all their stinkin' cheese. And do I get any credit for it? Nope. All I get is more cheese."

"I don't care," Jen hissed, a cracker crumbling in her hand. "I don't care if they have more cheese in the fridge. I don't care if the fridge is made of cheese. I don't care if you win an award for eating the most cheese at this party and your prize is a fridge made of cheese. I want you to stop yelling and stop eating all the fucking cheese."

"Why?" Jim asked, sliding three cubes of cheese into his mouth at once.

"Because *you are embarrassing yourself.*"

Jim ruminated. "You got your pronouns mixed up there," he said past the cheese in his teeth. "You meant *I* am embarrassing *you.*"

"Yes, that, too!"

Jim drained his fourth glass and set it upside down on the ravaged cheese plate. "I'm leaving." He maneuvered bluntly through the crowd toward the coat check. Meg and Pam were standing an arm's length away from Jen, studying the floor. Trickles of red wine wound and seeped around cheese ashes.

"I should go—go with him," Jen yelled apologetically to Meg and Pam.

Pam's mouth moved some more.

"Pam, I'm sorry, but I haven't heard a word you've said the whole time," Jen yelled, and Pam turned away.

"Okay," Meg said, pulling Jen into a hug. "Maybe you should go. Maybe not. Let's just take a moment together to think about it. But either way, do you want me to wrap up some cheese in a go-bag for you?"

Jen laughed into Meg's shoulder. They stood quietly in the din, Meg's fingers rubbing Jen's back as they watched the crowd, until Jen felt another hand grasping hers.

Pam was pulling Jen back to the cheese plate, where she had arranged the cheddar crumbs and cracker shards into letters that spelled out STAY WITH US.

Pam had coaxed the trickle of Jim's wine into a little underlining flourish on her message.

One of Jen's hands was held in Meg's and the other was held in Pam's.

"You know what, I will stay a bit longer," Jen yelled. "He needs to be alone. Meg, maybe I'll just go cry in a bedroom with your ancient charge until we fall asleep."

"You'll wake up as somebody's new wife," Meg said.

Submission

Ever since the commencement of the Project, Jen had mostly steered clear of drinking—even in small social doses, even just after a Monthly Adverse Development and at other times when she could be empirically certain that a bottle of beer after work or a glass of wine at a party could not possibly flood and scurry the nascent brain-cell choreography of a hypothetical tiny future boarder. Jen recognized the irony of this aversion, given how many Projects that alcohol must have rushed into production over the millennia. But the inflammatory effects of the Sermoxal—the bloating of face and midsection, the reddening of nose and cheeks, the attachment of an amplifier and rumbling-bass effects to her Monthly Adverse Developments—had led Jen to suspect that her body had been swarmed by volatile yeast metabolites, her flesh rising and folding into a ruddy, sluggish dough, distressing to the eye and bitter to the taste. Sermoxal was at least a kind of useful poison, Jen thought, while ethanol was a useless one. Her reproductive system—her body in its entirety—seemed already beleaguered and broken enough without the proximate demolition effects of alcohol as it took a power-sander to the stomach lining or the beveled teeth of a wrecking bar to the liver or a jackhammer to the bony labyrinth of the inner ear. Tonight it had smashed and crowbarred the barriers around the Thing That Happened, which Jen had disclosed to Meg and Pam as they'd sat together on the edge of the bed in Leora Infinitas's guest room: eggshells and sea greens, princess-and-the-pea stacks of linens, hotel-anonymous. Meg's ninety-four-year-old guest of honor slept beside them, emitting turtle-dove coos and snores. Jen's disclosure had come apropos of nothing but the liquefying effects of the wine, which had dissolved the border between Jen's public and private selves and poured out her inner life in a cascade of sloppy disinhibition. Fragments of this episode spotted her line of vision hours later; her body still felt warm from the four arms wrapped around her.

Soon, of course, Jen would feel embarrassed, and she would probably apologize to Meg and Pam. She knew that even now. For the moment, though, she enjoyed this period of reprieve from the symptoms of congenital shame. Her friends were supposed to know these things. And yet, Jen thought, if she were a better friend she wouldn't burden them. What, after all, were they supposed to do with such information?

As Jen tumbled out of the cab and into her building's lobby, as she slapped meatily at the elevator button a few times before noticing the OUT OF SERVICE sign, and as she galumphed up five flights of stairs, then down one flight, a matter-of-fact voice cutting in and out amid the jagged smear of her consciousness was asking Jen a familiar question.

Here is the swimmer.

Where is the shore?

"She drowned," Jen murmured wetly to her key as she stabbed it in the vicinity of the lock on the door to her apartment. "She *der-ow-ooooned*."

Inside the apartment, both the door to Jen and Jim's bedroom and the door to the nest for the hypothetical tiny future boarder were closed, and Jen wasn't sure which room Jim had chosen to fall asleep in. There were cinders in her mouth. Her legs were licorice. She bandied in her heels to the refrigerator, grabbed a pint of ice cream out of the freezer, and flopped down on the couch next to Franny, who leaped down and took up residence instead on the kitchen counter, five feet away, establishing that she would not take sides in any domestic conflict. Jen jumped at the sound of an admonishing voice. Her downstairs neighbor was scolding her for walking across the floor in heels, tapping her broomstick of judgment against her own ceiling. Without thinking, Jen yanked off her heels and threw one and then the other across the narrow room, where they left scuff marks on the lumpy-sealed fireplace and ejected a cry of infuriation from the downstairs neighbor, her broomstick-rapping now more insistent.

Jen had forgotten a bowl and spoon for her ice cream, but instead of risking the further wrath of her neighbor, she popped the lid on the container, licked off some butterscotch-and-chocolate-chunk swirls, and opened her laptop, clicking over to the Total Transformation Challenge submission page. She teethed and sucked more ice cream from the pint and sloppily wiped her mouth with the back of her hand. She considered the instructions for the seventh category and typed a response.

TTC CATEGORY 7: HEART

How can you challenge your heart to open itself to every possibility and spread its love and charity far and wide? How can you make your heart beat in perfect rhythm with that of your world, your friends, your partner, your children?

Your response here:

I challenge my heart to be a better, more understanding, less judgmental partner.

But can I vent for a second? It drives me crazy when Jim drops inside jokes in conversation with other people, and it drives both of us crazy that it drives me crazy. It's a stupid little thing that doesn't matter, but marriage has a way of magnifying those stupid little things—I know it's a cliché, but it's also like, if it's such a little thing, then it must be easy to fix—so why not just fix it? Whenever he drops the inside jokes without any sense of his audience, I feel this compulsion to explain what he's talking about, translate for him, not make the other person feel left out and awkward, even though the other person is by definition left out of a marriage and it just makes things more awkward to linger over it—oh, and also, just by the way, it makes Jim feel like shit, which seems relevant. Why do I fixate so much on stupid little things when he is (generally speaking in most respects not tonight but almost all the time) so great?

Anyway, this is how I would have explained the inside joke to Meg tonight. On our first date, we were in this wine bar, and it was too bright and too loud and too first-date-y, but then this song came on, "Burning Airlines," which is the first song on Taking Tiger Mountain (By Strategy), *the Brian Eno record. It was so random—the soundtrack to the date was, like, a Springsteen song and then the kind of lite bossa nova you'd hear in Starbucks and then boom ENO ART ROCK. And Jim and I started talking about that record title,* Taking Tiger Mountain (By Strategy), *how it's the best title of a record ever, and we didn't know at the time that Tiger Mountain is an actual place with an actual mythology, we thought maybe it was the name of Brian Eno's estate and it had tigers having pool parties in a moat and operating trebuchets and stuff, and we just started riffing about how tall Tiger Mountain might have been, and the weather conditions on Tiger Mountain, and the types of tigers populating Tiger Mountain, and different strategies for taking Tiger Mountain and winning the hearts and minds of native Tiger Mountainers—Mountaineers? Mountainites? Mountainians?—whom we'd assume would battle fiercely and to the death with any marauding infidels with plans for taking Tiger Mountain by strategy or otherwise. It was just the dumb, half-drunken bullshitting you do with someone when you're figuring out that you really, really like them and part of the reason you like them is that you like the same stuff.*

That following Monday, Jim mailed to me a beautiful replica of the illuminated manuscript of William Blake's "The Tyger," with this hilariously laconic note about "enjoying our time together," and I felt out of breath to be looking at this gift and thinking about what the gift meant and thinking about the thought that had been poured into the gift. So then I mailed to him a print of a lithograph by Paul Ranson, a French painter who died young, called "Tiger dans les jungles." And tigers and Tiger Mountain, however we were defining it, became the central metaphor or inside joke or whatever of our relationship.

That was our courtship—trading postcards of tigers through the mail, like we were exchanging handwritten love letters on parchment bundled in ribbon via furtive horseback messenger. I mean, that wasn't all of our courtship—we also had sex all the time, in fact, we had sex the night of our first date, and we had all three kinds of sex on our second date (or all four, depending on how you're counting)—which was a Saturday, so we also had breakfast the next day, eventually, around four p.m.—and by the third date we were skipping the date part and just having sex. I had it in my head that it wasn't going anywhere, that he was this wayward grad student with a shitty apartment and an impressive comic-book collection who couldn't possibly present a viable long-term "practical" option, and pretty soon the physical attraction would fade and I could go back to the real world and Meg could set me up with a banker-who-doesn't-act-like-a-banker and for now I could just enjoy this sex-and-tigers bubble before it burst. In fact, I remember our friend Lauren saying to me something like "Get out of the bubble, make sure to spend time outside the bubble"—like a warning, like she could see what was happening, like if I kept fucking this guy eventually the bubble would seal itself over with bodily fluids and force of habit. But I never did that thing that would happen sometimes with friends in college, where they'd become infatuated with someone and just fall off the grid for a while. I introduced Jim to Meg and Pam and Lauren right away. We did stuff together, even though sometimes we were late to whatever we were doing, because we were having sex. Everyone liked him a lot, except Lauren. Lauren thought Jim was "sketchy." I never see her anymore.

The tiger thing really stuck. We'd go to Prospect Park Zoo to look at the red pandas and be like "Look at all the tigers on the mountain!" Or he'd send me a text to ask me how a presentation went at work, and I'd text back TIGER MOUNTAIN I AM IN YOU, which would mean it went well. And then when I started working at LIFt, or, rather, when I realized that my job at LIFt was a total fucking farce, my job became Tiger Canyon, which was the exact opposite of the triumphant majesty of Tiger Mountain—Tiger Canyon was this arid, rocky depression with no tree shade or reliable sources of clean water, where wild animals stalked and disemboweled their prey. Jim would start getting texts from me when I was crying in the bathroom like MAULED BY TIGERS and TAKING TIGER CANYON (BY STRANGULATION).

Maybe all this sounds like precious gibberish, the language of twins. No one should ever attempt marital exegesis. It's like opening the door on a darkroom—better just to let this stuff slosh around in obscurity.

But maybe all the explaining and accommodating and apologizing I do—to my friends, to my colleagues, to this empty box—is a way of proving I'm real. I exist in three dimensions. I know that sounds weird. I can try to explain. So sometimes with Leora and Karina and people like that, I get the sense that their big problem is that they don't think of other *people as real—not every-one, but younger people, people outside their class or income bracket, people who don't "inspire" them somehow. And even the people who "inspire" them are abstractions—they exist as boxes to be ticked on their checklist of per-sonal growth. I have the opposite problem. My close friends, my real friends, become unknowable to me, paradoxically, because I know them well enough that their* lives *seem real and mine seems—not fake or imaginary, I don't mean it like that, but like a bluff, and that's the moment a fissure opens—and I actually don't think I've ever used the word* fissure *out loud, or* exegesis, *for that matter, which I guess means this email is a conversation I'm too embar-rassed to have out loud with anyone or anything more consequential than an empty box—but anyway, a fissure opens in the friendship because I start to feel sheepish and back away from this nice person who is just being nice and everything becomes awkward.*

I think that's why—stay with me here, this is connected—my heart drops into my stomach every time I find out that one of my friends has harvested from the Garden of Earthly Delights. It's never because I myself want to have a hypothetical tiny future boarder (although I do) or don't want to have a hypo-thetical tiny future boarder (although sometimes I think I shouldn't) or don't not want to have a hypothetical tiny future boarder (although that may be most accurate). It's because my friend has it together enough to have—to cre-ate and bake and provide for in all senses—a hypothetical tiny future boarder, and I do not. For whatever reason, I don't. It's like a metaphor, or a metonym, or symptomatic of a comprehensive incompetence: biological, psychological, financial, marital, "spiritual." It's gotten to the point that on the way to work in the mornings I look around at all the people crammed into the train car and think, How did all these people come to be? How did their parents time it out just right like that? How did they become alive? What do they know that I don't? Why won't anyone just tell me? *And I conclude that it's because whatever they're doing and however fucked-up their lives might be, at least they're not pretending. At least they're not faking that they're real people. That they're verified as authentic. Leora loves that word,* authentic. *Maybe if you raise the hem of their shirt you'll see a little gold seal stamped to the base of their spine, certifying their authenticity.*

It's weird because the realest thing I've ever done—and I can't believe I'm saying this, but I can trust you, empty box—is fall in love with Jim. It was undeniable and more or less instantaneous and I didn't have to do anything or figure anything out or strategize or hire experts to advise or intervene. It was not a choice. I did not choose him. I don't know if that is wonderful or terrible. Maybe a stronger person—a more pragmatic person, a person who doesn't bluff and fake her way through life, who thinks ahead and whose future is as formed as her present and who keeps a ledger of accounts—would have turned away from Jim, would have turned away from that love. She would have broken the love in two, because she was strong, not weak. Or her strength would have prevented the thing from forming that she'd have to break. She never would have wanted it so badly and continued to want it so badly endlessly forever and always with every

Jen stopped and sat back. Her lips were dry and her bladder was full and her head was full of ungulate children.

She pressed the delete key and watched the entry rewind on itself, first letter by letter, then word by word, then entire lines evaporating in one backward swipe. She made a mental note to ask LIFt's web developer to put character limits on TTC posts. She quit the browser, shut the laptop, and curled up on the couch without taking off her clothes, brushing her teeth, emptying her bladder, or switching off the lights. The dented tub of ice cream on the coffee table sagged and melted throughout what remained of the night. In the morning, the dried streak of ice cream had crusted over the back of Jen's hand. It looked like a blister, the remains of a burn that might not leave a scar.

Good News

Jen sat in her LIFt cubicle, spine straight, hands folded in front of her keyboard, eyes trained on her desk phone. She picked up the receiver, replaced it, and watched the phone some more. She broke off half an Animexa tablet and swallowed it dry, watching the phone. She picked up the receiver, dialed a number, replaced the receiver, and watched the phone some more. She walked to the vending machine, procured pretzels, ate the pretzels while watching the phone. She walked back to the vending machine, procured a diet soda, drank a diet soda while watching the phone.

Jen picked up the phone and dialed and chewed the edge of the mouthpiece as it rang.

"Hi, Dakota," Jen heard herself saying. "I'm sorry to bother you—I'm realizing that we never settled on my fee for Mrs. Durbin's portrait, and I was hoping we could discuss it now?"

Dakota said nothing.

"I admit I should have brought this up before, and I understand that the prestige of this project and the honor of being asked to do it are generous payment in themselves?"

Dakota said nothing.

"And I'm so very grateful to Mrs. Durbin for the opportunity?"

Dakota said nothing.

"And really with all that in mind I would be happy with any fee you thought was appropriate and again I do apologize for not raising this earlier?"

Dakota said nothing. Bertha Mason laughed, then slipped both hands around Jen's neck to silence her.

"I will discuss this with Mrs. Durbin," Dakota finally said. "In the meantime, could you send me your bank routing information?"

When Jen hung up the phone it immediately rang again.

"Hi, Jennifer. This is Shawna from Dr. Lee's office. We were expecting to see you during walk-in hours sometime last week. Just checking in to see that everything's all right?"

"Oh, yes," Jen stammered. "I've been meaning to—I mean—but everything's fine."

"We were hoping maybe—you'd had some good news on your own?" Shawna asked.

Daisy—it must have been Daisy—had pinned a photograph of a camel nuzzling a Komodo dragon to Jen's cubicle wall. Jen watched the camel and the dragon as a puddle of absurd despair spread inside her chest.

We were hoping

Jen wasn't even sure which one Shawna was. Nose-ring Shawna? Banana-clip Shawna? Shawna who had an expeditious rapport with the billing department? Or was that Sheila? Shana? It had never occurred to Jen that the generically pleasant people behind the henhouse desk had ever conceived of her in more than generically pleasant dimensions, certainly not to the extent that they could formulate expectations and desires on her behalf.

Good news

"Jennifer? Are you there?"

What is good news? Is a lack of good news equivalent to bad news? Is it good news if one doesn't actually spread the news? And what about last time? When good news turned into bad news? Wasn't the only way that bad news happened last time was because good news happened first? Doesn't good news—sometimes, maybe, last time yes—beget the worst news you could ever imagine?

Better no news
Say nothing
Thanks for nothing

"I'll keep you posted," Jen said.

Yes

Above Jen's bathroom ceiling, a hollering child repeatedly body-slammed himself to the tile, as he was scheduled to do every morning between six-fifteen and six-forty-five a.m., as Jen sat on the edge of the tub staring at the test, then at the small pile of broken tiles and unidentified black ooze collecting where the edge of the tub met the floor, then at the test again. It never seemed very scientific. It looked like something out of the play doctor's kits her brothers had as kids—alongside the plastic stethoscope and cartoonishly oversized bandages, maybe they'd find a popsicle stick attached to a pen cap, Magic Markered in blue with a positive or negative sign.

Jen walked down the hall from the bathroom to the room for the hypothetical tiny future boarder, opening the door for the first time since the night of the LIFt party. Jim was curled in a sleeping bag atop the naked futon, his curved back to the door. Jen molded her body to the shape of his and pressed her face into the back of his neck.

"I'm sorry," Jen said into Jim's hair.

"I'm sorry, too," Jim said into the sleeping bag.

"The answer is yes again," Jen said.

"I think I knew that," Jim said.

"I think the answer has been yes again for a while," Jen said, "and I ignored it."

"I think I knew that," Jim said.

"I shouldn't have," Jen said. "I've drunk alcohol. I've ingested hundreds of milligrams of central-nervous-system stimulants. I've been on a dangerous boat. The boat was very bouncy. I got a sunburn. I was obliquely threatened with an antique machete."

"It's okay," Jim said. "Early on, it's okay. You can do pretty much anything. It's a locked box."

"I want to forget," Jen said.

"Yolk sac," Jim said. "Hermetically sealed."

"I want to forget," Jen repeated. "Until we know for sure."

"Okay," Jim said.

"Until we know everything."

"Okay," Jim said. "We'll never know everything. But okay."

They exchanged more apologies and affirmations, and rose to brush their teeth, and returned to the room.

Let It All Hang Out

Re: Contact Jen!

Not to sound like a stalker and I know this isn't quite your aesthetic. But what if I gave you some photos of my ex and you did a Dorian Gray–style portrait of him? Rotting. Syphilitic. A corpse stuffed in a crawl space.

Only I want it for my walk-in closet, like a "skeleton in the closet." Like a dreamcatcher or a gargoyle, warding off harm and evil spirits. The scarier the better. Hope I'm not freaking you out!

Re: Contact Jen!

Hey Jennifer, it's Brian from *Politics + Psychology* magazine. We're doing a special issue that's a mash-up of history and contemporary psychology, where we'll try to answer the question "Who was the happiest President?" We thought you could revise iconic portraits of commanders-in-chief to happyfy them: G-Wash flashing those wooden chompers, Tommy Jeff saying "Cheese," Honest Abe cracking a grin for once in his life! If the idea appeals to you, I'd love to discuss further . . .

Re: Contact Jen!

3 questions 1) Do you do famous/fictitious people 2) Do you do site-specific work 3) Are you at ease in the spiritual dimension??!!? For my kitchen backsplash I would like a grid of painted "head shots" of hearth goddesses through the ages, Hestia the Greek, Frigg of Norse mythology, Julia Child, Martha Stewart, et al. I want the portraits to have a kind of dark pagan/Gothic feel. Do you know about the tradition of Slavic animism?

The words began to bob and weave on whitecaps of teary lethargy, and Jen, perched atop a closed toilet lid in a bathroom stall at LIFt, set her phone down on the tissue dispenser and rubbed her eyelids with her thumb and forefinger. During low-traffic intervals in the ladies' room, Jen could eke out a micro-nap in relative privacy and comfort, with elbows on knees and head in hands and immediate access to at least two viable receptacles for the contents of her stomach. Jen had been hunched in this position for twenty hazy minutes or more, her nauseated trance unbroken by Petra's wheezing breast pump or slamming stall doors or Donna's chatty bangles or the stifled cries of a freshly humiliated intern.

The fatigue had returned just as the Animexa had to be withdrawn, of course, transforming Jen's brain into a sulfurous swamp, wisps of anesthetic steam rising and veiling the half-submerged trees and clotted vegetation, curling in yellowish plumes around her head, then fragmenting and reassembling in an illegible typography of acid-rain skywriting.

MURFLE
MMMMPPHHHAH
MRRRGING
MTEETNNNGN

"Oh!" Jen blurted, the vowel bouncing against the stall walls and smacking her in the face as she stood up and scrabbled for the top of the door, clinging hard until the vertigo dissipated. She'd forgotten a mandatory all-hands meeting that had started a half-hour ago, a presentation based on LIFt-funded surveys demonstrating the negative psychological impacts of "emotional labor" on women. Jen pushed the stall door open, drank in the havoc in the mirror—the pink lab-rat eyes, the tetracycline-gray teeth, the tubercular pallor-and-flush—offered herself a queasy little salute, and pushed out the door onto an office floor denuded of people. The lack of their ebb and flow upped the volume on the *whhoooooossshhhhh* and heightened the treble frequencies on Jen's general sense of irreality, but it was only when she reached the conference room that she knew she was hallucinating.

There, gesticulating before a fully staffed and stocked conference table in a sharply tailored three-piece suit, clean-shaven and bright-eyed, holding not a machete but a PowerPoint laser wand, was Baz Angler.

"What these surveys are telling us is that organic honesty is the only answer," Baz was saying as Jen slipped through the door, the downward momentum of the closing statement in his voice. "It's a universal answer—everyone has access to organic honesty, no matter what stage of life. That's what's so empowering about it: There's no price tag or barrier to entry, no group you have to join. Everyone can benefit. I know I can. But nobody can benefit more from the organic-honesty concept than working moms!"

Baz Angler began tossing his pointer from palm to palm. Jen expected him at any moment to reveal its retractable blade.

"Let's be real for a moment. And don't think even a regular guy like me hasn't noticed. Society expects working moms to be happy, upbeat, positive, and uncritical at all times, in the workplace and at home and at all points in between," Baz Angler was saying. "And if the inside matches the outside, more power to you. But women are carrying a burden heavier than the child in their belly or on their hip, heavier than the paperwork and baby bottles spilling out of their handbags, and that burden is the burden of *the lie*."

A comic stock image appeared onscreen of a business-attired

woman at a computer, looking down in dismay at her mouse mat to see her hand gripping not her mouse but a supine sippy cup.

"When you smile and don't mean it, that's a lie. When you swallow your frustration or your disappointment, that's a lie. And when the lie becomes the habit, that's the boulder on your back and the chip on your shoulder. The lie can bend your spine and pull your muscles and corrode your insides. The lie wants to infect you!"

He paused, licked his lips, breathed in and breathed out. Just for a second, Jen could espy the blade-wielding-homesteader Baz beneath the smooth corporate friend-of-a-good-cause Baz.

"We have to fight back," Baz continued. "So let's stop lying to ourselves. Let's stop lying to each other. My God, let's stop lying to *our children*, above all. This is where you women have the edge on us men, because there's nothing like motherhood to make you honest. I'm no expert, but I've got a hunch that nobody ever told a lie in the throes of childbirth."

"Ho, ho," Karina said, as a discreetly pixelated image of a woman in active labor appeared onscreen.

"Motherhood—fatherhood, too, in its way, but especially motherhood—strips you down to your instincts and builds you back up again, and you're powerless to front and feint in the face of that love and that pain and that ultimate test of your endurance. That primal instinct—it can see right through you. Motherhood is labor enough, so stop taking on all this extra emotional labor. For women's sake, for men's sake, for children's sake. Let's stop trying to keep track of all these lies we've told. Let's set ourselves free."

Baz Angler held the laser pointer in a benedictory spirit toward Leora. "Leora, what have I missed?" Baz shrugged and grinned in a confident performance of diffidence as he took his seat.

"Now," Leora said from her seat, "this isn't opinion. This is all based on our own research, not to mention our own lived experience. We have the empathy gene. We have the nurturing gene. We have the gene of emotional openness. That's what makes us mothers, each and every one of us. Those are the essences of femininity, the roots and wellsprings of womanhood. Organic honesty helps us feel those roots and helps us draw from that wellspring. Organic honesty is an organic kindness that will break those chains that make us front and feint. Organic honesty will shatter that happy façade that becomes a prison. When you push down your true feelings, they rot and fester inside you, which can negatively impact not only your emotional health but your physical health, too."

"Don't invite that kind of negative energy into your life!" Baz added. "Don't seal yourself up and sicken yourself inside a prison of lies. Organic honesty. It's up to us to live a *real life.*"

"Just let it all hang *out!*" Sunny said, widening out her eyes and wagging her head approvingly. "Ayy-men, brother. Finally, it's like"—Sunny exhaled hard—"such a load off!"

"These ideas and thoughts should shape everything the foundation does going forward," Leora said. "They are the rock beneath our theory of change."

"So thought-provoking, Baz, really," Karina said. "We're so fortunate to have your perspective on this. And nice to hear these kinds of affirmations from a *man* for once, am I right, ladies?" Karina added, casting the rest of the room a roguish sidelong glance. The rest of the room tittered and cooed in abashed affirmation.

"My dear friend Baz and I have been talking about this concept of organic honesty for as long as we have known each other," Leora said. "But one of the many reasons I called upon him now is that we were starting to feel a bit—a bit *sequestered.*"

"Haha, boys don't have cooties!" Sunny giggled. Baz was staring at his phone.

"It's *such* an interesting perspective," Karina added. "I mean, we're out here living these truths every day, and—"

Leora was staring at her phone.

"We should open the floor for discussion," Karina said. "What's on everyone's mind, gang?"

Whhooooossshhhhh

"Wonderful, Baz, just wonderful," Leora said to her phone.

"Baz, looks like you got the first word, the middle word, *ay*-and the last word," Sunny said, shaking her head in amazement.

"But aren't you—we—basically talking about overthrowing the social order?"

Jen, subsiding against the wall, was as surprised as anyone in the room to find herself speaking. She leveraged her shoulder blades to push herself off the wall and inadvertently flipped off all the overhead lights.

"There's a difference between honesty and disclosure," Jen continued, one hand flapping behind her to switch the lights back on. "Just because I don't tell you everything I'm thinking at every second doesn't mean I'm lying to you. Privacy doesn't make you sick. I mean, Baz—"

"I remember you!" Baz exclaimed, fluorescent lights flickering on and off his face. "Julie!"

"Yes, it's me, Julie!" Jen said to the wall as she swatted at the light switches.

"Now *this*," Baz said to the rest of the room, his eyes wide with secret-disclosing excitement, his arm fully extended to waggle two proprietary fingers toward Jen's back, "this is a woman who tells it to you straight. Julie here is a role model for the kind of organic honesty that we're proposing."

"Such a role model she thinks she can just swan in and out whenever she feels like it," Donna said, not quite under her breath.

"But wait," Jen said. "If we were to do everything that you're proposing, Baz, could we even be sitting in this room with each other right now? We would kill each other!" Bertha Mason rattled weakly at the door, then retreated.

No one replied. Baz Angler's arm retracted in a dying fall. But she had begun, and she couldn't stop.

"Also, I'm wondering—kind of a more big-picture issue—when we say all these things about how women are more this and less that, even if we're praising women, isn't that kind of counterproductive?" Jen asked. "To say that women are categorically one thing or the other?

Part of the whole point of 'empowerment' or whatever we're going to call it—I know we're not on board with the word *feminism* as an institution—but the general idea is that women don't have to conform to prescribed roles. I mean, being empathetic and nurturing and emotionally open are great things, but I don't think a woman should beat herself up if those aren't her super-strongest qualities. Not every woman has to be a mother, you know?"

"You're misunderstanding the research," Sunny broke in. "What we mean is that the maternal instinct is a *metaphor* for—"

"But even in saying 'instinct' we're saying that motherliness is hard-wired into us," Jen interrupted. "Right? I don't think a tough, unmotherly woman is necessarily acting like a man or compensating for being a woman—maybe she's just a tough woman. I'm rambling, but it's just—feminism, sorry, I mean, *empowerment* isn't about backing ourselves into a corner with compliments, and it's not about anybody telling you who you're supposed to be or how you're supposed to act or policing your affect in order to win entry into the womanhood club. We're all already in the club. It's over. I mean, *you're* not in the club, Baz—"

Bertha Mason tapped one ragged fingernail against the door. Baz watched Jen impassively, chin cupped in palm, one finger tapping his temple.

"But the club—the club that *matters* is who has power, and—and um, sorry, I lost my train of thought—and people who say whatever they want, whenever they want, probably have power already," Jen said, her voice quavering and dipping steadily in volume. Her heart clapped at her throat, as if to dislodge the choking words. "Power and money and status. Saying exactly what's on your mind isn't empowering. It's just symptomatic of power."

Donna stared at the conference table with her head slightly cocked, as if she were receiving repeated blows to the skull and contemplating the best words with which to articulate the pain. Sunny was trying to make eye contact with Donna by drumming her fingernails on the table. Karina was wince-gazing over Jen's shoulder. Daisy's brow was knotted and she was nodding pensively. Leora and Baz scrolled their phones in tandem.

"Well," Donna said.

Leora, stirred by Donna, looked up from her phone. "You know, I agree with the group—that word, *feminism*, it limits us. I prefer *humanism*."

"*Toe* tally," Sunny said, headbanging.

Karina smiled. "Shall we wrap up?"

Jen walked back to her desk, cheeks ablaze, heart kickboxing. She sat without seeing at her monitor until a surge of nausea overtook her. She looked around wildly, saw that she would not have time to reach the ladies' room, lunged forward, and heaved into her wastepaper basket. Daisy appeared beside her with a half-full bottle of water and, over Jen's feeble protestations, draped a puce beach towel of unknown provenance over the wastepaper basket, replaced it with the basket from her own desk, and turned toward points unknown to deposit the contents of the used basket.

"It's going to be better this time," Daisy said to Jen's back a few moments later.

Jen twisted around to look at Daisy, hot cheek pressed against the open top of the water bottle. Daisy met her gaze. Jen knew that eye contact was hard for Daisy.

"I didn't know for a while, this time," Jen said. "Or I did but I didn't. I wasn't hoping. I wasn't paying attention. I should have been paying attention."

Daisy finally looked away as she arranged a stray strand of hair behind Jen's ear.

"How did you—how long have you known?" Jen asked.

Daisy shrugged. "I sit two feet away from you all day, every day," she said to Jen's earlobe. "You are the closest person in the world to me."

Statement of Accounts

Re: Contact Jen!

My girlfriend and I were just talking about how cool it might be to have our portraits painted, but instead of from the front, they could be done from the back—head/hair/back of the neck. It would still call on your amazing technical abilities, but the viewer of the portrait could project his/her own ideas onto it.

Re: Contact Jen!

Would you ever consider a commission to paint people's dreams? Not like people would describe their dreams to you. I mean, what if we hooked up sleeping people to a brain-wave scanner that decoded their dreams? Or maybe you could make a diptych of the dream and the scan?

Re: Contact Jen!

Hi, Jen, your payment should have come through via direct deposit by now. Please do let me know if there is any issue with the transfer. As always, it has been a pleasure for Mrs. Durbin to work with you. Warm wishes, Dakota

Jen tabbed over from email and opened her online bank account. Her lungs filled themselves with a muffled shrieking effort, and she clapped her hand over her mouth, her breath wooing back again through her fingers.

She folded her hands on her desk. She was comfortably seated in a still pocket of time, no turbulence, 70 degrees Fahrenheit, pH balance of seven. She had no idea when this pocket of time would expire.

Inside this space, as her amygdala dozed, as the volume and resolution of the world whirring around her faded out, Jen could not discern whether she was about to make a strong decision or was merely succumbing to impulse. What nudged her out of her seat and propelled her across the LIFt floor to Karina's office was the same prod that pinballed her back and forth across that floor hundreds of times before: a helpless sense of obligation.

In this case, though, the sense of obligation was to the idea that Mrs. Flossie Durbin had initiated a transaction and that it was up to Jen to complete it. Mrs. Flossie Durbin had rented the pocket of time for her.

Jen entered Karina's office and sat down without asking permission.

"So I just wanted to tell you, and this is such a hard thing to tell you, but that I've decided to leave the—".

"Bummer, we'll miss you," Karina broke in.

"—the foundation—oh! Yes, it's a difficult decision, obviously, but I—"

"*Bummer*, we'll *miss* you," Karina reiterated, raising her voice.

"Um," Jen said. "Do you need any other information from me?"

"I'm good, I'm good," Karina said. "Give us two weeks?"

"Right, sure."

"Should I tell Leora?" Jen asked.

"I can tell her," Karina said.

"Are you sure?" Jen asked

Karina blinked and beamed. "Is that all?"

"I think so," Jen said, getting up to leave. She hesitated. "It's just that—I just wanted to tell you that I'm leaving to try to do my art full-time. I did a portrait for Mrs. Flossie Durbin, the philanthropist—"

"Ah, yes, we tried to get her for our board of directors," Karina said. "Could the woman even *try* to return a phone call?"

"Right, yes, I'd heard that—and so, you know, that vote of confidence, it really seems to be opening some doors for me. I got a commission to do a magazine illustration of a reclusive mining heiress who's rarely photographed. I'm doing wedding portraits, baby portraits, someone even mentioned holiday cards to me, which seems so far away—"

"I think I got it!" Karina said.

Bertha Mason laughed. Bertha had rattled at the door all these years not seeking freedom from confinement or retribution. She rattled only for approval.

"Okay," Jen said. "Okay, this is great—I mean, not great in all senses, but—"

"Jen, what can I say—you're a real pull-yourself-up-by-the-bootstraps story," Karina said. "A real Horatio Alger tale."

"Actually—and most people don't know this—but Horatio Alger stories weren't really about pulling oneself up," Jen said. "They're more about being in the right place at the right time, about earnest young people happening to cross paths with a wealthy benefactor in a generous frame of mind."

"Aren't you Miss Smartypants," Karina said, grinning widely and crinkling her nose impishly. "I *will* miss all the ways you educate me. The foundation will, too."

"Also," Jen said as she turned to leave, "just FYI, Horatio Alger was a pedophile."

We've Met Many Times

"Julie."

Jen was standing in line at the coat check in the red-carpeted, red-walled arcade outside the ballroom where the annual Bluff Foundation Revel was winding down. Meg, her date, was in the ladies' room. Jen pulled her spangled black-cashmere wrap a bit tighter around her midsection and turned toward the voice to see Leora Infinitas. Structured mosaic-print dress and gladiator spikes. Smoky eye. Caramel-butter extensions. Shoulders thrown back, one hand on waist, hip turned and corresponding leg stepped out. Anxious handler—not Sunny, but Sunny-like in her force field of high-strung cheer, her flat-footed quickness—levitating nearby, BlackBerry in one palm and two handbags in the other.

"Oh, wow, Leora—Ms. Infinitas! Yes—it's Jen—but that's okay—what an amazing dress—it's so nice to finally meet you," Jen said, holding out her hand.

Leora Infinitas turned both palms upward, the cuffs and clatches encircling her wrists winking with light, in a gesture that Jen couldn't instantly decode as either a proposal for a hug, an invitation for a double hand grasp, or a dispensation with all tactile formalities. After a second's hesitation, Jen reached out her hand, knuckles to ceiling, and wrapped her fingers around Leora's limp right palm in a 90-degrees-turned handshake. The Sunny-like handler checked her watch.

"But we've met many times," Leora Infinitas said, extracting her hand and aiming her head in a quizzical tilt.

"We have?" Jen's voice squeaked. She felt as if she'd been caught committing a crime, but didn't know which one.

"Through our work," Leora said. Her eyes were black and bottomless, a sea seen churning through the pinholes of a painted porcelain mask. "Through the work that we do. Through the work we have done."

"Oh, of course, but we've never spoken—directly—I mean, with each other."

"But we have." Leora Infinitas did not break eye contact. She beamed like a hologram. "You have heard me. And I have heard you. I *see* what you do."

"Oh, of course. It's funny, isn't it? I totally feel that way, too, about you, and it's so cool to know that it goes both ways, Leora."

"We've got—the thing—" the Sunny-like handler said.

"We have always known each other," Leora Infinitas said. "We always will. I will always be with you. And you will always be with me." She turned and glided away, handler scurrying beside her, forever attended to and somehow alone.

Another Spring

Jen came home and sat down on the couch next to Jim and Franny.

"So. I think we can officially start talking about it now," Jen said.

"Yeah?"

"It's time," she said, rubbing her knuckles against Franny's brow. "We're out of the woods. The anatomy stuff. Testing. And it's becoming obvious. A lady gave me her seat on the train today. Although that happened once before."

"When it happened before, was it the yellow dress with the sailboats on it?"

"Yeah, good call. The waist kind of billows out."

"I love that dress. I wondered why you never wore it anymore."

"I guess now I can wear it again."

"How do you feel?"

"You have to be more specific."

"How do you feel about starting to talk about it?"

"I don't know. One time I blurted out to someone that we were 'trying,' and I felt like I was saying, 'We are having sex.' Now I'd be saying, 'We have had successful sex.'"

"But you don't have to say that. Your body will say it for you."

"Well, my body will start a conversation that I won't want to finish."

"Do people still say 'bump'?"

"Never under any circumstances ever say that again."

"Does starting to talk about it involve talking about all the unsuccessful sex-having?"

"When Genevieve from my old book club had her twins, everyone asked her if they were science babies."

"Did Genevieve make science babies?"

"I never asked her."

They sat silently for a moment.

"We should call some people in the morning," she said. "We should call my parents."

"We should definitely call your parents."

"They will be so happy," she said.

They sat silently some more.

"We are starting to talk about it," he said. "That's true. Does starting to talk about it involve you starting to talk about it with me?"

"Of course it does. I feel like I've been talking about it with you all along. I know I haven't—it's odd; something would happen and I'd just assume you would know, because if it happened to me it meant it was happening to you, too."

"Maybe someday we'll become so close that we won't have to talk to each other at all."

"I'm sorry, sweetie. It's weird that something can be so private and so public at the same time. It's like, inside and outside—I get confused about which is which."

"You're inside now."

"I know. I'm inside now."

They sat silently for a long time.

"How do you feel?" he asked.

She couldn't answer right away.

"Honey, look at me," he said. "Look at me. Come on. Look at those tears, so heavy with nutrients and minerals. They heal the sick and awaken sleeping princesses. They slake the thirsts and nourish the soil and moisturize the pores of Tiger Canyon."

"Stop," she said. "I appreciate what you're doing, honey, but stop."

They sat silently some more.

"I'm fine," she finally said. "I'm *fine*. I'm a little panicked. I'm extremely happy. I'm tired. I'm a moist, leaking grocery bag of wilted clichés and adjectives full of empty calories. I'm hungry."

"Do you want me to make some dinner?"

"Yes, that would be great. Thank you."

"While I make dinner, should we think about how everything is about to change, and soon we won't even remember the people that we are right now?"

"Yes, that would be great, too."

"Because we'll have amnesia associated with extreme sleep deprivation?"

"Yes."

"Which is, when you think about it, a kind of *psychic death*?"

"Yes!"

"Are you ready to stage a household coup d'état and then fall victim to it, and all the screaming mayhem and poverty and squalor that will follow?"

"Yes!"

"Are you ready to destroy your life?"

She climbed on top of her husband, wrapped her arms around his neck, and buried her face in him. "Yes. I am ready to destroy my life."

Acknowledgments

Thanks to Jynne Dilling Martin, this book's first reader and first champion, and to Katie Arnold-Ratliff, who dug through an early draft and made every line of it better. I am preposterously lucky to have such dear and brilliant and beautiful friends. I love you both with all my heart.

Thanks to Claudia Ballard, whose blazing intelligence, compassion, and generosity never cease to amaze me.

Thanks to Jordan Pavlin, for her keen editorial eye and boundless support and kindness. Thanks to Jordan, Josie Kals, Nicholas Thomson, and everyone at Knopf for believing in this book.

Thanks to Andrea Lynch, who schooled me in how charitable foundations work (and don't work). Thanks to Scott Indrisek, Ava Lubell, Dushko Petrovich, and John Swansburg for bringing their technical expertise to bear on specific sections of the manuscript. Thanks to Jesse Dorris, Dan Kellum, Josh Levin, Farah Miller, and Chandra Speeth for talking me through dilemmas and moments of doubt. Thanks to Julia Turner, David Plotz, and all of my colleagues at *Slate* for fostering a workplace that is as creative, congenial, and dissimilar to LIFt as an office can possibly be.

Most of all, thanks to Adrian Kinloch, without whom I never would have started writing this book, and to Devon Kinloch, without whom I never would have finished it.